JUSTIFYING THE MEANS

BRUCE MCLEOD

Justifying The Means
ISBN: 978-1-7642437-0-4

Cover design and photography: [Bruce McLeod]

Printed in Australia

First Edition

For permissions, inquiries, or rights, contact:
bruce.mcleod.author@gmail.com

CONTENT WARNING

This novel contains scenes depicting violence, trauma, suicide, self-harm, and strong language. Reader discretion is advised.

For Brian
Your friendship, loyalty, and laughter
will echo in these pages forever.

You always had my back — this time, I've got yours.

Based on actual events.

For all Prison Officers – The unsung heroes of the justice system.
You walk behind the wall, hold the line, and carry the weight few ever see.

CHAPTER 1: BEHIND THE WALLS

In Unit B, the sun still came through the bars—but the cold never left.

I stood at the officer's post, watching the Unit. Autumn had found its way through the window steel bars behind me, casting streaks of gold and shadow across the polished vinyl floor. Warm days. Cool nights. My favourite time of year. Brief reminders that life existed beyond concrete and steel.

Inside these walls, reminders were rare.

Metro Prison swallowed an entire city block in the heart of the CBD. People walked past it daily without a second glance. Just another slab of concrete in a city drowning it. But anyone who'd been inside knew the truth—this place didn't just hold criminals. It held tension. It held silence that could turn dangerous in seconds.

From the street, Metro looked like it held paperwork and photocopiers. Inside, it was razor wire, reinforced glass, and eyes – always watching. The officers. The prisoners. The cameras. The ghosts.

The Unit hummed with low-level motion—billets mopping the floor, someone laughing too loud over near the stairs. But underneath it all, I felt it. That low hum. The kind that means something's coming. Not yet. But soon.

My name's Jacob Daniels. Senior Prison Officer. Twenty years in the service. Twenty years of watching, measuring, anticipating. I'd transferred to Metro four years ago. Officially, it was a 'personal request'. Unofficially, I was escaping someone I no longer wanted in my life.

Unit B had become my territory. My rhythm. My battlefield.

They say prison turns you into someone else. They're wrong. It strips away the parts you pretend to be and leaves you with what you really are.

I wore the uniform—tactical boots with years of scuffs beneath a fresh polish. The belt sat lower now, belly pushing out more than it used to. I'd earned that weight the slow way. Night shifts. Shit food. Stress you don't talk about because no one wants to hear it.

People outside the job don't understand. For most, a bad day means a missed meeting or a cold coffee. In here, a bad day means a dead body and a week of lockdown.

Only one rule matters: everyone goes home.

I don't say much unless I have to. Learned early that most people talk just to hear themselves echo. Me? I listen. People show you who they are when they think you're quiet. Prisoners. Staff. Doesn't matter.

I'm old-school. Came up in a time when 'doing hard time' still meant something. Now? It's about managing behaviour and prisoner wellbeing. Nothing wrong with that—until someone gets hurt. That's the part the academics don't write into the policy papers. Written by people who never knew what it was like to deal with prisoners, especially on their worst days.

Downstairs, in Reception, the new arrivals were already banging on the cell doors—shouting to be processed. Some just wanted to get into general population to find their boys. Some had things tucked where you didn't want to imagine. Most just wanted to keep moving—staying in one place too long made them nervous. Nervous men make mistakes.

Reception was chaos on a good day. Every new prisoner assessed: offence, gang affiliations. Some came in amped on meth, wide-eyed and twitching. Others came in quiet, already calculating angles. Either way, we read them. Watched every tick, flinch, and breath. The experienced officers could clock danger in under thirty seconds.

Inside these walls, instinct kept you alive. That, and knowing when to act and when to hold the line.

I'd seen enough over the years to know the patterns. First-timers try to act tough. Lifers play it cool. The real threats don't say a word. They just watch. Wait. And when the time's right, they move.

I shifted my stance. My knees complained. So did my back. Long hours. Heavy keys. Heavy past. I'd been divorced twice. Married a third time. Emma, my current wife, was the only thing in my life that didn't feel like a war.

Somehow, she saw past the uniform—the silence, the thousand-yard stare, the blood that wasn't always mine. She never asked about work, and I never offered. It was the deal we didn't make but both understood. She saved the part of me I hadn't buried yet. The part I was starting to forget existed.

But the job took its toll. No amount of leave balances or EAP referrals changed that. You either found a way to cope, or you didn't. I'd seen good men buried. Sat through debriefs where no one said what they really felt. We were trained to be silent.

But that silence echoed.

I leaned against the desk, eyes sweeping across the Unit. Something was off. I couldn't name it yet. But after this long, I trusted the itch in my gut. A whisper under the surface.

Trouble was coming.

It always did.

CHAPTER 2: OFFICERS' POST

From where I stood at my desk, I scanned the Unit. Two levels of cells stretched out either side of me like rows of teeth. Upstairs—the Top Tier—was where we kept the doubles. Two prisoners per cell, jammed together like mismatched puzzle pieces. Downstairs to the left were the Billet cells. Single cells, for prisoners we trusted just enough to mop floors and serve food, but not enough to turn our backs on.

At the centre of it all, the Officers' Post sat halfway up a landing—a command perch overlooking the chaos.

My desk.

The bench was a relic. Laminated wood, scratched to hell, held together by habit and a few stubborn screws. Two mismatched office chairs sat behind it, threadbare and creaky, like the officers who used them. On the surface: the usual mess—paperwork trays, pens, a whiteboard marker stained with old ink, and a cracked mug half-filled with dead highlighters and Bic pens. That mug had outlasted four governors and more coffee than I could remember.

To the side, a little fridge. Half-working. It hummed louder than it cooled. It did its job—milk, leftover lunches, maybe an apple someone swore they'd eat one day. On top, a microwave covered in stains no one wanted to claim, and a kettle with a handle that burned you if you touched it too soon. Behind my chair sat a sagging couch with stuffing bleeding through the seams—shared by officers and prisoners alike. A piece of the outside world glimpsed through barred windows behind it. Not enough to feel free. Just enough to remember what you were missing.

The noise of the Unit had dropped into background static. A dull hum of footsteps, murmurs, doors creaking open. I wasn't really listening. Not yet. It was Monday afternoon, the draggiest part of a shift. Nothing new. Nothing interesting. The weekend had slipped by without anything worth remembering. All I felt was tired.

Opposite me, Bowden was on the phone, leaning back in his chair like he owned the place. He was new. Not fresh-out-of-training new, but new enough that he still thought the world might thank him for trying. Clean-cut. Trim frame. Sandy hair he insisted—I said it was light brown. He refused to accept that. We argued about it every few weeks, just to pass the time.

He reminded me of me, twenty years ago. Eager, curious, a little too open. I saw it in the way he leaned forward when people spoke. The way he wanted to help. It was the sort of energy the job would beat out of him, slowly and systematically. But I figured if I shaped him right—hardened the edges, kept the core—I could give him a chance. Not to be soft. Not in here. Just not to break.

Too many new officers walked in with a know-it-all strut. They didn't last. The real test wasn't how you handled prisoners—it was how you handled everything else. The noise. The silence. The creeping weight of knowing someone else's mistake could kill you. That's what I tried to teach Bowden. Because when things go bad, it's your partner who matters. Whether they freeze, flinch, or fight—that's what gets you home.

He closed the fridge with a click and held up a cup. "Daniels, want a coffee?"

I didn't answer. My mind was somewhere else, drifting in the usual fog of memory and monotony.

"Hey," he said again, louder. "Coffee?"

I blinked, then nodded. "Yeah. Thanks."

He busied himself at the bench while I let the background noise creep back in. Voices, metal clinks, the thud of stairs under footsteps. The unit was waking up again. I stretched my arms, careful not to knock the kettle out of his hand.

"Who was on the phone?" I asked, curling my fingers around the warm mug as he handed it over.

"Reception." He rifled through his papers, trying to find something he'd scribbled earlier.

"We've got five coming in. Two new. Three returns."

He passed me the list—names scrawled in hurried handwriting. I scanned it. Nothing jumped out. Just more bodies. More problems. More noise.

I raised my voice. "Billet!"

Johnno appeared like he'd been waiting for the call. John 'Johnno' Williams—mid-twenties, wired like a spring, always hovering nearby. Dressed in the usual: prison-issue t-shirt, black shorts, runners with laces double-knotted like he was expecting to sprint at any moment. His eyes flicked around the desk, cataloguing what he might be able to swipe when we weren't looking.

"Yeah, Boss?"

"Five bed packs," I said, not bothering to look up. My attention was on the cell allocation sheet. It was like playing a game of Tetris with violent men. Make the wrong move, and something explodes.

Johnno knew better than to dawdle. He was smart, in the way some prisoners are—always working an angle but never pushing too hard. He'd seen too many billets lose their spots because they got lazy or greedy. The job kept him out of the general mess. Kept him close to officers. Close to information. Close to safety.

He was back fast, bed packs stacked in his arms, dumped neatly on top of the battered filing cabinet near the couch. Then, curiosity had the better of him. It always did.

"So," he said, craning his neck to peek at the paper in my hand, "who we gettin?"

I didn't owe him an answer. But I gave him one anyway.

"Two new. Three coming back."

Johnno nodded like that told him everything he needed to know. Maybe it did. Some prisoners knew the system better than we did.

I glanced back at the list. One name. Couldn't quite place it.

Not yet.

CHAPTER 3: ARRIVAL AND ASSESSMENT

Johnno trotted down the stairs, keen to spread the news. Probably felt like he was in the know, passing intel to the other billets. His record—petty burglary mostly—would have made some officers flinch. But inside Unit B, he was solid. Reliable. That meant something. Finding a billet, you could trust wasn't just rare—it was gold.

The other four billets in the Unit? Similar offences. That wasn't coincidence. It was deliberate. I didn't hire drug addicts. Wouldn't. I'd seen too much damage—too much chaos wrapped in track marks and shaky lies. Addicts were a liability. Their hunger didn't just ruin themselves—it infected the Unit.

Addicts would do anything to score. That included leaning on their cellmates, pushing visitors to smuggle gear in, or bullying prisoners into hoarding and regurgitating meds. I'd seen it a hundred times—desperate men manipulating everyone around them like it was their right. Families included.

I once told Bowden about a guy who stole his daughter's birthday money. She was six. Her grandmother had tucked the cash into a card. He ripped it open the day it arrived, didn't blink, and spent it on heroin. That sort of person? You can keep your sympathy.

Addiction, in here, was a weapon. I didn't need it screwing up my routine. So, I kept my billet pool clean.

The Main Yard sat at the centre of the prison—a concrete hive segmented into six Units, all circling the Yard like wolves on the edge of a pack. Most prisoners didn't stay long. They were either waiting on sentencing, transfer, or classification. This was purgatory with fences.

By mid-afternoon, the Yard began to churn. You could feel it— movement, pacing, tension. They walked in loops, like animals in a cage. Some caught up with old mates. Others leaned against walls, eyes scanning like radar. Clusters formed—low murmurs, quiet chuckles, occasional side-eyes. The city hummed just beyond the walls, but in here, it might as well have been Mars.

Then came the shift.

The new prisoners arrived.

A steady flow of them were funnelled from Reception, escorted by officers with that look—half alert, half bored. Like bouncers at a party, they didn't want to be at.

Unit B's latest delivery came with heavy footsteps and plastic bags. Five of them, each clutching their gear—essentials, maybe a toothbrush. The escorting officer climbed the stairs and handed me the paperwork. I flipped through it while Bowden took position at the desk.

Names. DOBs. Charges. Repeat offenders. Nothing out of the ordinary.

I looked over the group. "Name?" I asked each one.

"Been here before?"

The three returnees all grunted some variation of "Yeah."

I nodded toward the bed packs Johnno had stacked earlier. "Grab one. Follow me."

Bowden dealt with the other two. He directed them to the couch behind the desk. It backed onto the barred windows that looked out onto the side street.

I escorted the returnees to their cells—no ceremony, no sympathy.

I already knew what would follow in the next few days: complaints.

"He snores."

"He stinks."

"He's trying to fuck me."

My response? Always the same: *'This isn't the Hilton. You don't like the accommodations, don't make a reservation.'*

Back at the desk, I dropped into my chair. It creaked under my weight. I rubbed my face once, exhaled slow. The Unit was humming again— radio static, voices, the clank of footsteps on steel stairs. I reached for the two remaining files. Bowden was scanning the yard. He'd learn to read it the way I did. Eventually.

I swivelled toward the couch.

The two new arrivals looked like they hadn't seen a shower in days. Shaggy hair, stained clothes, unshaven. One had acne scars that still looked raw. The other had a tremor in his left hand—nerves, probably, or coming down from something. Neither one looked ready for what was ahead.

I leaned to one side and flipped through their paperwork. Minor assaults. Theft. One was barely nineteen.

I had seen vulnerability like that before. It still haunted me that I couldn't prevent a suicide.

I placed the files behind me. I didn't need them for what came next.

"All right, listen up. This is Unit B, and from now on, until you're moved, this is your home. Stay within this Unit; don't invite your buddies from other Units in here. If you want to meet up, do it outside. Don't ask anyone about their charges, and don't disclose yours. If anyone asks, say it's for driving offences."

One of them starts looking around at other prisoners. I continued, just a bit louder.

"When it's time for a count, you'll hear the officers yell 'Muster Up'. That means you quickly move and stand by your open cell door, don't have anything in your hands, and no talking until we tell you to 'Break Off'. You'll clean your cell every day. Take a shower daily. Keep your clothes clean. We have a laundry billet here who will take care of your clothes. Just put them in a bag, mark your cell number on it, and place it next to the machine downstairs. Reception has provided you with milk and coffee, and you'll get more milk tomorrow morning during Let-Out. Your meals will be served downstairs in the Dayroom. Any questions?"

They looked at me like I'd just recited Shakespeare in another language.

They weren't listening. Not really. Too much fear in their eyes. Too much noise in their heads. That was fine. Repetition made routines stick. They'd figure it out.

I added, "Tomorrow, we'll sort out your money and visitor details. You both called home from Reception?"

They nodded, barely.

Collins. He reminded me of another kid—Kempsey, back in '08. Same wide eyes. Same tremor shakes. Found him swinging from a bedsheet after three days. I still wonder if I could've seen it coming. If I looked close enough. Or if I just didn't want to see it. Collins was the same shape of mistake. I wouldn't miss the signs this time.

"Good." I jabbed a finger toward the remaining bed packs. "Grab one each. Follow me."

And for them, day one had officially begun.

CHAPTER 4: SETTLING IN

The keys clinked against my belt as I hitched up my pants and led the way. Every step was automatic, each movement ingrained after thousands of times climbing those same steel stairs. But I was alert—always. My eyes scanned the Unit, catching glances, noting who was paying attention. You could tell a lot by who watched over the new prisoners and how.

We stopped outside Cell 22. My hand found the right key by muscle memory. *Click.* The lock gave way with that familiar metallic groan. I swung the door open and stepped aside.

"Right, you two will be sharing this cell." I stepped in, my voice steady, no room for negotiation.

"Around 10 AM every day, we do inspections. I expect this cell swept, mopped, beds stripped, sheets and blankets folded at the end. Questions?"

They just stood there—bags in hand, wide-eyed, still blinking from the change in air. Reality was starting to land. It always took a few hours.

I shifted to one side, giving them room to pass. They stepped in slowly, like they were entering someone else's nightmare. Their gear hit the floor—clear bags filled with whatever Reception allowed through. Not much. It never was.

Collins broke the silence first, voice thin, uncertain. "Uh… where do we get the cleaning stuff?"

Fair question. The cell was bare bones. A TV on a shelf. A plastic chair with a split in the seat. Two bunks, thin mattresses. Shower and toilet tucked into the corner. Peeling paint and scratched graffiti on the walls. Personal tags, dates, sometimes just the word *Fuck*. The noticeboard above the bench had nothing but a few torn scraps pinned in place. The ghosts of prisoners' past.

I scanned the tier—always watching, always wary. Words could travel. Eyes could lie. But silence? Silence had its own language in here.

"I'll get a billet to bring what you need," I said. Cleaning gear was the least of their concerns.

I squared up in the doorway, hands on hips, elbows out—classic power stance. You had to make yourself the largest thing in the room. Let them know exactly who was in charge.

"Two more things," I continued, tone edged now. "Every night at lockup, you'll hear us yell: 'Muster Up, by-your-doors, lights on, TVs off.' That means exactly what it says. You stand here, in your cell, nothing in your hands, lights on, and don't speak. We check you against your ID photo, then you're locked in."

Collins nodded like a schoolboy being lectured—wide-eyed and soaking it in.

Dodd, on the other hand, leaned back a little, wearing indifference like a coat. "Yeah, and what's the other thing?" he asked, voice flat, testing.

I didn't blink. "My name is Mr. Daniels. Sir or Boss. And don't piss me off."

Silence.

I turned and stepped out, the door creaking behind me as I left them to it. I heard muffled conversation—Dodd's voice mostly. Might've been a 'fuck off' under his breath. Wouldn't be the first, wouldn't be the last. In here, attitude was often armour. Some wore it loud. Some just waited until they thought no one was watching.

Some of them came in looking for a fight. I just wasn't in the mood to give them one. Yet.

I moved down the tier. Prisoners passed me with nods and muttered "Boss" under their breath. Not respect, not really. Acknowledgment. Recognition. That I had the keys. That I could make their day easy—or hard.

Respect wasn't a right in here. It was a currency. Earned. Traded. Tested. Most of these blokes thought it came with the sentence. It didn't.

I glanced down at Bowden at the desk. He was swamped, calls coming in, trip passes scattered, papers everywhere. I'd been drilling patience into him since day one. Not everything was urgent, no matter what the prisoners thought. They'd get their turn when it came. Same as everyone.

I moved on, keys gripped tight in my right hand, not letting them swing to make noise. No sound? That was the point. Any sound would make prisoners sit up, quiet down.

I moved down the tier. Not rushed, not slow. Just present. Just enough to catch something if it was happening. Most of the time, I didn't need to say a word. Just being there was enough.

The carpet told its own story—thin, stained, worn bare in spots. The places where prisoners stood, argued, waited. Some faded blood spots. Some deliberate. Some not.

Walls marked with years of history—scuffed, dented, and battered. Anger made physical. Doors slammed; fists thrown, plastic chairs weaponised when backs were turned. Each mark a memory someone didn't want to leave behind.

At the end of the tier, I leaned casually against the doorframe. Cold steel against my palm. Eyes forward. A silent warning. I didn't need to say a word. Anyone stepping out of line would feel the temperature change the second they saw me.

Some prisoners thought they ran the show. That the pecking order on the inside worked like it did on the street.

They were always surprised to find me waiting.

CHAPTER 5: CLASH OF TITANS

From my post at the top tier, I scanned the Unit like I always did—steady, patient, assessing. And then I saw him.

Osbourne.

Moving with that overcompensating swagger, like he owned the place. Like he'd never taken a beating in his life.

Osbourne was trouble wrapped in muscle. A walking problem with a rap sheet longer than his attention span. He was the type that mistook intimidation for respect, force for authority. A standover man from a gang with roots buried deep in drug turf. His game was control—through fists, threats, and connections. Didn't matter what colour skin you had—unless you were paying. Then your race didn't exist. You were just a wallet.

Couldn't pay?

That's when things got interesting. Osbourne loved that part—the punishment. Especially if the debtor wasn't white. He didn't say it, but he didn't need to. It was in how he acted. The quiet glee when someone fell behind. When he had to make an example.

He wasn't stupid either. Not the sort of thug that couldn't spell his name. He knew the system. Knew how to play it. Knew how to read officers and manipulate the weak ones. The dangerous ones aren't loud—they're strategic. Osbourne was both.

He walked right up to me, smirking like he thought he had me figured out.

"Boss, did you see the new guys?" he asked, dragging out the words like they tasted bitter. "I was hoping to get a new cellmate. Or a fucking single."

Here we go.

Osbourne always wanted something. Never happy. Never grateful. His entitlement filled whatever room he was in. His arms flared wide as he talked—more show than substance. His neck and arms were inked up with crude tattoos, his head shaved to the skin. Scars crisscrossed beneath the surface—a life lived hard and mean.

I didn't blink. Arms crossed, right hand on top. Ready. Always ready. Because if Osbourne ever snapped—and one day he would—I'd need to be faster.

"You gave Harrison a single last week," he snapped, volume rising. "I was ahead of him on the fucking list!"

There it was. The spark. Power struggle in motion.

I leaned forward just slightly. Voice low, calm. Not for him—he didn't deserve it. For the prisoners listening from nearby cells. Osbourne loved an audience. But I wasn't about to give him the show he wanted.

"I don't owe you an explanation about cell allocations," I said, barely above a whisper. "But if a single's that important to you, we can arrange it. Twenty-three hours a day. Management cell. You can count the bricks one by one."

Our eyes locked. Neither of us flinched. His jaw twitched.

"Fuck off with that shit! Get fucked, ya fucking dog! Just get me that fucking single!" he barked, then turned and stormed back toward his cell—loud, dramatic, and very aware he was being watched over.

I didn't follow. Didn't need to. Several heads peeked from behind cell doors, watching it all play out.

I didn't smile. Not exactly. But I let the calm return to my face. Message delivered. Loud and clear.

Back at the desk, I motioned to Bowden. "Outside. Keep your eyes on the yard."

He nodded, slipping past the office threshold, taking up his post.

"Billet!" I called out, voice raised just enough to command.

Johnno appeared within seconds, reliable as ever. "Yes, Boss?"

I picked up the folded newspaper sitting on the desk, weighing it in my hand like it meant something. Maybe it did.

"I need you and the other boys to have a word with Osbourne. He's getting a little too comfortable. Thinks he runs the place."

Johnno raised an eyebrow, the question in his silence.

"How much of a chat are we talking about?"

A faint grin touched my face. "Just make sure I don't see any blood."

I handed him the newspaper.

Johnno tucked it under his arm like it was some sacred scroll and slipped away, eager. Not because he liked violence—Johnno wasn't built like that. But because he understood balance. And Osbourne was tipping the scale.

From where I stood, I watched over the other billets—move with purpose. They didn't need instructions. Johnno led them to Osbourne's cell. Nguyen stood sentry; door closed.

I didn't need to hear what was said. I'd seen this scene play out before. Not violence. Not really. Just correction. Prison-style diplomacy.

Johnno could stand his ground with Osbourne, so long as it was private and in his favour.

The old days, when officers dealt with these things directly. Those were over. Cameras saw too much. Paperwork dragged officers down. Now? We adapted.

Didn't make it cleaner. Just quieter.

If someone like Osbourne became too bold, the whole Unit suffered. Osbourne would standover other prisoners for anything, clothing, coffee, drugs. It didn't matter.

He'd take the hit now. But men like Osbourne? They never forget. They'd file it away like a debt. And debts always come due.

The billets understood the stakes. Their job was to keep order. Warnings and reminders.

I leaned back in my chair. In this world, real control doesn't come from shouting.

It comes from knowing exactly when to whisper.

CHAPTER 6: LOCKUP

"Ten minutes until Lock-Up. All prisoners return to your Units—ten minutes until Lock-Up."

The announcement echoed across the yard like a dropped gavel. Radios buzzed. The last of the day's noise picked up pace as prisoners drifted back through the front door, some jogging, others dragging their feet like it might win them another minute of freedom. They darted for milk from the fridge, made last-ditch deals, shared smokes, and barked their final jokes of the day.

Bowden was moving with purpose now, joined by two security officers. Herding stragglers with the right mix of calm and authority, the kind you need in a place where the wrong tone can spark a fight.

Upstairs, I stood at the desk, watching the chaos wind itself down. Prisoners rushed by some asking if their mail had arrived, others looking for a receipt that might signal money sent from home. The billets shuffled back downstairs, laughing about something—probably nothing.

"Five minutes until Lock-Up."

I pushed back from the desk and straightened my uniform with slow precision. Routine was its own armour in here. I ran through the notes I'd scrawled throughout the day—cell changes, behaviour issues, Osbourne's little tantrum. Bowden was downstairs, locking the front door and doing his sweep. Kitchen wiped. Common area clear.

He returned to the desk, scooping up the Unit's admin folder and his bag. "I'll drop this off on the way out," he said, stacking the papers with practiced ease.

He moved like he'd finally figured out the rhythm. Not fast, not frantic—just right. The sort of pace that keeps you alive in here.

The radio snapped to life again. "All staff, commence Lock-Up."

I didn't wait.

"Stand by your doors!" I shouted, my voice sharp and loud enough to slice through the Unit.

I led the charge upstairs, my boots thudding one step ahead of the other. Prisoners scrambled into cells, calling last words down to mates before the snib of steel locks cut the conversation short. I paused briefly at each door—count two heads, close it, snib it, move on. The billets were always last to be locked—one of the only perks that came with the job. First out. Last in.

Once Unit B was sealed, Bowden and I moved through the inter-connecting door near Cell 1, into Unit A. Same routine. Same rhythm. Quick nods to the staff already there. We helped with their lockdown and security checks, then turned back toward Unit B to complete our own.

I stopped the senior officer just before we re-entered. Kept my tone low.

"If Osbourne's sporting any new bruises," I said, "he slipped in the shower. All good."

He didn't need the details. Just nodded once, a smile twitching at the edge of his mouth. The kind that said, *Understood.*

The process was well-oiled: two officers unlocking and checking IDs, Bowden locking the cell, me running the final sweep behind them. No surprises. Until we reached Osbourne's cell.

I stayed out of sight behind the door.

"Name?" the senior officer asked, eyes already on the photo book.

"Osbourne," came the reply, less venom than usual. His eyes dipped slightly, as if the Unit had finally reminded him where he stood.

The officer spotted the swelling—left cheek, corner of the lip—and didn't blink. Just gave a smirk, shut the door, and let it slam louder than needed. Statement made.

We wrapped the checks and waited at the top of the stairs with the other officers for the official count. Talk turned light. Dumbest prisoner of the day. Weirdest excuse someone gave for hiding contraband. Laughter filled the space in place of alarms.

"Lock-Up Count correct," came the final call over the PA.

The others peeled away fast, racing to get their gear logged and keys returned before someone else made them late. Outside the Key Room, the line was already forming—uniforms half-unbuttoned, accoutrements in hand, the day shedding like old skin. Everyone had a story. Everyone had something to laugh at.

In the locker room, it was more of the same. Doors slammed, bags zipped, deodorant sprayed like fog. Phones came out. Some texted partners, others checked the news or just scrolled social media in a daze. It was the transition zone. The halfway step between prisoner screams and city streetlights.

Out front, the cool night hit different. A few huddled near the corner lighting smokes, eyes adjusting to freedom. Buses hissed past. Trams clanged. The contrast between chaos and normalcy was jarring, like stepping out of a warzone and into a shopping mall.

Then a thumb's-up from the Gatehouse. Final checks complete. Day officially done.

We didn't linger.

We never did.

I used to think walking away meant leaving it behind. But not anymore. These days, I carried everything out with me. In my head. In my chest. In the little black notebook, I kept hidden in a locked drawer at home— names, times, patterns. Not for therapy. For something else. Something coming.

CHAPTER 7: THE JOURNEY HOME

Among the sea of post-work commuters on the train platform, I stood still—alone yet surrounded. A strange sense of isolation crept in. We'd all clocked off, but the shift didn't just end at the gate—it clung to you like sweat.

A few prison officers passed by. We exchanged the usual nods. The kind that said, *Yeah, long day*, but nothing more. No one stopped. Once you stepped off prison grounds, the unspoken rule kicked in: colleagues became strangers. Everyone just wanted to disappear into their own little world and forget.

The PA system crackled overhead, warning that the next train was on approach. That was the cue for movement. The crowd surged forward, all elbows and backpacks. A fight for space. For air. For the chance to sit instead of sway.

I managed to snag a window seat halfway down the carriage. Not exactly luxury, but it would do. Plugged in my headphones, flicked through my messages—nothing urgent—and hit play on an '80s playlist that always managed to settle my head. The train jerked forward with that slow, reluctant start. A sigh on wheels.

Shoulder to shoulder, the carriage was packed tight. Human sardines in work shirts and winter jackets. Those who didn't find seats were left to hang onto metal poles, swaying like drunks with each lurch of the train. Across from me, a man buried his face in the daily paper. The woman beside me pressed her oversized handbag into my ribs, silently demanding more space. I obliged with a half-shuffle—not out of politeness, but because I didn't feel like pausing to start a conversation, I had no interest in.

Instead, I did what I'd always done. Watched.

People-watching was a skill in my line of work. On the train, it passed the time. In prison, it could save your life. My eyes moved from face to face. Two men in animated debate. A woman laughing too hard at her phone. A teenager pretending not to notice the older guy ogling her. And a couple near the door—arguing, not shouting, but sharp enough that you didn't need audio to catch the tension.

The woman wore a sharp grey suit. Hair pulled back tight. Lips even tighter. She jabbed a finger at the man beside her—mid-thirties, slouched into a black jacket that hung on him like regret. He kept his eyes low, scanning the floor, pretending to care about shoes. That argument was either about something he'd done, or something he hadn't. Probably both.

I'd seen that look a thousand times. On prisoners when they learnt they were caught. On partners during visits when the trust finally snapped. Same body language. Same story. It was just the clothing that changed.

As the train left the city behind, the pressure eased. Each stop peeled away another layer of bodies until the carriage felt less like a box of tension and more like quiet. The world outside shifted, too. High-rises gave way to rooftops. Streets widened. The pulse slowed.

By the time we reached my stop—about an hour from the city—the carriage was on the verge of half empty. I slung my backpack over one shoulder, jammed my hands into my jacket pockets, and stepped out into the fading light.

The streets here were wide and tree-lined, suburban in that picture-perfect way real estate agents love to pitch. Neat fences. Single-story homes. Everyone's lawns trimmed just enough to look effortless. This was Emma's sort of place—quiet, stable, connected to everything that mattered. And after the days I had, I didn't mind the stillness either.

The walk home was familiar. Automatic. A stretch of silence between two worlds.

Somewhere in front of me, I heard the faint rattle of the train echo into the distance.

And just like that, the prison was behind me.

CHAPTER 8: HOMECOMING

Our modest three-bedroom place wasn't flashy, but it was ours. A weathered little sanctuary tucked into a quiet street. The timber floors creaked just enough to feel lived-in, and the kitchen—renovated on a budget but sharp as hell—handled everything from Sunday roasts to late-night snacks. Out back, a yard big enough for the dog to patrol, but not so big it turned into a second job.

The spare room was always made up for Adam, my son from my first marriage. He stayed with us on weekends and holidays. Emma insisted we keep it ready. Same doona cover, same posters on the wall, just the way he liked it. A subtle reminder that even if he didn't live here full-time, he belonged.

The low hum of trains rolling past had become part of the soundtrack of our lives. It was a sort of white noise that made everything else feel still. Peaceful. But I'll admit—some nights I'd lie in bed, listening to the steel-on-steel rhythm and imagine something more. A forever place. One we could grow old in without neighbours too close or walls too thin.

It had been ten years since Emma, and I met. We found each other online—two broken people trying to connect. She pulled me out of the pit after my second divorce. Not with grand gestures, but with steady hands and kind words.

Emma had this uncanny way of making everything make sense. Music, footy, cooking—whatever we bonded over, it stuck. I didn't just love her. I respected her. And when she called me her rock, I understood what she meant. I was the ballast, the counterweight. And she was the spark.

As I approached the front door, the glow through the glass told me she was already home. Her car sat tucked under the carport. As I opened the door, a burst of energy from inside.

Dougal.

Our Jack Russell. All four paws skating on the floor, tail spinning like a propeller. A blur of pure joy. He launched at me, excitement like I'd been gone for a year.

I knelt and scratched behind his ears. "You miss me, mate?" His body wiggled with the sort of happiness only a dog can manage.

"I'll be there in a minute," I called out to Emma, her voice drifting in from the kitchen.

But first—the ritual.

Before I spoke, before I ate, before I even smiled properly—I had to get the uniform off. Not just the clothes, but the weight of the day. Every step from the front door to the bedroom was part of that process. That mental reset.

In the bedroom, I peeled it all off. Jacket, shirt, boots, socks—dumped in the basket. My shoulders slumped as the tension started to fade. I sat on the edge of the bed, still patting Dougal who had flopped beside me like a sentry on leave. That quiet moment, just me and the dog, did more to heal the day than anything else.

I slipped into track pants and a faded band tee—comfort armour. Tossed the rest in the laundry and headed to the kitchen.

Emma was already unpacking groceries. On the bench, a folded sheet of paper—a new recipe. She grinned as I entered and kissed me, quick and warm.

"How was your day?"

I shrugged. "Yeah, good." I lied.

She arched an eyebrow. "Anything exciting?"

She knew the game. I never gave much away unless I needed to.

"Nah, all good," I said, already pulling ingredients from the fridge and running water over my hands.

Emma didn't push. She never did. She didn't need to hear about prisoners threatening staff, or the smell of blood in a cell, or the look in someone's eyes right before they tried to take a swing at you.

Knowing I was home—that was enough for her.

I'd always made a choice to protect her from the worst of it. Not because she couldn't handle it, but because I didn't want the grime of my job to bleed into our life.

Some things needed a firewall. The violence, the filth, the darkness—I left it all at the door. So, we could just… be.

Together.

CHAPTER 9: SHADOWS OF THE MIND

Sometimes, without warning, my mind would drift—snagged on some invisible thread. Eyes fixed on nothing. Body present, but somewhere deep inside, I was back behind the wall. Back in the noise. The stink. The chaos.

Reliving past assaults, arguments, bloody scenes, death.

Prison doesn't just clock off when you do. It hangs around. Leaks into your pores. Follows you home like smoke after a fire.

Emma sat at the kitchen counter, adjusting the sleeves on her work jumper, the company logo stitched cleanly over her chest. She tucked a strand of hair behind her ear and kept talking—soft, steady, comforting. Stories from her day rolled out in little waves. Office politics, a new manager who didn't know his arse from his elbow, some harmless gossip over salad bowls at lunch.

I grasped every word like a life raft.

This—*this*—was what normal sounded like. What I craved. A conversation not coloured by violence or power games or the smell of blood in the air.

I stirred the pan, turning the sizzling meat with just enough focus to stop it burning. Veggies on the board, knife in hand, fingers moving with rhythm and purpose. Cooking was my escape hatch. My therapy. My way to scrub the day off my skin. Some people golfed. Some meditated. I diced onions and seared meat.

Dinner was plated. Nothing fancy, just good food made with care. We sat down, ate, and talked about nothing. That was the best sort of talk.

Emma took over cleanup duty—as she always did, insisting it was her way of saying thank you for cooking. I didn't argue. I sank into the couch, letting the cushions swallow me, remote in hand. I scrolled through a mess of recorded shows before landing on an old favourite. Something familiar. Predictable.

Dougal flopped beside me with his chewed-up toy between his paws. He gave it one lazy gnaw before drifting into that half-alert Jack Russell doze.
Emma came back in with a glass of water, placed it on the table, then curled up beside me, her head resting against my shoulder.

The three of us sat there—me, Emma, Dougal—watching a crime drama. Ironic, really.

For a moment, it was perfect. Too perfect. That's when my brain betrayed me.

My thoughts had already shifted. Back to work.

To the unit. To the prisoners I'd see tomorrow. The ones nursing bruised egos or plotting petty revenge. I thought about how I'd juggle movement schedules, how I'd head off brewing trouble before it lit up.

There was always something ticking. Some minor grievance that could explode if you weren't ahead of it.

Even in the calm, I was already planning.

Running scenarios in my head.

Anticipating every angle. Every tell.

Because when tomorrow came, I'd be stepping back into the storm.

And in that world, survival meant staying three moves ahead.

CHAPTER 10: SHADOWS OF THE YARD

I took my usual place—back corner of the Parade Room, where the senior officers gravitated like moths to a flickering light. I checked my keys, double-tugged at the belt clip to be sure. Smoothed my shirt. Adjusted my badge. Every detail locked in. Presentation mattered. It wasn't vanity—it was discipline. Control.

The other seniors were already cracking jokes, leaning into their routines like stand-up comics in uniform. They took shots at the day ahead, the prisoners they could mess with, and the newbies too green to see it coming. They were seasoned, sharp—always ready with a snarky comeback or a perfectly timed sledge.

They didn't need fists. Wit was a weapon. And they wielded it with precision.

The room hummed, officers scattered across seating, half reading newspapers or paperwork, half chatting like it was a reunion. But the vibe shifted the second Phil Hunter walked in. Security Supervisor. Battle-worn. Loud. Built like a retired footy player who hadn't let go of the post-game beers.

We didn't always agree—Hunter and I—but we respected each other. He might've gotten softer around the middle, but he still had our backs when it counted. Especially when things turned ugly.

He dumped a stack of folders at the lectern. The murmur of conversation ebbed. Names rolled off his tongue for Roll Call. One after another, officers answered with a crisp "Sir," like it was muscle memory.

Then came Operations Manager Steve Tourney. Slim, average height—but he had that look. The sort of guy who could walk into any room and command it without raising his voice. His posture said it all: power without trying.

He rattled off the night's incidents. Mentioned a fresh crop of prisoners coming through Reception. Nothing unusual. Just the day's dirty laundry, pressed and folded.

"Dismissed!" Hunter barked.

A thunderclap of movement followed. Bags slung over shoulders, boots stomping toward Units. Another shift in the pressure cooker.

Bowden was already waiting for me at the top of the stairs. The wind cut across the yard, lifting small spirals of dust and grit. Empty for now—eerily so. A rare moment of stillness before the storm.

"You ready for a big day?" he asked with a lopsided grin.

"Sure," I muttered, silently praying for a boring day. Just the usual complaints, mind games, and petty dramas. No lockdowns. No blood. No paperwork. And definitely no one saying the cursed word: *quiet*. Everyone in the job knew better. Say it out loud, and the universe would spit in your face.

We walked the length of the yard and unlocked the Unit. The lights flickered on—harsh and sterile. The smell of old dust and stale air settled over us like a blanket. We unpacked our gear like clockwork. Bags down. Kettle on. Caffeine was the only religion we all subscribed to.

While the kettle hissed, I started the Trap Count. One by one, I ticked off each name. Some doubled up in tight bunks. Others sprawled like kings on the bottom. All accounted for—barely.

Bowden swept through the dayroom and kitchen. Methodical. Eyes sharp. Searching for contraband or things that shouldn't exist. Prisoners were crafty. Hide a sharpened toothbrush in plain sight and call it art.

I handed him a handful of ID cards—prisoners marked for transfer. Notes scribbled beside names: where they were headed, what Unit was expecting them. Bowden moved with efficiency. Into the cells. "Pack your shit. I'll be back in five."

"Attention: Trap Count is Correct," the PA droned.

Right on cue, Bowden opened the billets' cells. The rest of the prisoners were still rubbing sleep from their eyes, dragging their feet out from under blankets.

"Who's doing milk run?" he asked.

Johnno tipped his head toward Nguyen, and just like that, the decision was made.

With a nod from me, Bowden cracked the front door. Nguyen wheeled the trolley out, heading for the kitchen like a kid on a milk run. He was back in minutes with crates of cartons stacked high.

Bowden opened each door one by one. Nguyen placed a carton just inside—no words, no fuss.

Meanwhile, I brewed the morning coffee. A ritual. The only thing separating us from sanity.

Once the milk run was done, Bowden made his way downstairs, and I gave him a quick nod. "Good job."

He'd stopped asking questions and started anticipating them. That was good. That meant he was watching.

We stood at the desk, coffee in hand, watching the Unit slowly stir to life.

Prisoners drifted past. Some offered a respectful "Morning, Boss." Others hovered near the desk, checking for mail, receipts, or any gossip. Who was leaving? Any single cells? Could they get moved? I listened, offered the usual line— "I'll think about it." Which really meant, "Depends if you act like a dickhead today."

A few of them were too quiet this morning. That's when you start paying closer attention.

Mornings were the sweet spot. Before the attitudes kicked in. Before the bullshit started.

I noticed a few hats—caps pulled low to dodge the cameras. I didn't give warnings. I just snatched it. If they wanted it back, they could ask like a grown-up. Otherwise, it was "Fuck off. Come back tomorrow."

They knew the rules. Hats screwed with ID on camera, and ID meant accountability. No faces, no consequences. Not on my watch.

I sipped my coffee. Watched them move.

It was early, but the game had already started.

CHAPTER 11: A DELICATE BALANCE

By mid-morning, the Unit had settled into its usual rhythm—part tension, part routine. Bowden and I stood at the desk, sipping lukewarm coffee and watching the Unit breathe. He tapped the corner of a list he'd been holding, his eyes tracking Osbourne's name.

"Jacob," he said, tone cautious. "You thinking of giving Osbourne a single cell? He's been at the top of the list for a while."

I slid the list in front of me, scanning it slowly, more for show than necessity. "What do *you* think?"

Bowden let out a reluctant sigh. "I know he's a pain in the arse, but…"

I cut him off.

I arched an eyebrow. "He hit you up yesterday, didn't he? After I turned him down."

He gave a slight nod. "Sort of. Just said he's done with doubles."

I leaned back, my chair giving a low groan. "Fine. Call him up. Tell him he can have Cell 9."

Bowden blinked, surprised. "Seriously?"

I didn't answer right away. Just returned to flipping through my newspaper like it was a Sunday morning at a café. I listened as Bowden gave Osbourne the news. No thanks, no emotion—just a grunt and a shuffle toward the stairs.

Once he was out of earshot, I leaned in. "It's not about giving him a single. It's about not risking another prisoner in a cell with Osbourne."

Bowden frowned. "You think he'd go that far?"

"I know he would," I said flatly. "Osbourne doesn't want privacy. He wants control. Guys like him… they don't rape for sex. They do it for power. It's violence, plain and simple. A statement. If he can dominate someone, he owns them—and everyone else watches and learns who *not* to cross."

Bowden shook his head. "And we just give him what he wants?"

"On the surface? Yeah, but we'll see." I replied cryptically.

Bowden didn't push it further. He knew when I was playing a longer game.

The rest of the morning passed in a blur of movement and paperwork. I juggled transfers, updated bed allocations, and fielded a call about six new prisoners scheduled to arrive later that afternoon. Bowden dealt with a dozen interruptions—medical escorts, visits, and prisoners angling for last-minute favours.

But Osbourne lingered. He was like a bad smell—strutting around the Unit with that smug grin, chest puffed out like a prize rooster. Acting untouchable. Acting *seen*.

I hated him.

Not just because of what he did, but because of how he did it. Calculated. Cold. He didn't lose control—he *used* it.

I'd seen the aftermath of what he did to young blokes. The silence. The look in his eyes. That was power. Not the kind you earn—the kind you take.

I pulled his file from the cabinet, flipping through the pages. He had a court appearance in three months—enough of a buffer to avoid any transfers in the meantime. Typical. He'd played Management like a fiddle, claiming he had enemies at the Remand Prison to avoid relocation. It was bullshit. Manufactured paranoia. Just another way to keep hold of his little empire here.

Once he was sentenced, he'd go to Yarra Prison, where his gang associates ran deep. That was the plan. Stay here until then. Build his network. Intimidate, threaten, increase drug activity. Manipulate staff and prisoners. Create a web of loyalty and fear thick enough to follow him to the next prison.

Even the billets—hard-working prisoners we usually relied on—kept their heads down around him. They hated that he threw his weight around, but no one was stepping up to challenge him, at least not in front of other prisoners. Not in here. Not while Osbourne still had the backing of names that carried real consequences.

He never bragged. That was the thing. Just dropped hints. A name here. A smirk there. Let the fear do the rest. He didn't *have* to prove anything—he just had to maintain the illusion that he could.

But I'd been watching. Recording every interaction, every whisper, every time he encountered someone vulnerable. I wasn't building a case. I was building leverage.

And when the time came, I'd bury him with it.

Bowden walked past and glanced toward Osbourne, now lounging near the microwave like he owned the place.

"You'll deal with him soon, yeah?" he asked.

I took a sip of coffee. "Soon," I said, eyes still fixed on Osbourne. "I just need the right opening."

What I didn't say was: I was already building it. Piece by piece. Making sure when he fell, he wouldn't get back up. Not here. Not anywhere."

He nodded, satisfied—for now.

Because in here, power didn't come from yelling or throwing punches.

It came from waiting. Watching. Knowing when to strike.

And I was almost there.

CHAPTER 12: THE FRAGILE ONES

The billets knew how to walk the line. They were careful around Osbourne—challenging him just enough to hold their ground, never in the Unit. Behind a cell door. It was like watching men work a live fuse, trying to keep the system running without blowing up the Unit.

The air was thick. Like the moment before a storm hits.

Around mid-morning, Collins approached the desk.

He didn't walk. He *drifted*. Eyes down, shoulders rounded, like he was trying to shrink into the background. I knew the type. Nervous energy, twitchy hands, that hollowed out look in his eyes. The look of someone who realised too late that he didn't belong here.

I gestured to the couch. "What's on your mind?"

He sat down, perching on the edge like the fabric might bite. There was ink still fresh on his wrist—remnants of hospital bands. The kind you didn't ask about.

"Mr. Daniels… I was wondering if I could get a single cell?"

His voice barely rose above a whisper. Young. Barely shaving. Face unmarked, like he hadn't been here long enough to collect the scars that came standard issue in prison.

"We'll put your name on the list," I said, keeping my tone flat. "But it's not first come, first served. If I think someone else needs one more than you, they'll get it. That's how it works."

His eyes darted across the room, tracking every twitch, every whisper. He was watching the other prisoners—watching them watch us. Fear held to him like sweat.

I rolled my chair forward, lowered my voice. "You're in here because you fucked up. That's the truth. You want to avoid coming back? Start making better decisions."

Then, louder, for everyone else's benefit: "Alright, that's enough. Go away."

He stood, gave a tight nod, and slipped away. Just another prisoner. Just another number.

But I kept my eye on Collins.

He was the sort of prisoner who didn't need a cellmate to make his life hell. The pressure would come in other ways—guys leaning on him to get family to mule in drugs, testing him to see if he'd break. If he cracked, he'd find himself asking for razor blades just to get transferred. Or worse—he wouldn't ask at all.

Remand prisons were notorious for suicides. You walk in thinking it's a few days in holding, and then the charges hit. The reality sets in. You're not going anywhere for a long time. And that's when the darkness starts whispering.

I'd told Bowden once, when he was hesitant about a young kid: *Don't feel sorry for them. They weren't crying when they were doing the crime. They cry when they get caught. That's not remorse. That's panic.*

Still, I watched over the fragile ones. You had to.

That morning, Bowden was elbow-deep in paperwork. Normally, he'd do the cell inspections. This time, I volunteered. Told him to keep at it— I'd Walk the Unit.

Truth was, I wanted eyes on Osbourne.

I grabbed the busted broomstick from behind the filing cabinet. No head, just the handle. Perfect for poking around without touching anything. I started with the billets.

Then I saw it—Osbourne's cell.

He wasn't alone.

Some poor bastard was on hands and knees scrubbing the toilet like it owed him money. Osbourne sat at the desk sipping instant coffee like a king. When he saw me, he grinned. Big, crooked teeth. A leer that said, *look what I can do. Look what I own.*

I didn't stop. Just moved on. But I filed that moment away. Another prisoner being dominated by Osbourne.

Upstairs, I hit the other cells.

"Dust in the vents," I barked at one guy. "You're breathing that shit in every night. Get up there and clean it."

Tone mattered. You couldn't be too friendly. Not in front of the others. You had to be the parent who never smiled unless it hurt.

I used the broomstick to tap window frames, rattle vents, make sure nothing was tampered with. The smell in some of those cells could knock you sideways—sweat, piss, mildew. I flagged down the laundry billet and told him to remind the guys about hygiene.

Not for their sake.

For everyone else's.

No one wanted to bunk next to a guy who reeked. And prison justice had a way of resolving those issues—with fists and boots.

I checked sheets and blankets. If they weren't folded right, I dumped them in a heap. Let them come back to a mess. They'd whinge, sure. But I had a line ready.

"You like burglary so much? Now you know how your victims felt."

It shut them up. Every time.

That was the thing most prisoners couldn't stomach—having their own crimes reflected at them. They could handle the sentence. The food. The noise. But being reminded of the damage they'd caused? That hit somewhere deeper.

They'd glare. But they'd clean. Because they knew: argue with me, and it only gets worse.

CHAPTER 13: TENSION RISING

Back at the desk, I dropped the broomstick into its usual resting place behind the filing cabinet and flicked the kettle on. Bowden looked unsettled. Still chewing on the fact that Osbourne had landed himself a single cell. His silence said more than any protest would've.

I handed him a coffee and gave his shoulder a firm pat. "Don't worry about Osbourne," I said. "His time will come."

I settled onto the couch, letting the cushions take some of the weight off my back, just as Security Senior Mark Hawkins strolled into the Unit.

He scanned the space like he always did—eyes landing on prisoners, checking their positions, their movements, their faces. Calculating. Assessing. Then he locked in on me and headed over, cutting across the floor like he owned it.

Mark Hawkins and I went back years. Not friends in the beer-and-banter sense, but allies. We understood each other—how to handle pressure, when to show force, when to let silence do the talking. He was leaner than me—probably from constantly being on the move—but no less dangerous. Metro was all he'd ever known. He bled routine and ran tighter than the security logs.

He gave Bowden a quick backslap before turning to me. "How's the circus?"

I gave a tired smile. "Spinning. Osbourne's flapping his feathers. Got a single cell, so we're keeping tabs."

Hawkins wiped sweat from his forehead with the back of his hand. "It's a bloody zoo out there. Had ten piss tests before lunch. And a management prisoner tried staging a fucking protest in his cell. Refused to come out unless we gave him a PlayStation." He chuckled. "I figured I'd grab a coffee before Reception turns into a flood zone."

Bowden started moving toward the kitchenette to make him one, but Hawkins waved him off and grabbed a paper cup himself. "I've got it, mate."

As the water hissed into his cup, he glanced back over his shoulder. "So… Osbourne. Any trouble?"

I kept my voice flat. "He's quiet. Too quiet."

Hawkins grinned. Not the friendly kind. The sort of grin that came with clenched fists and old scores. "Well, if he kicks off, let me know. I'd love to punch the fuck out of him while he's 'resisting'."

We both laughed—loud enough to carry, subtle enough to keep them guessing. A few prisoners turned their heads; ears tilted toward us like dogs hearing a whistle. Let them wonder.

We talked a bit longer. Nothing heavy. Updates. Unit gossip. Which prisoner was likely to crack. Who'd thrown a tantrum over toast. The usual.

Then the radio on Hawkins' belt crackled to life. Reception needed him. Didn't sound urgent, but he gave a quick nod and vanished with the ease of a man who lived in motion.

The Unit fell quiet again.

I watched over the yard through the reinforced window. Count time was closing in, and the space outside filled like clockwork. Some of the blokes were barely out of high school, still with acne on their chins. Others looked like grandfathers—wrinkled, weary, defeated. Crime didn't discriminate. It welcomed everyone with open arms and cold steel.

My mind circled back to Osbourne.

That smug, calculated arsehole had stirred the pot just enough to set the Unit off balance. The atmosphere felt different now. Brittle. Like the air itself had turned sharp at the edges. One shove, one wrong word, and the whole thing could tip.

Someone would push back. It was only a matter of time. And when it happened, I didn't know if I could stop it.

I leaned forward, elbows on knees, dragging my hand slowly down my face like I was trying to scrape off the tension. It didn't help.

This wasn't sustainable. Not with Osbourne walking around like he owned the place. Not with vulnerable kids like Collins eyeing the floor every time he passed.

Collins flinched when Osbourne passed him in the kitchen this morning—like a dog expecting the boot. I noticed. So, did Osbourne.

I wondered if I'd waited too long already. If someone like Collins would be the price for my patience.

I just needed the right opening.

Osbourne was going to go.

One way or another.

CHAPTER 14: INTRUDERS AND BLOODSHED

By mid-afternoon, the Unit had settled into a deceptive calm. Most of the prisoners loitered in the yard, eyes peeled for fresh meat. Nothing stirred them quite like the arrival of new prisoners—they watched over, judged, and weighed them with the cold calculus of predators sizing up prey.

I'd cleared the bulk of the morning's paperwork, and Bowden was off near the kitchen, chatting with the billets about a stores order that would no doubt arrive short-staffed and over-inventoried. My desk was mostly cleared—just a single prisoner file left open, enough to look convincingly busy if an operations manager wandered through.

But beneath that surface calm, Osbourne still lurked in my thoughts like a bad smell under the floorboards.

I stood and grabbed a roll of paper towels, and the spray bottle stashed beneath the desk. The billets were supposed to clean the area, but I didn't trust them around my files. Or anything that wasn't nailed down. Give them five minutes and half the desk would vanish.

I wiped down the desktop with focused precision. Cleaning helped me think. Helped me control the chaos, even if just in this one small corner of the world.

That's when I noticed it—too many prisoners clustered near the front of the Unit. A few lounged on the old garden bed, others blocked the window. The hair on my arms stood up. They weren't loitering. They were waiting.

Then the door exploded open.

Three Sudanese prisoners barrelled in, fast and wild-eyed. The Unit shifted instantly. The men in the dayroom backed away, forming a hesitant ring, unsure of what was coming next.

I moved. Quick down the stairs, boots slapping vinyl.

That's when I saw it—blood. The middle guy was holding his thigh, both hands clamped over the wound. Blood between his fingers, starting to soak his jeans. The other two flanked him, half-supporting, half-dragging him into the dayroom like they were walking wounded from a war zone.

"What the hell happened?" I barked.

The tallest one, dreadlocks tight to his scalp, stepped forward. His voice was thick with accent but drenched in urgency.

"Boss, someone cut him. Outside. We weren't looking for trouble."

I snapped my fingers at a nearby billet. "Towel. Now."

The injured one—tried to sit at a table, but I stopped him with a raised hand. "No one sits. Not yet."

The towel came fast. I handed it over. "Press on it. Hard." He did. Jaw clenched, knuckles white.

I herded them up the stairs to the officers' post, sat them on the couch under my direct line of sight, then grabbed the radio from my belt. My voice was clipped, tight.

"Security Supervisor and Security Senior to Unit B. MSO can you attend Unit B. Over?"

I pulled my chair close, sat directly across from the three. They were scared. Even the tall one who'd done all the talking had a tremble in his jaw. The third was damn near vibrating—eyes darting like a cornered animal.

"What's your name?" I asked, voice low but firm.

"Achebe," said the tall one.

I nodded toward the injured man. "And him?"

"Badawi."

I jotted both names down on the notepad I always kept inside my shirt pocket.

"Tell me exactly what happened."

Achebe swallowed hard. "We were just sitting there. Minding our own business. Couple of guys walked past, and one of them just... cut him. No words. Just swung his arm and kept walking."

Badawi sat hunched, towel clutched tight. His face was twisted in agony, sweat pouring down his forehead.

The third guy looked like he might shit himself.

Outside, I could see the prisoners crowding again. Faces pressed to the glass. Nothing attracted attention like blood.

I stood abruptly to address prisoners in the Unit and pointed. "Get the fuck outta here, now!"

They slowly scattered.

Back to Achebe. "You sure you didn't provoke it?"

"No, I swear," he said, shaking his head furiously. "We didn't even look at them."

That's when MSO Baker arrived with a nurse and a medical bag. I pushed my chair back, cleared space. Bowden grabbed gloves and started putting them on.

I kept my eyes on the others while the nurse dropped to her knees beside Badawi. Latex snapped, antiseptic stung, and low murmurs passed between them.

I leaned toward Achebe again. "Who did it?"

His face tightened with frustration. "We don't fucking know. You've got fucking cameras. Look at them. You'll see."

I could hear the panic rising in his voice. He was angry—but underneath, a real fear. The kind that came from knowing that the rules of the yard didn't apply when someone decided you were prey.

"Listen," I said, voice steel now. "I don't give a fuck where you're from or what you've done. But if you come into my Unit and start screaming at staff like an arsehole, I'll treat you like an arsehole. You understand me?"

Achebe glared. Then nodded. Slow and bitter.

"Good," I said, standing tall. "Now shut up and sit still."

I turned to Bowden, "Lock down the Unit. Everyone outside."

The Unit had slipped into chaos for just a moment—but that's all it ever needed.

And deep down, I knew this wasn't the end of it.

This was just the start of the blood trail.

I'd seen this play out before—blood spilt over a look, a rumour, a name misspoken in the wrong tone. But this? This felt more deliberate. Calculated. Like someone out there was marking territory. And inside this place, blood wasn't just violence. It was language. A way of saying: *This is mine now.*

CHAPTER 15: MISTAKEN IDENTITY

Hawkins stormed into the Unit like a man on a mission, flanked by two security officers who looked just as wired. Without missing a beat, he started issuing orders. One officer peeled off to assist Bowden: the other swept upstairs to clear out any stragglers. Hawkins nodded toward the far side of the dayroom.

"Let's talk," he said, low and clipped.

The nurse was still tending to Badawi's thigh, now crusted with blood and tension. I descended the stairs to speak with Hawkins, watched over by prying eyes pressed against the reinforced glass.

"What the hell happened?" he asked, eyes scanning the room even as his voice dropped. Concern lurked beneath his usual steel.

I took a breath, exhaled slowly. "From what I've gathered, these three were sitting outside when someone walked past and sliced one of them— clean across the thigh. Shiv or blade couldn't say. It's not deep, but it'll need a few stitches."

He frowned. "Random attack?"

I shrugged. "That's what they're claiming. Just sitting there, minding their business. Personally, I think that's bullshit."

We turned to watch the three prisoners on the couch. They were jumpy. Achebe's leg bounced restlessly. Badawi's face was pale, sweat plastering his dreadlocks to his forehead. The third looked like he wanted to be anywhere else but here.

"Got names?" Hawkins asked.

I tore a page from my notepad and handed it over. "Achebe. Badawi. The other one didn't speak."

Hawkins took the paper and ducked into the Unit office to make a call. I sat at the edge of a table, eyes on the prisoners in the yard. They were watching, as always. The scent of blood drew them in like sharks.

Hawkins returned, voice low. "Intel flagged them this morning. Apparently, they were preparing an Alert. Some of the prisoners thought these three matched CCTV footage from a gang assault in a train station tunnel last week. Vicious attack. Last night's news all over it."

I raised a brow. "But?"

"But they were wrong. Dead wrong. Not the same guys. It's a case of mistaken identity."

I snorted. "Doesn't matter in here. Truth doesn't matter when someone sees an opportunity to score street cred. Someone out there wanted a trophy. And now they've got blood on the board."

We walked back toward the injured trio. MSO Baker was still with Badawi, assisting the nurse. The cut wasn't life-threatening, but the message behind it was loud and clear. You're marked.

"How's it looking?" I asked.

Baker didn't look up. "Clean cut, a couple stitches. Lucky it wasn't deeper. We'll take him upstairs. Doc's still around."

A rookie officer behind me muttered, "Should've called a Code Black."

I turned; eyebrows raised. "For what? A small cut? Code Black's for death or serious injury. You want us calling codes every time someone sneezes? You'd be chasing your arse all day."

Hawkins smirked behind me. He would've said the same thing.

I signalled to Bowden. "Grab a Haz Waste bag for that towel."

Hawkins directed one of his men to escort the nurse and MSO to Medical. "Take the top-tier route. Use the lift near my office. Avoid the main floor. Last thing we need is for things to escalate."

I nodded. "Bowden—radio Unit A. Let them know we're coming through with a prisoner and staff."

They moved quickly, leading Badawi up the stairs and out, with as much dignity as the situation allowed. The towel was placed into the Haz Waste Bag, folded tight like a wet bandage of secrets.

Two more security officers entered the Unit as they left. Hawkins stayed behind while I addressed the two remaining prisoners on the couch.

"You're going back to your Unit," I said flatly. "You'll be locked down until further notice. For your own protection."

Achebe's eyes flashed. "But we didn't do anything!"

I stepped closer, jaw tight. "I don't give a fuck what you did or didn't do. You walk into that yard now, someone's going to finish what the last guy started. And I'm not risking staff because you think it's unfair."

I signalled to the guards. "Let's go."

The prisoners stood and followed, heads low, shoulders tense. As they crossed the yard, the crowd erupted—taunts, slurs, animal sounds. It was a show now. The predators had scented weakness and wouldn't let it go.

Through the chaos, Supervisor Hunter pushed through the crowd and into the Unit. I gave him the rundown—clean, sharp, no sugarcoating. Just the facts and the tension buzzing behind them.

Hunter nodded grimly. "I'll head over there myself. Make sure they're locked down properly. I'll need a report from you before shift's end."

"Yeah, I figured."

Then he was gone, striding into the madness like a man walking into a storm, knowing damn well he couldn't stop the rain—only contain the flood.

And me? I went to the office.

And started typing the report.

I didn't need to type it. I could've dictated the whole thing from memory—each movement, each mistake, each fucking drop of blood.

But typed reports made it official. Sanitised. Like we could turn trauma into bullet points and close the file.

CHAPTER 16: LOCKDOWN UNLEASHED

The yard had turned into a seething, stirring thing. Whispering with a hundred mouths and no conscience. The sky overhead was darkening, but the real storm was still inside.

Each prisoner passed along the tale of the stabbing, shaping it like wet clay—exaggerating, distorting, injecting venom until the original truth was just a shadow, flickering behind a wall of rumour and paranoia. By the time it reached the second tier, the attacker had a machete, and the victim had lost a leg.

You could feel it in the air, thick and electric, like the charge before lightning hits.

All it would take was a wrong look. A misstep. One bump of the shoulder and half the yard would go up like dry grass.

I finished my report just as the PA system cracked to life—two monotone words that meant everything and nothing: "Commence Lockup."

Security reinforcements poured into the yard, dispersing into Units. No smiles. No banter. Every step tight, eyes scanning, nerves wound to snapping point. Upstairs, Bowden and another officer began locking down the top tier. A third stood sentinel on the landing, arms folded, daring anyone to try a last-minute dash downstairs. Anyone caught trying would be out of luck—and out of patience from us.

I moved with purpose through the billets' cells. No extra time. No favours tonight.

"Want me to bin your paper, Boss?" Johnno offered with that tired smirk.

"Not tonight," I snapped, shutting his door before he could draw breath to follow up. I wasn't in the mood for conversation. I was in the mood for locked doors and silence.

And soon, we had it.

The crash of metal doors slammed shut across the Unit like dominoes—one after the other—until silence. No voices. No laughter. Just stillness, thick and brittle.

It was like a war zone after the air raid—the eerie calm that follows screaming. The tension didn't vanish; it just shifted, buried itself under the surface like an unexploded mine.

The Sudanese prisoners would be gone in the morning. Quietly transferred out, one more incident wrapped up in the usual bureaucratic packaging. A fresh start for them. A cold reset for us. We'd survived the day, and nobody had been sent to hospital. A technical win.

Lock-up complete, Bowden and I moved to Unit A to assist with the final checks. My limbs ached with fatigue. The adrenaline had burned out hours ago, leaving only the weight of everything that had almost happened.

Each step toward Hunter's office felt heavier than the last. My report—gripped tight in my hand.

Inside the locker room, the hum of post-incident chatter filled the space like background static. Officers threw around half-baked retellings of the stabbing, some claiming to have heard early radio chatter, others adding dramatic colour to their versions. Bowden was deep into storytelling mode, animated and gesturing wildly. His version made it sound like a scene from a prison riot movie.

I didn't correct anyone. Let them have their narratives. I'd lived the real thing. That was enough.

I kept my head down, changed quickly, and made for the door. I knew the same scenes were playing out in the women's locker room. Same questions. Same whispers. Everyone wanted the same thing: to make sense of the chaos.

Outside, the cold smacked me clean across the face. The same air as inside, but it felt different now, unfiltered. No walls. No steel. No keys. Just streetlights, shadows, and the wind.

A few others spilled out behind me, forming little knots on the pavement—laughing too loudly, checking their phones, killing time until the next train. The false normality of it all made me feel even more detached.

I drifted a few steps away, grateful for the isolation.

Then, like a ghost materialising out of the gloom, Senior Officer Walsh appeared. Walsh—the hardliner. Ran Unit D like a boot camp. Older than me. Colder too.

"You better have a word with Osbourne tomorrow," he barked. "Tell him to stay the fuck out of my Unit."

His voice was flat. No invitation for discussion. He wasn't asking—he was warning.

I gave him a nod. "Yeah, no problem."

Wasn't the time to argue. Walsh didn't care about nuance. He saw a problem. He wanted it gone. Couldn't blame him. I felt the same way most days.

Still, it took everything in me not to tell him to piss off. But what would've been the point?

I watched him walk away.

Then I looked up at the sky—blank and brooding. Storm clouds churned like ink in water, swallowing what little light remained.

The prison was locked up tight.

But the storm?

That was still coming.

CHAPTER 17: A MOMENT OF RESPITE

The train ride home was my decompression chamber—metal walls, worn seats, and a rhythm that numbed the edges of the day. I slumped into the corner seat, slapped on my headphones, and let the music bleed out the noise. Not just the hum of the train—but the prison, the blood, the lies, the twisted power plays. Gone. For now.

Eyes closed, I let the momentum lull me. Each stop a faint buzz in the back of my mind. The overhead sign blinked station names, but I didn't look. Tonight, the faces around me didn't matter. I wasn't in the mood to share a smile or nod with strangers. I didn't want the world. I wanted silence. I wanted home.

When the train finally screeched into my stop, I peeled off the headphones, shoved them into my bag, and joined the quiet herd spilling out into the night. Down the ramp, into the streets. Homes lit soft yellow behind drawn curtains. The smell of garlic and something baking drifted on the wind. Comfort food. Comfort lives.

I walked alone, as always. I'd grown used to the solitary silhouette I cast under the streetlights. But tonight, it felt heavier.

The image of Osbourne. I couldn't shake the grin. Or the blood. Both stuck with me the whole walk home. But up ahead, the soft porch light of home waited—like a lighthouse through fog.

Key in the lock. Door open. And then—Dougal.

He launched himself at me with a bark that shook the hallway. Tail wagging like a malfunctioning metronome. His energy hit me like a shot of adrenaline. Dogs know. He could smell the prison on me. The tension. The ghosts.

"Yeah, alright, mate," I muttered, bending to ruffle his fur. "Miss me, huh?"

I peeled off the uniform and folded it with the same methodical habit that had become second nature. That act alone—packing away the prison—always felt like stepping out of armour. Dougal jumped onto the bed, watching every move. His eyes said it all: *You're safe now.*

I sat down beside him, giving him a proper pat. Not the rushed kind from the morning. This was slower. Honest. Needed.

His ears perked up again, and before I could ask why, I heard Emma's keys jingle at the front door.

She stepped inside, makeup slightly faded, a tired smile that still worked its magic. Her bag hit the table. "Long day?" she asked.

"You could say that" I muttered.

She looked at me, really looked, then nodded. "I'll get dinner tonight."

But before she moved, she said, "Let's take him for a walk. He's been waiting. Might do you both some good."

I hesitated. Not because I didn't want to—but because I wasn't sure I had the energy. Still, I found myself saying, "Yeah. Alright. Just need a jacket."

As I ducked into the bedroom, Dougal followed like a shadow, only turning back when Emma called him into the lounge. She was right—the backyard wasn't enough. He needed to run. I needed air.

I threw on my jacket, zipped it halfway. The wind had picked up. Emma stood at the door now, a scarf loose around her neck, that same tired but knowing look in her eyes.

She didn't say anything—didn't need to. There was something she wanted to tell me. I could see it brimming behind her lips. But she held it, letting the moment breathe.

But she had that cheeky look in her eyes, which always made me wonder.

Dougal's paws clicked across the timber floor as he bolted for the door, barking with a joy that was unapologetic.

I clipped on the lead, and just like that, the three of us slipped into the darkened streets, where the silence didn't judge, and the shadows asked nothing.

CHAPTER 18: THE BURDENED MIND

The footpath stretched ahead of us in silence, slick with the faint sheen of late-evening dew. A few streetlights flickered indecisively, casting uneven shadows across the footpath. Emma's voice cut through the quiet—light, excited, untethered by the weight pressing on my shoulders.

"Guess where we're going Friday night?" she blurted, barely containing her grin.

I blinked. My brain, still locked in the prison's gears, struggled to downshift. "Umm?" was all I managed.

Emma bounced a little with the reveal. "An '80s tribute band at the pub—dinner and the show. Booked it earlier."

She was expecting a grin. Maybe even a kiss. I gave her a tired smile instead.

"Sounds great," I said, doing a terrible job of faking energy.

She tilted her head, reading me too easily. "You, okay? You've been off all evening."

"Long day," I muttered. "Just a lot going on upstairs."

You can't explain prison to someone who's never tasted its air. It's like trying to describe drowning to someone who's never seen the ocean. There's only so much you can say without dragging them under with you. And there are things—dark, rotting things—you don't speak aloud.

We turned into the park, Dougal trotting ahead on the lead, tail up, alert. I unclipped him, pulled a ball from my jacket pocket, and let it fly. Dougal shot off like a missile, the grass slick beneath his paws.

That dog had a sixth sense for timing. Emma reached for my hand as we watched him vanish into the shadows and reappear with the ball like some furry magician.

Under the orange glow of a single streetlight, she squeezed my hand a little tighter. No words, just the sort of look that said *I'm here*, even if she didn't know what *here* meant.

For a few minutes, the weight in my chest lifted. Out here, I wasn't Senior Officer Daniels. I wasn't balancing psychopaths and paperwork, politics and predators. I was just Jacob. Husband. Dog dad. Civilian.

"Dougal!" I called out as he edged too close to the dark. He reemerged; the ball clenched tight. He dropped it near my feet, took a few paces back, ready for another round.

We played until the air turned colder, and Dougal's panting slowed. Then we walked home, hand in hand, slipping into the sort of quiet only couples who really *know* each other can manage.

Back inside, Dougal beelined for the water bowl while I helped Emma with her coat. The fridge door opened with a soft hiss—cold air on my face, momentarily washing away the day. My eyes landed on the magnet-hung tickets. *Friday night. Music. Normalcy.* Maybe even joy.

I nodded to myself. "Friday night, looking forward to it," I said.

Dinner was simple, warm, real. Dougal took up position like a landmine between us, waiting for a dropped scrap that never came. We talked about her day. Laughed about something mundane. Pretended, just for a while, that the outside world stayed outside.

Later, we cleaned up together, then migrated to the couch. TV on. Lights low. Dougal wedged himself in, nose nudging my hand. I scratched behind his ears, letting the rhythm settle my nerves.

The news rolled in like a punch. Another drug-fuelled rampage. A stolen car. A house fire. A family shattered. The warning on the screen was pointless. I'd seen worse. Smelled it. Stepped over it in steel-capped boots.

Emma winced at the images. I didn't flinch.

These people… these stories… some of them were coming to me. Tomorrow. Or next week. Or the week after. The system's rinse cycle never stopped.

Emma kissed me goodnight and disappeared into the bedroom. I stayed on the couch, channel surfing with no real interest. Just white noise to push back the memories.

But they came anyway.

Osbourne.

A name that had burned into my consciousness like acid. A predator in plain sight, playing the game like, he owned the board. And everyone on it.

Yeah, he'd be moved eventually—after court, after sentencing, after all the boxes were ticked. But I couldn't wait. Not when the threat was that real. That dangerous.

He had to go.

And I knew exactly how to make that happen.

CHAPTER 19: SHADOWS OF THE MORNING

The bathroom mirror didn't lie.

Grey streaks threaded through my hair, like cracks in concrete. The lines under my eyes were deeper than yesterday—etched there by years of noise, pressure, and watching my back. The mirror wasn't showing age. It was showing erosion. Piece by piece, prison life was wearing me down.

I threw on my jacket and eased open the front door, careful not to wake Emma. The world outside was drowned in fog, the kind that swallowed light and blurred reality. A chill hung in the air—one that bit through fabric and into bone. I crouched beside Dougal, whispering a quiet goodbye and rubbing behind his ears. He nuzzled me once, then padded back to bed, unconcerned by the ghosts that haunted my mornings.

The street was deserted. Just me, the fog, and the low hum of lights throwing warped glows onto the pavement. I walked toward the train station like a ghost on autopilot.

In the carriage, I buried myself in music. Noise to drown the silence. Eyes half-lidded, I observed the other commuters. Tradies. Office drones. A kid with too many piercings. Some were easy to read. Others made me twitch.

It's a habit now—profiling people. A reflex. Like checking exits in a restaurant or standing with my back to a wall. Working in prison rewires your instincts. Trust becomes a relic. Suspicion is your new oxygen.

My thoughts drifted—inevitably—to Osbourne.

There was already heat between him and the billets. Johnno wasn't a pushover, but Osbourne was calculated, patient. The sort of guy who'd gut you with a smile and call it foreplay. And Johnno? He was standing in the wrong shadow. Johnno wouldn't see it coming, not from Osbourne. From other prisoners doing Osbourne's bidding, then Osbourne would step in for the final blow.

Osbourne held grudges the way others held religion—close to the chest, eternal, and always ready to be weaponised.

By the time I stepped into the prison yard, the wind had picked up. Brutal. Unseasonal. The kind that cut sideways through your clothes and reminded you just how exposed you really were in this fortress of steel and glass.

Inside the Unit, Bowden and I slipped into routine like old cogs in a grinding machine. I called in the trap count while Bowden swept the dayroom for contraband.

Five prisoners were set for transfer that morning. Their cells would be filled again before sunset—just the way the machine liked it. Whatever I'd been nursing would have to wait. I had movement lists to adjust, meal tallies to update, and enough bureaucratic detours to keep me spinning until midday.

Still… coffee first.

I made two cups. Bowden returned from his rounds, sweat on his brow and that rookie-hunger for approval still flickering behind his eyes. He looked at the steaming mug like it was gold.

"Cheers, Jacob," he said, almost surprised.

Most seniors didn't bother with small gestures. But I knew the currency of trust. Bowden had potential. More importantly, he listened. I gave him just enough rope to learn the job—and not hang himself.

"Good job," I offered, keeping it casual.

He beamed like a teenager who just got handed the car keys. That was enough for now.

I leafed through the day's newspaper while the P.A. crackled to life, announcing the trap count. Bowden abandoned his mug, descending the stairs to let the billets out. The Unit shifted. Slow. Restless. Like trouble wasn't far off.

Mid-morning. The chaos dipped just enough to breathe. A lull before the next punch.

It was time.

"Hey, grab Johnno and get him to vacuum around the desk," I said, pointing to the scuffed carpet beneath my feet. "And keep an eye on the yard while you're there—just in case I miss any codes."

Bowden nodded and disappeared.

Minutes later, Johnno rolled up with the vacuum cleaner like it was one more job. Which, for him, it was. Most seniors hated having billets near the desk—paranoid about files going missing or prisoners overhearing something they shouldn't. But I saw it differently.

Letting prisoners handle the mundane meant I could focus on the real threats. And besides—if we're busy cleaning, no one's watching the wolves.

Today, the desk wasn't the real cleaning job.

The real target was Osbourne.

And the stage was finally set.

CHAPTER 20: THE CALCULATED MANOEUVRE

I stood near the filing cabinet, arms crossed, watching Johnno crawl beneath the desk to plug in the vacuum. The machine came to life with a guttural roar, drowning out everything but my own thoughts—and just enough of them.

Perfect cover.

I stepped over to the desk and picked up the phone. Didn't need to dial. Just raised it and started talking—loud enough for Johnno to hear over the hum of the vacuum. Loud enough to bury the hook deep.

"Yeah... prisoner had a note dropped on him," I said, my tone urgent, measured. "Management had no choice. Moved him out of the Unit. Transferred to another prison for his safety."

The bait dangled in the air, and I didn't need to see Johnno's face to know he was listening. The slight pause in his vacuuming said it all. I kept going, laying it on just thick enough.

"Who found the note? Staff pulling the mail from the Unit box," I added, injecting just the right amount of disbelief. "Yeah, I bet the billets were relieved. Probably glad to see the back of him."

I glanced around. No other prisoners in earshot. The rest were still milling in the yard or sprawled out in the dayroom, half-asleep or half-scheming.

I finished the fake call and hung up with a clack.

Johnno killed the vacuum and crawled out from under the desk. I gave him a nod. "Good job—appreciate it."

He didn't say anything, just coiled the extension lead like he had somewhere more important to be. Which, judging by the twitch in his movements and the way he descended the stairs, he did.

I watched as he dropped the vacuum at the bottom landing, then whistled for the other billets. Four of them peeled off from their corners and followed him into his cell.

I didn't move. Didn't interfere. I'd already done my part. The rest would play out on its own.

Twenty minutes passed. Slowly. Deliberately. One by one, the billets re-emerged. Loitering by their cells. Wiping benches. Checking the dayroom. All of them keeping an eye on the other prisoners. Calculating who was watching—and who wasn't.

Then, like actors hitting their marks, it began.

The first billet made his way to the mailbox and dropped something inside. Casual. No hurry. Just another envelope. Then another followed. Then another. Until finally, Johnno strolled over and did the same. I didn't smile. Didn't blink. Just logged the moment and let it pass.

Smooth. Measured. Too clean to be coincidence.

If anyone reviewed the footage later, it'd look like a blur of movement—too many hands, too many shadows. Nothing definitive. Just smoke and suggestion.

Exactly how I wanted it.

It was in motion now. The note had been 'dropped'. Or five of them had. Didn't matter which one stuck—only that it stuck enough to raise a flag. I wouldn't need to push much further. Just lean back and let the system do what it does best: overreact.

I wasn't naive. I knew the ethical line had been erased the moment I picked up that phone and started talking to no one. But in this place, where every prisoner was playing a game, I couldn't afford to keep both hands tied behind my back.

Osbourne was a threat, to everyone. And threats had to be managed—quietly, strategically, and without fingerprints.

In here, prisoners play the game. I just played it back. That was survival.

And this time, survival had a plan. One step closer to making Osbourne someone else's problem.

CHAPTER 21: THE MENACE

Bowden sat at the desk, head down, scribbling out another trip pass. Meanwhile, I leaned against the filing cabinet, arms folded, eyes locked on Osbourne. He lounged in the dayroom like he owned it. Laughing with a couple of prisoners, flashing that smug little smirk of his whenever our eyes met.

He knew I was watching. That was the point.

What Osbourne didn't know—or maybe just didn't care about—was that I'd read more than his file. I'd lived it. The parts that never made it into reports. Whispers traded in locker rooms. Warnings, not rumours.

His rap sheet was long, sure—multiple incarcerations, violent assaults, trafficking. But those were just facts on paper. The reality? He was something else entirely.

Osbourne wasn't just a criminal. He was a predator. A sadist. A parasite with a punch that could shatter bone and a grin that said he liked doing it.

There were no laws in his world—only opportunities. No remorse, no guilt, just an endless hunger to manipulate, exploit, dominate.

He used women as stash-houses, hiding drugs where no warrant would reach. They didn't dare cross him—not unless they wanted to wake up missing teeth, or worse. He didn't beat them out of impulse. It was strategic. A lesson. One that kept him untouchable.

His clientele? Tradesmen and celebrities. The first gave him leverage—debts settled in labour. He once bragged about getting an electrician to install a full CCTV setup in his house. Payment? A couple grand worth of ice, handed out like party favours.

But it was the celebrities he loved. Big money. Bigger egos. Perfect prey.

He'd bait them in with discount bags—then jack up the price once the hook was in. His only condition? Invitations. A-list parties. Red carpet events. He treated them like open bars for new clients. Coke. MDMA. LSD. Whatever they wanted, Osbourne would get it. And he expected access in return.

He wanted the high life. Not the drugs. The attention. The power. He used fame like his fists—fast, dirty, unapologetic.

I'd seen it all. Heard the aftermath. Officers whispering in locker rooms. Prisoners limping after 'accidents'. Osbourne's signature was unmistakable.

He didn't fight to defend himself. He fought to destroy.

He'd fake a handshake, drop a joke, lean in—then slam a fist beneath your ear or smash the back of your skull with a king-hit. If you hit the floor, you didn't get back up without bruises that turned yellow before the pain faded.

He kicked low—kidneys, ribs. Targeted. Calculated. He didn't want you just to hurt. He wanted you broken. Something to remember him by.

Inside these walls, he stirred chaos like a chef with a recipe for destruction. He'd get two prisoners wound up, push them into a fight, then jump the third from behind. He was never just one-on-one. He was never fair. He was efficient.

There was a reason no one stepped to him. Not without backup. And even then, you better hope he didn't see you coming. Or worse—he did.

He had gang ties too. Serious ones. He trafficked for them. Collected debts. Broke bones on command. They kept him protected. In return, he kept them feared.

Even he knew the limits. He talked tough, but he never refused an order. Not from the crew. Disobedience wasn't punished—it was erased. Quietly. Permanently.

No funeral. No goodbye. Just... gone.

The other prisoners knew what he was. They avoided him or flocked to him depending on how desperate they were. Most kept their heads down. A few tried to earn favour. None lasted.

Me? I didn't play those games.

I knew what he was. And I knew what had to happen.

By this time tomorrow, he'd be gone.

Transferred. Dislodged from this Unit like a tumour cut clean. I had no illusions about justice—but I believed in consequence. And it was long overdue.

That smirk? It wouldn't survive the bus ride.

CHAPTER 22: SHADOWS OF CHANGE

The file sat in front of me like a tombstone.

I stared at it. Not reading—just absorbing its weight. A name scrawled across the tab. A neat summary of chaos, wrapped in paper and ink. Every file told the same story in a different dialect—violence, failure, trauma, addiction. Repeat.

These weren't just case notes; they were autopsies of lost lives. Each one a quiet obituary pretending to be procedure.

Unit B had become a holding cell for the worst parts of humanity. The desperate, the broken, the violent. You didn't work here—you endured it. Peace wasn't expected. It was a fragile illusion that shattered the moment someone blinked the wrong way.

Blood on concrete. Screams behind steel. That was our daily rhythm.

But you couldn't completely shut down—not if you wanted to survive it. You had to find slivers of connection where you could. Not because they deserved it. But because it stopped you from becoming what they were.

Sometimes, that connection felt like a nod. A warning. A single word said calmly in the right tone. Other times, it was just listening to a man who hadn't been heard in years. You didn't excuse what they did—but you recognised what they'd become.

I was still staring at the file when the phone rang. Sharp. Shrill. Like it was cutting through the fog in my head.

Bowden answered. He listened, nodded, then looked at me. "You're being relieved. Ops Manager wants to see you."

That was all.

No reason. No tone. Just enough vagueness to set off alarms in my gut.

I stood up slowly, my body heavy with that creeping sense of consequence. The kind that lives in the pit of your stomach in this job. Was this about Osbourne? About the mail? Had someone talked?

Or was it something worse?

I crossed the yard. The wind was biting again. Same as yesterday. Same as always. The fog hadn't lifted. It had just settled into the bones.

Up the stairs. Each step sounded like a sentence being passed.

Tourney's office was a bureaucratic coffin—files stacked like bricks, plaques pretending this place had soul. He didn't look up when I entered. Just gestured at the chair. I sat. Waited.

He finally spoke without fanfare. "Jacob, Senior Officer Jones is going on leave. You're taking his place in Unit A."

That was it. One sentence. One shove into the deep end.

Unit A wasn't like the rest of the prison. It didn't run on routine or fear. It was a psych ward with bars. A place where the air always felt wrong. Where silence didn't mean calm—it meant something was brewing.

I didn't respond straight away. I processed. Assessed. Tried to bury the spike of dread rising in my chest.

"So, when do I start?"

"Tomorrow." He was already looking past me. Back to his mountain of paperwork. "You'll be with Davis until the roster adjusts."

Dismissed.

I nodded, rose, and walked out of that office with a weight pressing on my shoulders. I wasn't afraid of prisoners. But Unit A was different. It wasn't about control. It was about instability. And walking that line between keeping someone alive… or watching them burn.

Crossing the yard back to Unit B, my eyes flicked toward the grey outline of Unit A. The building loomed. Not just physically—but in what it represented. A threshold. A point of no return.

I dropped into my seat at the desk and broke the news to Bowden. He masked the disappointment, but it was there in his posture. We'd become a tight team—steady in the storm. Now we were being split.

He nodded. Gave me the only response that made sense. "You'll smash it."

But even he knew Unit A didn't get "smashed." It just tried to break you slower than the others.

The rest of the day passed like molasses. Conversations, observations, decisions—all filtered through the growing shadow of what tomorrow meant.

Unit A would demand more than just vigilance. It would demand patience. Clarity. Humanity. And a willingness to stare down the abyss every damn day—and not flinch.

It wasn't about rules in there. It was about thresholds.

Mental illness didn't follow a script. Neither did trauma. But both had teeth. And I'd need to keep mine sharp.

Tomorrow, the real test would begin.

CHAPTER 23: THE WHISPERING SHADOWS

Unit A wasn't like the rest of the prison.

It was quieter. But not the sort of quiet that brought peace. It was the sort of quiet that warned you something was wrong—like the air before a lightning strike.

Officers here weren't psychologists. We didn't have degrees in trauma or advanced diplomas in de-escalation. We had instincts. Gut reactions honed by chaos. Raising your voice only made things worse. Shouting fractured the fragile stillness and turned it into something dangerous.

In this place, you spoke low. You moved slow. You watched for the twitch—the flicker behind the eyes that told you someone's meds had stopped working or that the voices in their head were screaming again.

That was the real problem. We weren't always told when the meds wore off. When psych reports were absent. When someone flushed their Seroquel to feel the edge again. We had to figure it out ourselves. Privacy reasons. And if you missed the signs… you paid for it in blood and broken bones.

Unit A was a cocktail of untreated psychosis and trauma—minds scorched by ICE, stripped of reason. The other half was vulnerable prisoners—men who'd been prey all their lives and wore the trauma like a second skin. Mixing them together was like stacking dynamite beside a leaking gas line. And yet, that's what we did. Every day.

I called the Billets to the desk to break the news—I was being transferred to Unit A. Johnno leaned in; his usual cocky smirk slightly faded. "Who's taking your spot here?"

I shook my head. "Not sure yet. But I'll speak up—push for you blokes to stay put."

He nodded. "Appreciate that. Maybe I could follow you over there?"

I chuckled. "I think one headcase per Unit is enough, don't you?"

He smiled but looked away, aware of how it might look if he followed me into a psych Unit. Prisoners didn't forget things like that. Loyalty was admirable—but it could get you branded soft or worse. And Johnno was too smart for that.

Before we could say more, the radio cracked to life—Code Black, Unit 5.

Fucking perfect.

I turned to Bowden. "Go. I'll stay here."

He didn't hesitate. That was something I respected about him—when it counted, he ran into the fire.

I descended the stairs slowly, bracing against the door with my foot. Outside, the yard had ignited; officers heading toward Unit E with urgency in their stride. Prisoners loitering outside the Unit spotted me watching.

"What's wrong, Boss? Too fat and lazy to run to a code?" one called out. Laughter followed—jagged and eager, like hyenas testing the fence.

I didn't blink. Just stared at them until the laughter started to taper off. Then I replied—low, flat, controlled.

"Someone's got to keep an eye on you fucking pricks, just in case I need to put you on the ground, and fucking sit on you till help arrives."

Silence.

I shut the door and walked back to the desk, sliding into my seat without another word.

In this job, it wasn't enough to be in control. You had to look like you *wanted* the fight—and that you'd finish it without flinching. That was how respect worked in here. Not through fear. Not through kindness. Through certainty—the unshakable knowledge that you'd do what needed to be done when the moment came.

I glanced around Unit B, committing it to memory.

Soon, I'd be crossing the threshold into something darker. Something more unpredictable.

Unit A didn't just house the broken—it echoed with their nightmares.

And tomorrow, I'd be walking in.

Not as a guest.

But as a keeper of shadows.

CHAPTER 24: SHADOWS OF THE PAST

Bowden returned to Unit B, winded but charged, like a man still shaking off the scent of blood. His boots hit the stairs with heavy thuds, the kind that said something serious had gone down. I didn't even look up from my paperwork.

"So," I said dryly, "someone get a papercut?"

He dropped into the chair like he'd run a marathon. "Nah. Seizure. Unit 5. Bloke dropped like a stone. Smashed his head on the bed frame— blood everywhere."

There was a flicker of excitement in his voice. That low-grade adrenaline hum. You don't walk into chaos and leave it behind untouched.

I gave a subtle nod. "Officers alright?"

"Yeah. Kept my distance. Let medical handle it."

I glanced at his hands—still trembling slightly. He tried to hide it with his coffee cup, but I saw it. I didn't say anything. No point rattling the cage while the storm was still passing through.

Once the Unit resumed its rhythm, we both leaned into the ritual that made mornings bearable—a hot coffee in hand, a moment's peace before the next fire lit itself. Five new prisoners were due today. On paper, anyway. I'd learned not to trust 'expected arrivals'. Especially when half the blokes turning up were still riding the tail end of an ICE comedown. Reception could be a war zone.

One memory bubbled to the surface—some bloke years ago, wide-eyed and tweaking, took a swing at four officers and a nurse before we managed to secure the cuffs on him. Bit into his own forearm like he could chew his way back to reality. There was always one like that— lurking just beyond the doors.

And speak of the devil…

The sound of boots echoed up the stairs. Prisoners escorted in like livestock. I watched as the last one climb the steps—bald, bulked out under the weight of time. And then the voice hit me. Familiar. Rough around the edges. That same slow, prison drawl.

"Hey, Mr Daniels. How you doin'?"

My face cracked into a grin before I could stop it. "Mark Rogers. Holy shit. What the fuck are you doing here?"

Rogers. Nineteen years since Yarra Prison. We'd shared more stories— and scars—than I could count.

"Just fillin' in some time. Got parole coming. Waiting on a spot in rehab," he said with that easy shrug, like prison was one more roadside motel.

We processed the new arrivals quickly, handed out bed numbers, and showed them their cells. Rogers dropped his gear, then made a beeline back to the desk. Old habits.

I introduced him to Bowden, who looked at Rogers like he was seeing an extinct species up close. In a way, he was. Bald, gut pushing at his shirt, scars stitched across his knuckles like a war medal collection. Age had softened him, but not too much. You could still sense it—the heat under the ash. The kind of guy who could level a room if the mood took him.

"I'll be out soon, Mr Daniels," Rogers said, half-sincere. "Just killin' time till I get that bed in rehab. Probably a couple of weeks."

Then, the old Rogers peeked through.

"So, when do I get my single cell and a Billets job?" he grinned.

I rolled my eyes. "Still the same old Rogers."

He chuckled, and for a moment, it was like nothing had changed. But something had.

Rogers was slowing down. His edges dulling. Time had caught up. The bravado was still there, but the venom had faded. Or maybe been redirected.

"I'm done with all this," he said, quieter now. "Too old to be punchin' on with these young fuckwits. Every one of 'em thinks they gotta prove something by taking a swing at the biggest cunt in the Unit."

His voice dropped—low, raw. This wasn't about prison politics. "Mum's sick. Not long now. I just wanna be there... for whatever time's left."

I nodded. There wasn't anything else to say. I'd seen the wear in his bones. The way he moved like each step had weight.

We had an understanding, him and I. Nothing written, nothing owed. But it meant something in here. I could tell him to fuck off, and he'd grin. Anyone else tried it—they'd be lucky to walk away without a broken jaw. That's what mutual respect felt like behind these walls. A handshake made of barbed wire.

I never bent the rules for him. Not officially. But I'd turn a blind eye to things—if it didn't hurt staff, if it saved me paperwork. Rogers never pushed it. That's why it worked.

Then the radio snapped us back.

"Code Purple, Unit 9."

Both of us froze. Unit 9 was the protection Unit. Housing the worst of the worst—paedophiles, rapists, sex offenders. The ones too cowardly or too hated to mix with general population.

I muttered, "Probably a couple of creeps arguing over whose turn it is to suck the others cock."

Dark humour. It was how we survived in here.

But the mood shifted fast.

"Code Black, Unit 9. Code Black, Unit 9."

That was no argument.

I reached over and turned up the volume. Bowden stared at the speaker, concern tightening around his jaw.

"Hope none of the staff got hurt," he said.

"Yeah," I murmured. "Hope."

Rogers drifted back to his cell, cool as ever. Meanwhile, Bowden and I stayed sharp. Radios on. Eyes up.

Twilight in prison is a dangerous hour. The light dims. Tension rises. Everything feels like it could go sideways in an instant.

Deals were made. Debts settled. Grudges sparked. A dirty look, missing milk, a comment about someone's sister—any of it could explode into fists, or worse.

Even if we locked down early, the routine didn't change. Dinner. Meds. Yard cleared. Cells shut. Always in that order. Officers stationed at the corners, watching for the twitch. The whisper. The first flash of trouble.

In that dusk hour, prison throbbed like a living thing—angry, restless, coiled to strike.

And we were the line.

The last thin thread holding back the dark.

CHAPTER 25: SHADOWS OF THE NIGHT

With the incident still unfolding up on Level 5, the rest of the prison slipped back into the familiar routine of nightly lockdown. A system running on muscle memory—automatic, mechanical, and necessary. Bowden and I moved through Unit B with silent efficiency, securing cells, finalising paperwork, double-checking for any discrepancies before the new Senior Officer took over tomorrow.

Before stepping out, I paused at the Unit's threshold and glanced back.

My Unit.

Everything where it should be. Nothing out of place. But it still felt like I was leaving something behind—like this grim, steel box had become more than just bricks and noise. It had become part of me.

Later, in Unit A for a security check, a few prisoners weren't standing at their doors. That sort of subtle defiance always carried weight. It wasn't about laziness—it was about testing boundaries.

I didn't raise my voice.

I didn't need to.

Just stepped into their space, cool and deliberate. "Starting tomorrow," I said, locking eyes with one of them, "I'm your new Senior. Fail to follow instructions and you'll lose privileges. TV's the first to go."

I let the silence hang there, like a blade resting just above their heads.

I would always give a warning first, but the message was clear.

"Sometimes you just have to remind them who's in charge," I said to Bowden as we walked out. "And not to fuck with you."

He grinned, but there was unease behind it. He was going to miss the dynamic we'd built—and I would too, though I wouldn't say it out loud.

Back in the locker room, I thanked him. Told him we'd cross paths again, and if he ever needed to talk—work stuff or otherwise—he could find me. No ranks. Just one bloke helping another.

He nodded. "Appreciate that."

Outside, the air was sharp with that post-lockdown buzz. Officers lingered, waiting for final checks. Everyone's ears pricked when Unit 9 staff finally emerged.

We didn't need to ask. The story was already on the wind.

Some prisoner lost his dessert. Accused another of taking it. A verbal spat became a push. The push became a punch. Then both men were on the floor, restrained and cuffed. One had a fractured eye socket and a concussion. The Emergency Response Group took him to hospital. The other was dragged off to a management cell.

No staff injured. Just bruised knuckles, rattled nerves, and another cautionary tale to stick in the mental filing cabinet.

Still, adrenaline was a stubborn thing. The Unit 9 crew buzzed like they'd walked away from a car crash. Some officers vented about management; others were already making weekend plans, as if we hadn't just been inches from another serious use-of-force review.

It always amazed me—how quickly the weight lifted once you stepped outside those walls. How the mask came off. The wariness. The edge. Some of us became almost human again.

Once the last signatures were inked and logs finalised, everyone scattered. A few peeled off towards carparks. Others moved like shadows toward the train station.

I walked alone.

Didn't mind it.

There was something grounding about walking at your own pace, even with the night biting at your heels. The sort of solitude that reminded you the job hadn't claimed all of you. Not yet.

At the platform, I flicked through playlists. Something low and brooding.

When the train arrived, I found a window seat. A small win.

The carriage was full of tired faces—eyes down, minds elsewhere. Just like me. Trying to make it home with the pieces still intact. I let the city blur past in streaks of amber and black. The train moved. My thoughts didn't.

Osbourne would be gone by morning. That smirk finally wiped from his face. Bowden would be fine. The new guy was solid. And me—I'd walk into Unit A ready. I always did.

But readiness wasn't the same as peace.

At home, Emma and I sat at the table. I told her a filtered version of the day. She didn't ask for more. She never did. She just listened, her eyes flicking between mine, reading the spaces between the lines.

Later, we curled into the couch. The television flickered in the background, but my thoughts were miles away.

When we finally made it to bed, Dougal was already there, curled up on the bed.

Emma was asleep within minutes.

I lay there in the dark, staring at the ceiling, phone in hand. Opened a rain sounds app. A digital downpour hummed softly into the room. A poor substitute for peace, but it would do. Sometimes it wasn't about feeling calm. It was about quieting the noise long enough to sleep.

I closed my eyes. The job would still be there tomorrow.

But for now, this moment—this thin, fragile sliver of calm—belonged to me.

CHAPTER 26: PAYDAY BLUES

Thursday. Payday.

The one day that made swallowing the daily grind of abuse, manipulation, and manufactured chaos feel almost… justifiable. I stood in front of my locker, eyes half-dead, already mentally allocating every dollar of my wage like a junkie rationing a hit. Rent. Groceries. Fuel. Takeaway and a brief delusion of freedom.

Good thing stupid people keep me employed, I muttered internally, smirking at the irony.

I stared at the fading image taped inside the locker door. We'd circled a photo of our dream home months ago—clean lines, fresh plaster. A life that didn't creak like a cell door. We were done renting. Done bleeding our pay into someone else's mortgage.

But the dream felt distant now. Distant and fragile. New or old didn't matter anymore. I didn't want a fixer upper. I wanted clean walls that hadn't seen violence. Floorboards that didn't creak like cell doors. I wanted peace—whatever that felt like. And I wanted Emma to have something pure. Something untouched by this place.

I adjusted my name badge. Made sure it sat straight on my chest. The mirror on the inside of the locker door gave me a distorted reflection. I shut it with a click and followed the crowd to the Parade Room.

Metal detectors. Scanner wands. Casual nods and tight-lipped smiles. The usual theatre of civility before stepping into hell. I took my usual place in the back corner. From here, I could see everything. Every fidget, every smirk, every glance that lasted a second too long.

The mood was lighter than usual. Weekend coming up. Pay in the account. Everyone pretended it wasn't wearing them down.

Supervisor Hunter began roll call in his usual tone—one octave short of drill sergeant. I tuned out, eyes drifting toward the front where Operations Managers Tourney and Reed were having a whispered exchange. Something simmered behind those clipped voices.

Then Hunter nodded toward Tourney. "Your parade, sir."

Tourney stepped up to the lectern. Didn't even look at us.

"Busy day and night yesterday," he started, eyes scanning his paper. The same tired script, but the subtext was never just routine—it was a warning shot.

"Hardy in Unit G threatened staff—police notified. Ibrahim swallowed something in Visits. Balloon suspected. He's under 15-minute OBS in Medical. Police attended."

Tourney didn't pause. Just kept peeling through the ugliness like he was reading the ingredients on a cereal box.

"Corwin in Reception was non-compliant—minor use of force. Murphy in Unit H has a fractured eye socket. Prisoner Fuller who assaulted him is now management. Police notified"

And then—

"In Unit B, a note was found stating prisoner Osbourne would be stabbed if not removed. Osbourne was relocated to Reception earlier this morning before Let-out, where he threatened staff before being transferred to Wendarra Prison."

There it was. The name.

Osbourne.

Gone.

A flicker of satisfaction twitched behind my eyes. Not joy—there's no joy in this place. Just relief. Like releasing the breath, you didn't realise you'd been holding for weeks. Someone else could deal with his bullshit now.

Tourney stepped back. Hunter resumed control.

"Daniels, see me after. The rest of you, dismissed."

The crowd began to scatter. Chatter erupted. Plans for the weekend. Jokes about the latest screw-ups. I waited, giving Hunter space to wrap up whatever nonsense was coming out of someone's mouth. Eventually, he looked up.

"Jacob," he said. "Watch staff said Green caused a disturbance last night—screaming, yelling. Find out what's going on."

"Sure," I said. At least it wasn't about Osbourne. That storm had passed.

I made my way out of the building, up the stairwell and into the yard. That open sky always looked out of place—like freedom was mocking us. Brick walls climbed around me like cliffs. Slit windows stared down like watchtowers. Shadows stretched long across the pavement.

Ahead, I spotted Bowden crossing toward Unit B, slinging his bag over his shoulder. We exchanged a nod—something unspoken in the look. Solidarity. Closure.

I turned the key and stepped into Unit A.

"Morning, Daniels," came a voice behind me. Davis. Officer Ryan Davis. Ex-finance guy. Three years in. Still had soft hands and a habit of overexplaining. But he was steady, and in this job, steady was good.

"Ready for a big day?" he asked.

"Depends. Let's hope not."

I dumped my gear at the desk and threw my lunch in the fridge. The post in Unit A was cramped. Barely enough room for two officers and the weight we carried. But we had a private office downstairs for interviews— one of the few luxuries.

Davis hit the PA. "Stand by for a trap count."

Before he moved, I stopped him. "I'll speak with Green. You cover the rest."

He raised a brow but nodded. "Sure. You okay with that?"

I didn't answer. Just climbed the stairs.

The air on the top tier always felt thinner. Tense. Like something unseen was holding its breath.

As I walked, I listened. For muttering. Footsteps. Breathing. Nothing. The Unit quiet.

I stopped outside Green's cell. Raised the trap, slow and cautious.

He stood near the TV. Old white T-shirt, more nicotine than cotton. A few holes—hard to tell if they were earned or inherited. Grey trackies, stained in places you didn't want to ask about.

His fingers twitched slightly near the TV remote—but he didn't blink. Didn't acknowledge me. Like I wasn't real.

That sort of calm only ever followed a storm—or foreshadowed one.

I unlocked the door but kept my foot against the door. Not all the way open.

Just enough for a conversation.

Or a warning.

CHAPTER 27: FRAGMENTS OF THE MIND

Green was already a ghost before I opened the cell door—just a meat puppet hollowed out by years of chemicals and chaos. One of the 'Drug-Fucked'. That's the brutal term we used behind the walls—no time for tact when you're dealing with broken circuitry. Guys like Green weren't dangerous in the traditional sense. Not unless the voices told them to be. But you never knew when the switch would flip. And that made him dangerous enough.

I stood at his door, key cold in hand, listening—footsteps, muttering, maybe a scream caught in the walls. Nothing. Just the eerie hum of the fluorescent lights and the metallic tick of my heartbeat in my ears.

I spoke low, steady. "What's going on, Green?"

Thin. Sallow. A thousand-yard stare aimed at a flickering TV screen. He turned slowly, like he was underwater. Movements lagged by a full second. His eyes were glassy, haunted. Like he wasn't here anymore—just a body held together by leftover drugs and institutional glue.

"What're you talking about, Boss?"

His voice was cracked porcelain. Barely held together.

"Staff reported yelling. Screaming last night. Just wanted to check on you." I didn't move. Just stood with the door cracked open, one foot anchoring it like a dam against the flood.

He blinked. Took longer than it should've. "Nah… I'm okay, Boss."

I wanted to believe that. I wanted to file him under *not today* and walk away.

But I'd seen what happens when belief overrides instinct. I'd seen a prisoner scoop out his own eye with a toothbrush. I'd seen an officer stabbed six times before his radio ever hit the ground. The calm ones—the ones who said "I'm fine"—were the ones you watched over closer.

"You sure?" I asked, my voice the edge of a knife. "I can call the Chief. Move you upstairs. Psych Unit."

He tensed. Just a flicker. But enough. Even Green didn't want to be tossed in with the droolers and the screamers. The ones who shit on their hands and paint the walls. The ones who saw things that weren't there—and sometimes made you see them too.

"No, Boss. I'm alright."

I held his gaze. Tried to see through the fog in his eyes. Nothing there. Just a shattered mirror reflecting the static of some other world.

I gave him a tight nod. "Alright. Don't make me regret it."

He didn't answer. Didn't need to. The silence said enough.

I shut the door and locked it. One more soul deferred. One more crack papered over with duct tape and routine.

I walked back to the top of the stairs, every step vibrating in my knees. Davis was waiting below. I gave the nod—one prisoner for the count.

He called it in while I leaned against the wall, watching cells.

Let-out began.

Prisoners emerged. Sluggish. Suspicious. I moved behind the desk and picked up the phone. Called Hunter.

"Green's fine," I said, lying like it was one more part of the job. Because it was.

Hunter didn't question it.

The Unit found its rhythm again—if you could call it that. Like a haunted orchestra playing the same tired song. Shuffling feet. Clinking cutlery. The quiet tension of men living with too much time and too little hope.

I scanned the Unit with dead eyes, seeing more than I wanted. Noticing who walked like prey. Who viewed them like a predator. You didn't *learn* that. It became instinct. You *developed* it the way calluses grow—pain first, then numb.

Davis tried small talk. A joke that didn't land. I offered half a smile and returned to the burnt sludge pretending to be coffee.

The phone rang.

"Daniels," I answered.

McNamara's voice came through, clipped. All business. "You've got a special prisoner coming up. Get ready."

My stomach twisted.

Special.

A word that tasted like blood.

Special meant high risk. Special meant *problem*. Not mine, not yours—just *ours*. A burden shared by whoever drew the short straw.

I hung up the phone.

Stared out over the Unit.

Concrete. Steel. Rust and resentment. The hum of the overhead lights sounded like flies circling a carcass. My eyes drifted across the tier. The prisoners felt it too. The shift. Something was coming. They always knew. The animals could smell the storm before the sky changed colour.

Davis glanced at my arms, ink peeking from under my sleeves.

"So," he asked cautiously, "what's with the tatts?"

I gave him a half-smile. One with more teeth than warmth.

"Memories. Mistakes."

He didn't ask again.

I checked my coffee cup. Empty. Couldn't even remember finishing it.

The phone rang. McNamara again. "They're bringing him now."

I stood. Coffee will have to wait.

My muscles ached with fatigue that no sleep could cure. Years of this place had worn me thin. I felt like old wire stretched too tight, waiting to snap. And I knew, deep down, this special prisoner was going to test me.

They all did.

Twenty years inside these walls.

Twenty years watching men rot from the inside out.

And the day was just beginning.

CHAPTER 28: FRAIL SHADOWS

He shuffled in like a gust of forgotten air.

George Anderson. Eighty-five. Looked ninety-five. Moved like he'd died five years ago but no one had told him yet. His shoes were cracked leather slippers with no laces, his trousers clung to him like they were afraid to fall apart, and his shirt was stained with memory.

The Escorting Officer held the Unit door open. I stepped forward and froze.

"He shouldn't be here," I muttered, quiet but hard.

The other prisoners had gone silent. Even the loudmouths. Every eye in the Unit latched onto Anderson like they were trying to figure out what the hell they were looking at. Some relic from another era.

I didn't ask him to climb the stairs. One look told me he wouldn't make it. His bones were already negotiating surrender.

"Cell Seven," I said to the escorting officer.

Anderson didn't need prompting. He staggered inside like the cell had been waiting for him. Sat on the bed with the weight of a life lived too long. Shoulders slumped. Hands trembling. Eyes cracked glass—full of red veins and haunted things.

I turned to the Escorting Officer. "What's his story?"

He didn't blink. Just sighed like he'd already told it too many times.

"Murder charge. Came straight from police cells. Quiet transport. No media. No fuss."

"Murder?" I echoed, disbelieving.

He nodded; jaw clenched. "Wife had terminal cancer. Years of it. They made a pact—go out together. Pills. Gas on. Laid down in the kitchen, holding hands."

I closed my eyes for half a second. That was all I could afford.

"She didn't make it," he continued. "He did. Home Care nurse found them. Called it in. Police broke in, Ambos brought him back. Wife was gone."

The silence between us thickened. Like a noose.

"Police charged him?" I asked.

"Didn't want to. Had to. Law doesn't care about promises whispered in the dark."

I shook my head. "That's fucked."

"Yeah," the officer agreed. "Lawyer's working on bail. But until then— he's yours."

No trial yet. Just a number and a charge. The system didn't pause to ask *why*. Only *how many*.

I called over Carter, one of the Billets I trusted.

"Boss?" he said, already moving.

I pointed toward George.

"He's yours. Meals. Laundry. Any issue—you let me know."

Carter nodded, then stopped when I stepped closer, my voice dropping into the basement.

"If anyone touches him... if anyone even *thinks* about fucking messing with him, I'll make fucking sure they wish they'd never been born."

He didn't smile. He just said, "Understood."

I walked back to the cell, crouched in front of Anderson, met those broken eyes.

"How are you George, my name is Mr Daniels" I told him. "This is Carter, he'll help you out. You need anything, you let me know."

He nodded slowly, like each movement was a negotiation between flesh and bone.

"Okay." His voice rasped like parchment scraping glass.

I wanted to believe he'd be okay.

But this place didn't care how old you were. Wolves still tore meat from the weak.

Back at the desk, I scanned through his paperwork. Not much. Sparse history. Daughter listed as next of kin. Probably hasn't spoken to her in years. Probably didn't want her seeing what's left of him.

The kettle clicked behind me. One of the few sounds in here that still felt human. I offered Davis a coffee. He lifted a tin of tea bags and shrugged. "Tea, thanks."

I sipped mine slow. Strong. Just how I liked it.

The Unit moved with its usual sluggish menace. Prisoners drifted between tasks—mopping, folding, pretending to be busy. But every so often, I'd catch someone sneaking a glance toward Cell Seven. Gauging. Calculating.

I didn't miss those looks.

You didn't have to throw a punch to commit violence in here. Sometimes it started with a stare. A whisper. A rumour passed like poison down the line.

George smiled at the Billets as they brought him fresh bedding. He didn't really know what was going on. But maybe that was a blessing.

I sat at the desk and waited.

Because the quiet in prison doesn't last. It's not peace—it's pressure. Pressure that swells in silence. That creeps behind eyes and under doors.

And pressure always builds toward something.

Something loud.

Something sharp.

Something bleeding.

CHAPTER 29: DIRTY SECRETS, BURIED DEEPER

Mid-morning light crawled through reinforced glass like it was ashamed to be here. Weak. Washed-out. Cold. Doing nothing to warm the chill that had settled in my gut.

That's when Sharron Price walked in.

She didn't knock. Never did. Just appeared like a blade in the dark.

Thirteen years in Corrections, seven of those buried deep in Intelligence. Whatever softness she might've carried into the job had been boiled off years ago. What was left behind was steel. Lean. Precise. Unapologetic.

I respected her. Always had. She didn't give a fuck about what management thought, didn't fake pleasantries, and never wasted a breath on bullshit. She moved like someone who'd seen things she couldn't unsee—and survived every one of them.

She gave me a look. Subtle tilt of the head toward the office. No words, no theatrics. Just a signal.

I caught Davis's eye. "Watch the Unit," I muttered, already halfway down the stairs.

Inside, I shut the door behind us. Sharron tossed a folder onto the desk. It landed with a slap that echoed louder than it should've.

"This stays between us," she said. "Intel only."

Her voice had that clipped edge—the kind you only ever heard when things were about to go bad.

"You ever see Officer Nicky Kostavoski spending time with Osbourne? Unit B?"

I kept my face still. Professional calm, even as her words slammed into me.

"No," I said. Lie. "Didn't pay much attention to Osbourne."

Sharron stared right through me. She didn't push, didn't call me on it. Just opened the folder.

"They searched Osbourne's property after the transfer. Found photos."

"What kind?"

"Her. Nicky. In lingerie. Full-on shit. Like something ripped from a fucking men's mag."

My stomach flipped.

"Holy shit."

She nodded grimly. "Letters too. Handwritten. Love stuff. Obsessive stuff. Hidden in his legal papers. We think it's been going on for months."

I dragged a hand down my face. Betrayal's one thing. Stupidity is another. This wasn't crossing a line. It was dragging a bloody axe through the whole goddamn rulebook.

"She's off today," Sharron continued, "but tomorrow morning she'll be in front of Joslin Read. HR will walk her out before lunch. Quiet. Clean."

I stared at the desk, numb. I thought about every conversation I'd ever had with Nicky. What I'd said. What she could've passed on. Whether Osbourne knew more about me than I was comfortable with.

In prison, the prisoners study you. Watch every move. Catalogue every habit. Every silence. They wait. Until they don't.

Then Sharron pulled a photo from the folder. Slid it across the desk.

Kyle Duncan Phillips.

Even on cheap paper, the image bled menace. Shaved scalp. Tattoos choking his neck. Eyes like cold slate. No posing. No smile. Just that lifer smirk—the look of a man who'd seen the edge and made it kneel.

"Osbourne's handler," she said. "He's the one pulling the strings."

I stared at the photo, my thumb hovering but not touching. It felt radioactive.

"Drugs. Extortion. Assaults. Hits. All from inside. He doesn't shout. He doesn't need to. Even patched bikies give him space. And he never leaves fingerprints."

I nodded once, slow. "Don't know him," I said.

Another lie. I'd heard whispers. You don't work this long in the system without hearing certain names.

Sharron saw through it but didn't call me out. She started packing the folder.

At the door, she paused.

"One last thing," she said. "Osbourne thinks you're the one who had him moved."

I snorted. "I didn't write the fucking note."

I hadn't. But in this place, perception beats truth every time.

"I know," she said. "But it doesn't matter. He believes you did."

And then she was gone.

I didn't move. Just sat there in the silence.

In prison, facts mean nothing. Belief is everything. It fuels grudges. Builds narratives. Justifies revenge.

Osbourne had written a new chapter. And I was the villain.

Eventually, I stood. My legs felt heavier than they should've. Back at the desk, Davis looked up.

"All good?" he asked.

"Just new arrival paperwork," I said, waving it off.

He nodded, went back to his tea.

But I knew better.

The ground had shifted beneath my boots.

The balance of power had changed.

And somewhere—maybe soon, maybe not—someone was going to bleed for it.

Maybe Osbourne.

Maybe me.

CHAPTER 30: CHOICES AND CONSEQUENCES

Next Day.

The platform rattled as the train pulled in, like the whole city was shivering. Rain crept through my jacket, cold fingers down my spine. I ducked under the iron roof, letting the sound of the rain hammering the metal drown out the world.

The express train hissed to a stop. Doors slid open. A moment's reprieve.

I slid into a seat by the window, plugged in my headphones, and closed my eyes. The music thrummed low in my ears. The city slid past the window — wet, hollow, pretending to shine.

There was something about the way rain stripped everything back — the fake gloss, the dirt — leaving nothing but the raw underneath. I stepped off the train and into streets that smelled cleaner than they deserved. For a moment, it almost felt like hope.

Almost.

The Parade Room was already filling up when I arrived there. I stayed in my usual spot, near the back wall. Out of reach. Out of questions.

As names were called out, I kept my head down. The briefings rattled on. New prisoners. Old problems. Same shit, different day.

Through it all, my frustration simmered. Not just with the job. With everything. It all boiled down to one thing.

Consequences.

We teach kids that choices have consequences. That every decision leads somewhere.

But these prisoners — most of them never learned that. Or they never cared. They lived in the moment. Grabbed whatever they could. Fast money, fast highs, fast escapes.

And when it all came crashing down, they played the victim.

Blamed their upbringing. Blamed society. Blamed the world. Anyone but themselves.

It wasn't just a prison thing. It was everywhere now. This disease of entitlement. No one wanted to own their mistakes anymore.

I thought about the drug dealer we'd had a few months back. He used to brag about how he'd 'helped more families than Centrelink'. Said it with a straight face. He always whined about being locked up. Like it was some unfair penalty for a career choice. He justified it, said he was providing for his family.

Never mind the families he tore apart peddling his poison. Never mind the overdoses, the broken kids, the destroyed lives. He didn't care. None of them did.

I'd seen a young girl detoxing near a train station. Screamed for her mum all night. Nobody came. Not until I called an ambulance.

And sitting there, in that freezing room that stank of wet uniforms and cheap coffee, I made myself a promise.

I wouldn't forget.

Wouldn't forget the real victims. Wouldn't forget what this place tried to grind out of you.

Accountability. Responsibility. Truth.

No matter how many lies they told themselves, no matter how many excuses they screamed from behind those bars, some things didn't change.

Choices mattered.

And the consequences never went away.

CHAPTER 31: SHADOW OF EMPATHY

Mid-morning finally gave me a breather. I slumped into the battered chair behind the desk, a cup of coffee cradled between my hands like it was something sacred.

Another day treating a wound that didn't want to clot.

I closed my eyes for a second, listening to the hum of the Unit, the occasional bark of orders, the shuffling of prisoners trying to kill time.

Three days off coming. A lifeline. A deep breath escaped me. And then, right on cue, the phone rang.

I checked the clock — 09:50. It was SPO Johnson from Unit 3. They had a bed ready for George Anderson. Two Billets already on their way to move him. Duty called.

I sat the coffee down and headed downstairs to George's cell. He sat on the edge of his bed, looking even smaller than I remembered. His face lifted when he saw me.

"Morning, George," I said, keeping my voice light. "How are you feeling?"

"Fine," he said, voice dry as dust.

The Billets showed up, nodding toward George.

"We're here for him, Mr. Daniels," one said. "Got a few old blokes in Unit 3. Closer to his age."

I knelt beside George.

"Alright, George. These two will walk you across the yard. You're moving into a new Unit."

George rose slowly, tugging at his pants with one hand, the other reaching out — grabbing my arm without thinking.

The Billets stiffened, waiting for my reaction. There was an unwritten rule — prisoners didn't touch staff. But I didn't pull away. I let him steady himself.

He shuffled out of the cell, slow and fragile. In the Dayroom, George paused, voice rough.

"Do I come back here for meals?"

I smiled at him.

"No, mate. You'll eat over there. I'll let the kitchen know."

The Billets hovered close, patient. I knew Johnson would have all the paperwork sorted. Meal lists. Medications. The works.

I wasn't just blowing smoke when I promised George he'd be alright. I meant it.

Because empathy mattered in this job. Sympathy was a death sentence in here. Empathy—that was your shield. You didn't carry their pain. You just refused to ignore it. You could respect the wreckage they carried without letting it pull you under.

George deserved that. Even if most didn't know it.

I glanced back at my desk, where my coffee sat stone cold. Not that it mattered anymore.

I flicked the kettle on, needing something to fill the dead air. But before the water even boiled, the radio shattered the calm.

"Code Black Unit B, Code Black Unit B."

I was already moving.

"Davis, stay put!" I barked, sprinting for the door.

Running towards Unit B.

I tore across the yard. Unit B's door blew open ahead of me. Prisoners burst out, shoving and running, chaos spilling into the yard.

I didn't slow down. Didn't hesitate.

The radio crackled in my hand, keys slamming against my hip.

"Get out of the fucking way! Move! Fucking Move!"

Faces at the windows watched over us.

Hungry for blood.

I hit Unit B just as the real shitstorm broke loose.

CHAPTER 32: PAYBACK

Entering the Unit, my attention locked onto the commotion at the officers' desk. The Senior Prison Officer stood there, jabbing his finger urgently toward the Billets' cells.

No hesitation. Instinct took over.

I moved fast, still barking at prisoners to keep their distance, pushing through the tide of noise and confusion. When I reached the cell, Bowden was already inside, kneeling beside Johnno. The sight hit me like a punch to the gut.

Not him. Not now.

Johnno was slumped on the floor, bloodied and bruised; his back wedged into the corner between the bed and the wall. Blood soaked the left side of his shirt, dripping into his jeans, pooling across the cold floor.

The cell looked torn open — clothes and papers scattered like storm debris. An upturned plastic chair teetered on the edge of the bed. Broken chaos everywhere.

Urgency kicked my voice sharper. "Johnno, stay there, don't move."

I snapped my fingers at Bowden, pointing at a towel discarded across the floor.

"Grab that towel. Now."

Johnno shifted, instinct clashing with shock. His right hand clawed for something, anything, to pull himself up — but the blood and debris sent his foot skidding.

Bowden snatched the towel and flung it across the cell with a quick, practiced throw. It landed near Johnno's trembling hand.

Johnno pulled his blood-slicked palm away from his face — and the injury underneath froze me for a half-second.

A deep gash, running from the corner of his mouth to his ear. His earlobe barely hanging by a strip of torn skin.

Thick blood grasped his hand, starting to clot in patches. He pressed the towel against his face, the cloth turning dark almost instantly.

Blood pooled at the corners of his mouth, bubbling each time he tried to breathe. A wet, ragged sound.

Bowden and I didn't waste time. We both yanked latex gloves from our belts, snapping them on.

Johnno tried to speak — I cut him off, voice harsh.

"Don't try to talk, for fuck's sake! Just stay where you are."

Johnno trembled harder. Shock setting in. His eyes wide and glassy, breath hitching in shallow, panicked bursts.

"Bowden, grab the chair for Johnno." I said, pointing where to place it next to the bed. We eased Johnno up and into the chair. He pressed the towel to his face, shaking.

The Unit buzzed and churned around us. More officers pouring in, pushing prisoners toward the yard. Yelling, shouts, threats spat back and forth. Radios screeching like broken alarms. Security formed a line at the cell door.

I stepped back, leaving them to shield Johnno.

The Security Supervisor arrived at a near-run. Hunter approached the door, sharp-eyed and stone-faced. Together, Bowden and I stepped out into the Dayroom, the bloody towel still pressed to Johnno's face, his body shuddering in the chair.

"Right," he barked. "What happened?" He pushed toward the cell, taking a glance inside.

Then motioned Bowden and me over, dragging us into the middle of the Dayroom where we could talk away from the chaos.

Bowden, catching his breath, put his hands on his hips, staring back at the wrecked cell.

"Sir, we were at the desk when we heard something smash — plates, maybe a chair. Then the real noise started. I sprinted downstairs. About six prisoners burst out of Johnno's cell, made a run for the Unit door."

He swallowed hard. "I found Johnno lying there, bleeding bad. Called Code Black straight away."

Hunter scribbled notes fast, head flicking between Bowden, me, and the slow migration of prisoners being corralled out into the yard.

Outside, the noise picked up — prisoners clustering near the entrance like scavengers around a carcass.

Reed stormed in, red vest flashing like a warning flare amid a sea of blue. She pulled Hunter aside, exchanging clipped, fast words.

Both scanning the crowd that pressed harder against the barriers outside.

The MSO and the Nurse rushed in with a medical trolley. Officers pointed them toward Johnno's cell without needing to be asked.

Inside, they went to work.

No drama. Just cold, precise action.

Then Reed's voice barked over the radio.

"Control, call Code Aqua."

Lockdown.

Full. Total.

The prison ground itself into stillness, like a machine shutting down.

CHAPTER 33: A DESCENT INTO CHAOS

Security burst from the Unit, voices cutting through the prison yard like blades. Their commands slammed into the air, slicing through the tension, demanding immediate compliance.

The prisoners shuffled backward, reluctant, muttering curses under their breath, hurling insults at the officers who pushed them toward their respective Units.

Supervisor Hunter and Security Senior Hawkins stepped forward without hesitation, taking the lead, barking out orders with the sort of authority you didn't argue with. They directed their officers back to their Units, reinforcing the Code Aqua lockdown.

The response was fast, efficient — a tightly wound machine snapping into place under pressure.

The prisoners from Unit B, still buzzing with adrenaline, were escorted down toward the gymnasium. The once-chaotic yard emptied. Left behind was the stark, ugly truth — Unit B, now a locked-down crime scene, the epicentre of the violence.

My gut clenched.

I flagged down a passing Security Officer, sending him straight to Davis in Unit A to assist with the prisoner lockdown. Another officer followed without needing to be told. They disappeared into the shadows.

Inside Unit B, the Nurse and MSO Baker, moving with brutal efficiency, eased Johnno out of his cell and settled him into a chair in the Dayroom. Nobody moved. Nobody spoke.

The towel was soaked. When the Nurse peeled it back, gasps followed automatically.

The wound was vicious — a deep, jagged gash torn from the corner of Johnno's mouth clear to his ear.

Flesh hung loose, raw and gaping, a chunk missing where his face should've been whole.

Other bruises, other cuts, were barely noticed. The savagery of the main wound eclipsed everything.

Without pause, the Nurse and MSO sprang into action, ripping open gauze pads, applying pressure, trying to stop the bleeding. Baker, glancing at the Johnno's face, barked towards Reed, calling for an ambulance.

Reed, moved like a pivot point — information flowed to and from her at speed, funnelling straight into the ECC headquarters.

No panic. Just cold, hard control.

I pushed toward the Officer's Desk, asking permission to use the phone.

The Senior Officer nodded, tight-lipped. I called Davis.

"You good?" I asked.

"All locked down," Davis said. "The boys are finishing the final count."

It helped. A little.

I hung up, glanced at the officers at the desk. "Time of the Code?"

"10:09hrs," one replied.

I scrawled it onto the back of my latex glove.

No time to lose. I grabbed Bowden and headed back toward the bloodstained cell.

The smell hit first — coppery, thick, clinging to the back of my throat. We stood at the entrance, eyes sweeping the floor.

"Looking for a shiv?" Bowden asked, half-knowing. I said nothing, moved a pile of clothing with my boot.

There it was.

A blood-soaked tuna can lid, folded and honed into a razor's curve. Sharpened hate into metal.

Classic jailhouse weapon.

I grabbed a scrap piece of paper, nudged the weapon onto it carefully, and left it untouched on the floor.

"We'll leave it for Intel," I said. "They'll want photos before they bag it."

Back in the Dayroom, Reed stood at the centre, a clipboard clutched tight, relaying updates over her mobile to the ECC. Bowden and I approached her, reporting what we'd found. Hunter, nearby, listened while still coordinating Units and the response.

I told him I was heading back to Unit A to start my report. Hunter just nodded — he already knew the paperwork storm about to hit.

I walked toward the Unit door, yellow crime scene tape already stretched across the entrance like a wound dressing.

Before I stepped through, I paused.

Turned back.

Johnno was still there, barely conscious, wrapped in bloodied bandages. Nurse and MSO Baker working to keep him stable. I clenched my fists, jaw tight.

This wasn't just about Johnno. It was about all of us.

A reminder — brutal, simple — that fairness didn't exist here. That mercy was a dead language behind these walls.

At the Unit door, a Prison Officer logged my departure for the record.

I caught a glimpse of Sharron Price, Intel bag slung over her shoulder, striding in across the yard. I flagged her down, gave her a quick debrief about the weapon, the blood trail, the cell.

She didn't say much. Just looked at the towel, then at me. One second too long. And I knew — she'd seen worse, but not by much.

Standing in the open doorway, I watched over the last few officers being pulled out of the Unit. Some shared a laugh about something that had happened during the chaos.

A coping mechanism. I didn't blame them.

But I didn't feel it.

Didn't want to laugh.

Six against one wasn't a fight.

It was a message.

And tonight, every man inside these walls would hear it loud and clear.

CHAPTER 34: A SINISTER REMINDER

Johnno had always maintained a respectful demeanour toward me, and while we weren't exactly friends, there was an understanding between us. I trusted him — trusted him enough to share the occasional joke.

Johnno took it on himself to keep the Unit in order, helping with new prisoners, sometimes putting a few unruly ones back in their place when they stepped out of line.

I made my way up to the desk, hoping to check in with Davis. To my relief, everything was under control. Davis, curious about the chaos, tried fishing for details. But my mood had sunk too far. Too heavy after what I'd just seen.

I told him I'd be in my office working on the report, and if he needed anything, he knew where to find me.

Just as I turned away, I spotted officers escorting two paramedics, pushing a stretcher between them.

I observed them move through the yard, slow, steady — a grim procession.

I unlocked my office door, sat at the computer. Still wearing my gloves, I peeled the right one off before logging in. The bloodstain on the left glove caught my eye — a few small drops near where I'd jotted the time of the Code.

I stared at it longer than I should have. Couldn't look away.

The nagging feeling returned — a suspicion already taking root. This wasn't random.

Something about the attack smelled like Osbourne.

Osbourne didn't need to lift a finger. He had others to sharpen the blades. That's what made him dangerous.

Sure, the Billets had clashed with him before, but not like this. Not brutal. Not coordinated. This felt different.

Flashes from my early days flooded back — faces torn by razor blades, calculated slashes that weren't about killing. They were about sending a message.

Prison gang tactics.

The purpose wasn't death. It was control.

Leave them breathing — but mark them.

Every time Johnno looked in the mirror, he'd remember exactly who owned this place. And everyone else would too.

The realisation slammed into me hard. Gang violence was rising again. They were taking the prison back — piece by bloody piece.

Didn't matter which prison. Didn't matter how many walls we threw up.

Inside, tobacco was worth its weight in gold. And heroin or meth? Beyond price.

Smoking bans had made sure of that — commodities turned into currencies of blood.

I finished the report, printed it, and signed it. One more piece of paper in a system that barely held the chaos back.

The prison stayed eerily silent under lockdown. Johnno's blood on the floor was a warning none of them missed.

Davis must've seen the weight on my face. Without a word, he made me a coffee. It was his way of giving me space — a small kindness in a place that usually demanded hard edges.

I wasn't ready for banter or distractions. Not today. I walked to the Unit door, pushed it open, and stepped outside. I needed air, something real.

The yard stretched out before me, quiet and still. The prison seemed almost beautiful— if you ignored the barbed wire and what was locked behind it.

I sipped my coffee, my eyes dropping to my boots — bloodstained again.

Someone else's blood soaking into the leather. You could scrub the boots clean. The mind? Not so much.

Inside Unit B, officers still moved through the aftermath.

Johnno lay on a stretcher now, hands cuffed to each side, his head wrapped in heavy bandages. Only his eyes were visible.

Tears filled his eyes as he closed them tight.

Pain? Shock? Or maybe he understood, even then, that he was done here. Johnno wouldn't be coming back to this Unit.

Hours in the hospital getting stitched up, then a Management Cell — a cold holding — before relocation to another prison far from here.

I viewed the scene until the paramedics and Security Officers slowly and silently walked past me. Then they disappeared. Leaving nothing but cold wind curling around me.

Hunter emerged from Unit B, his head bent over a folder, scribbling notes as he walked.

"Thanks for the report," he said, reaching out.

I handed him the page, neatly folded. He flattened it against his clipboard, securing it down. He said he was heading to the Parade Room for the hot debrief. Management would decide when the prison could resume normal operations.

I knew Reed had moved into the Gatehouse. A television van had parked outside. They picked up the ambulance attending on a scanner. And now the world outside wanted a story. They were circling, eager for blood.

The kind that made careers and ruined lives.

Intel officers combed through footage, trying to piece together who ran, who fought, who struck first. Without witness statements, it would be like chasing smoke.

During the Code Aqua lockdown, prisoners had time to swap clothes, mix back into the crowd. Disappear.

I sat through the hot debrief in the Parade Room.

Reed stood at the lectern, cool and composed. Officers involved in the incident filed in behind her.

Operations Managers clustered at the front, talking low among themselves. Hunter slipped into the back just before it started.

Reed laid out the basics — the incident, the Code Aqua, the discovery of a weapon. Intel had bagged the evidence, taken crime scene photos. The injured prisoner — Johnno — transported under escort. Police contacted.

That was it. Polite thanks to the officers involved. Then we were dismissed.

Security Officers moved the prisoners from the gym back to Unit B. Fifteen officers overseeing the return. The prisoners were herded straight to their cells — no chances to grab belongings or pass messages. The Unit went silent, like a graveyard.

Johnno's cell stood sealed, wrapped in crime scene tape.

Later that night, after Lock-Up, the cleaners would come. They'd scrub the blood off the floor, wipe the walls, bleach the cell. Make it ready for the next occupant. As if it never happened.

Two hours later, the radio crackled alive, shattering the fragile silence. The voice came through clipped and urgent — all Security Officers to the yard. No explanation. Just a command that pulled your gut tight.

Five minutes later. "Code Aqua All Clear," the voice declared. I turned to Davis, coffee long forgotten in my hand. I took a breath.

"Fuck," I muttered. "Here we go."

And we both knew — the day wasn't over yet.

CHAPTER 35: TENSION IN THE SHADOWS

The tension in the prison had barely begun to settle after the violent incident. Prisoners moved cautiously now, heads down, instincts kicking in. Staff stayed sharp, senses wired tight, knowing it wouldn't take much for the place to erupt again.

The yard wasn't its usual bustling mess. A few prisoners jogged toward the kitchen: heads low. Security officers scanned the yard with that constant predator gaze — hunting trouble before it could even breathe.

No one knew yet what had really sparked the attack. Racial tensions? Unpaid debts? Someone refusing to play ball with the wrong crew?

I had my own theory.

It stank of Osbourne. Johnno had never been the type to back down — but even he was smart enough not to pick a fight without reason and to his advantage.

Outside Unit B, small clusters of prisoners gathered. Gossip spread faster than blood in water. All eyes pointed toward Johnno's cell, the scene of it all. Whoever had jumped Johnno wasn't far.

Lurking. Waiting. Checking if they'd been spotted.

I stood outside my unit, watching them. Every move. Every glance. Among the group were a couple of prisoners with serious psychological problems — the kind who could snap without warning. Two Security Officers threaded through the yard, joining me, forming a solid wall. None of us spoke.

My face stayed blank. But inside, my mind kept replaying the attack like a film on repeat.

Somewhere from the yard, a voice barked out: "Fucking dogs." Anonymous. The sort of coward who hides behind a crowd.

I didn't even flinch. Let them bark.

Prisoners shuffled past us, throwing side glances sharp enough to cut. The contempt was thick enough to choke on.

Out of the corner of my eye, I caught Rogers. He gave a nod — a signal. I nodded back. Something was brewing.

I left the officers standing guard and walked toward Unit B, where Rogers was already slipping inside. Rogers waited near the Top Tier, just outside his cell. I made a detour to the officers' desk, masking my real purpose.

"Can I borrow Bowden to search a couple of cells in here?" I asked the Senior Officer.

The request raised an eyebrow, but no argument. They knew my calls were rarely wrong. Bowden geared up with latex gloves, following me upstairs. Before we hit Rogers' cell, I held Bowden back.

"Stand outside for a minute," I muttered.

He didn't question it. He knew better.

Inside the cell, I closed the door behind me. Confidentiality was survival in this place.

I kept it light. "Mark, how's things?"

Rogers looked like he hadn't slept. Face pale. The Johnno incident had rattled him too.

"Hey, Mr. Daniels," he said, voice low and raw. "This thing with Johnno... fucking pisses me off. Six blokes jumping one? Back in my day, you fucking punch on one-on-one, till someone was left standing. None of this pack dog bullshit."

I moved closer, settling into a half-sit against the wall, keeping it casual.

"I'm listening, Mark. Whatever you tell me stays between us. You know that. You know I don't throw names around."

Rogers shifted, tension bleeding off him like steam. He wrestled with it, trying to stay true to the old code.

"I ain't no fucking rat, Mr. Daniels. Never have been in thirty years, and I ain't fucking starting now. But this... this is different. And I owe you. You've always looked out for me."

I stayed still, giving him the space.

"I can't name 'em. But I'll tell you this — the ones who did it? They're not random. They're playing from someone's script. And it smells like Osbourne," he said, shaking his head.

Inside, my gut clenched. It was the confirmation I'd expected — and dreaded.

I locked my jaw, kept my face neutral. Let him talk.

"If someone greenlit this, it didn't come from Osbourne. He's too fucking stupid for that," Rogers added.

I thanked him quietly, left the cell, finding Bowden still on watch. To keep up appearances, I picked a random cell.

"Let's search this one," I said aloud, like it was one more part of the job.

As we moved through the motions, Bowden gave me a sideways glance.

"That wasn't just a chat. What info did he drop?" he asked.

I knew I couldn't lie. Not outright. But the truth could wait.

"Don't worry about it," I said, shrugging. "Just old history between me and Rogers."

It was enough. For now.

Sometimes, silence wasn't just protection.

It was survival.

Especially when dangerous truths were hanging in the air, waiting to cut you down.

CHAPTER 36: SHADOW OF FEAR

I returned to the Unit, my demeanour a mask — covering the weight of what I'd just learned. The revelations from Rogers, dark and heavy, echoed in my mind like the last tick before a detonation.

If this was a hit arranged against Johnno, like Rogers suggested, it confirmed every suspicion that had been clawing at my gut. But it wasn't just personal vendettas crossing paths anymore.

This was something bigger. Something colder. Something that could spiral fast.

Routine had been replaced with something heavier — the sort of quiet that made you reach for your radio without knowing why. A tension you could almost taste.

Prisoners went through the motions — cleaning, moving about — pretending normalcy. But their eyes gave them away. Quick flicks toward the yard. Short, sharp glances that said they were just as wired as we were.

The billets, supposedly focused on their chores, observed too. They cleaned benches, wiped tables — but it was all a front. Underneath, they were waiting, ready.

Fear hung in the air, thick and oppressive.

The attack had left a shadow across the yard — across all of us. More security officers flooded in, dragged from Reception and other Units, a desperate push to show strength, to choke out the chaos before it could flare again.

The yard, once a swirling chaos of prisoners walking endless loops, now huddled in tight knots. Each knot of prisoners had a centre — someone who kept their eyes forward while the rest took cues.

Whispers replaced shouting. Side glances replaced bold stares. Prisoners stalked prisoners. Officers observed prisoners.

It was a staring contest waiting for a spark. The tension felt alive, a thing with teeth. Every breath seemed too loud.

A crackle broke the tension — the radio static coming to life, the voice scratchy:

"Ten minutes to lockup."

A countdown. A race to contain the day's wreckage before the dark settled in. But even lockup wouldn't scrub away the ghosts.

Johnno's bloodied face stayed burned into my brain. The rage behind it. The message it carried. It was more than just prison violence. It was a warning.

It wasn't random. It was orchestration under the surface — a dark tide building strength.

The radio clicked again, the final signal. Lockup.

The Unit shifted, prisoners shuffling toward their cells, moving slower, shoulders hunched. The doors slammed shut, one after another, steel locking steel. The sound ricocheted down the tiers, hammering out the end of the day.

Outside, darkness began to swallow the yard. Inside, the Unit settled into a brittle quiet.

I felt frustration simmering under my skin — barely contained.

Today proved a hard truth. Any one of us could be next. Any one of us could've been Johnno.

The Unit secured; a slow procession of officers gathered at the top of the stairs. We stood there, the silence pressing down like a heavy blanket. A fellow officer, voice cautious, broke the stillness with a question — asking about the day, the attack.

My jaw tightened. I stared down at my boots.

"Not talking about it," I said flatly. My voice left no room for argument.

"Ask someone else."

And that was the end of it.

CHAPTER 37: NEON RHYTHMS OF THE NIGHT

The rhythmic rattle of the train echoed my mood as I slouched into my seat, staring absently through the window. My thoughts blurred, like scenery behind glass — visible, but distant.

A sigh slipped out as I pulled my phone from my pocket, my thumb dragging through playlists in search of something, anything, to drown out the noise in my head. Not the usual upbeat stuff. Tonight needed something different. Something to numb the storm inside.

As music streamed into my headphones, I leaned back, closing my eyes. The rocking of the train was oddly soothing, a temporary reprieve. Still, the journey stretched, each station crawling by. Each minute stretching longer than it should.

The train's routine rhythm felt off — like the universe was deliberately dragging out my return to normality. Around me, passengers fidgeted and shifted, desperate to escape the working week. I shared their desperation, but for reasons they could never understand.

Finally, finally, the train gave up its grip and spilled me onto familiar ground. Home.

Dougal's excited bark cut through the haze, my little friend crashing into me. His enthusiasm pulled me across the threshold; it almost felt like peace.

"I'm hopping in the shower," I called to Emma, catching sight of her appearing in the hallway.

Her voice floated back, light and warm — a reminder that tonight was mapped out already. A fragile truce between the day I was leaving behind and the night ahead.

Under the spray of hot water, the grime of the prison washed away. For a few stolen minutes, I could almost pretend none of it had happened.

Behind the wheel on the way to the venue, Emma's excitement filled the car like sunshine cracking through a storm. Her laugh pulled a rare smile from me — small, but real. I placed a hand on her arm, the unspoken reassurance clear between us.

The car park was overflowing when we arrived, the buzz of anticipation thick in the air. Emma brushed dog hair from her dress, fussing without real concern. My eyes scanned the shadows automatically — old habits, impossible to switch off. Tonight, I wasn't just her date. I was her shield.

Inside, we found our table in a sea of strangers and flashing lights. Emma's smile lit the room, but my mind stayed locked on the crowd, scanning every corner, every movement.

As dinner faded, the lights dimmed, and a low hum of excitement built around us.

The announcement cut through the darkness, and the crowd erupted. *Pure 80's* hit the stage in a blast of neon and sound, the lead singer — a retro fever dream — commanding every eye in the house. The rhythm section churned, the bass and guitars punching through the noise, the piano weaving nostalgia into the air.

For a moment, I let the music take me. My fingers tapped the table. My mind uncoiled just a little.

Emma swayed beside me, lost in the moment. When her eyes caught mine, a spark passed between us. For once, the weight I carried didn't feel so heavy.

The band's first set ended, and Emma made her way to the bar for a refill. I watched over her, weave through the crowd. Her figure swallowed by the bodies moving to the pulse of the music.

After a few minutes, I pushed off from the table, threading my way after her, my eyes locked on her hair bobbing among the sea of strangers. She was deep in conversation with a woman when I finally reached her, their words lost in the surge of noise. Emma's face lit up when she saw me.

"Jacob, this is Brianna," she said, her smile so wide.

Brianna leaned in close, her voice cutting through the chaos like a secret.

"Hi Jacob, Emma's been telling me all about you."

A wry smile tugged at my mouth.

"Not too much, I hope."

Emma's hand found my shoulder, grounding me. "Just how much you love 80's music," she teased.

Emma passed me a drink. I took it, glancing between the two of them — Emma laughing, Brianna smiling — when I felt it.

A force slammed into my back. Hard. My drink exploded across my sleeve. I staggered half a step, heart already locking into fight mode.

Then breath on my ear. Hot. Tainted with alcohol and venom.

"You screw dog, maggot, cunt."

The words sliced through the neon haze.

Everything else vanished — the noise, the lights, the music.

All gone.

The world narrowed to a pinpoint focus.

And I knew without even turning that the night was about to tear itself wide open.

CHAPTER 38: BROTHERHOOD UNDER THE LIGHTS

My gaze stayed locked on Emma, making sure she saw nothing, sensed nothing, as I slowly pivoted to face the presence behind me. A towering figure loomed there — massive arms, cropped black hair, a stern, unreadable face.

My whole body braced. Fist starting to clench. Jaw locked. And then—
"Jacob, this is my husband, Chris."

"So, you're in public warehousing security too," the man said, his serious mask cracking into a wide, almost ridiculous grin.

The coil of tension inside my chest loosened. I shook Chris's hand, firm and solid, and he slugged back a mouthful of his drink. Relief rolled through me, quiet and sure. There was an understanding between men who'd spent too many hours in places like mine.

Chris chuckled, his eyes alive with mischief, reading my momentary panic for what it was. The misunderstanding dissolved into laughter, the kind that only comes after adrenaline spikes for no damn reason.

Chris's curiosity surfaced naturally, a sideways grin on his face. "Which prison do you work at?"

I let my posture relax a little.

"Metro Prison," I answered, "in the city."

Chris fished a pack of cigarettes from his pocket, offering one with a tilt of his head. "Need a smoke?"

I shook him off with a small smile but agreed to follow him outside — away from the pulsing noise.

The night air wrapped around us, cooler, cleaner, cutting through the neon haze we'd left behind.

"That's the second time I've been caught like that," I said, shaking my head. "Another time, standing in line at a supermarket. Colleague sneaks up behind me: 'Hi Boss.' Nearly fucking shit myself."

We laughed together, the sound rough and easy, a release of tension we both understood too well. Chris leaned against the wall, flicking ash from his cigarette.

"How long you been on the job?" he asked, genuine interest in his voice.

I took up a post beside him, stealing a quick glance toward the venue's doors. "Twenty years," I said. "Not all at Metro. Started at Yarra Prison. Shifted here after the divorce."

Chris took a drag, nodding. "I'm at Wendarra Prison. Six years now. Was a Chippie before that."

Stories spilled between us in quick beats — scars traded like old soldiers comparing wounds.

Something unexpected settled over me — ease. The usual division between government and private, between employers, between prisons — none of it mattered here. Not with Chris.

I found myself saying things I usually kept buried. Old stories. Opinions too sharp for anyone else. It was easy, knowing he worked somewhere else, far enough away from my mess.

It was like finding a long-lost friend, I never knew was missing.

We drifted back inside eventually, the bond between us solidified in the space of a few cigarettes and too many shared truths.

Chris stopped me. "You want a drink?"

"Yeah, thanks. Bundy and Coke." I said, voice casual. Watching Chris move through the crowd toward the bar, I stayed planted — eyes scanning, posture relaxed but ready. Standing watch while he ordered drinks didn't feel like a habit anymore. It felt normal.

Back at the table, Emma and Brianna peppered us with questions about where we'd vanished. My answer was simple and happy.

A smile — real this time — found its way to my face without effort.

Emma tugged me down beside her; Chris dropped into the chair next to me. The conversation flowed smooth as water. For the first time in a long time, I felt lighter.

Chris and I fell back into the rhythm easily, picking apart the realities of the job. We circled the subject of remand prisoners — that special breed of chaos — trading strategies, trading stories.

Chris grinned, shaking his head. "Like when you find a shiv stashed in their cell and they swear they've got no fucking idea how it got there."

I laughed, the sound low and knowing. The look we exchanged said it all — we understood this world in ways few others ever could.

Numbers were swapped. No big deal, no promises. Just a thread of brotherhood tied between us.

As the band kicked back into gear, Emma dragged me toward the dance floor, her hand warm and insistent. Chris and Brianna followed without hesitation.

The four of us moved into the heart of the music.

Laughter rose, merging with the beat, the neon lights spinning and blending around us like some wild, reckless dream. Singing loud to songs we all knew.

For once, the weight of the world slipped off my shoulders.

And under those pulsing lights, for just a little while, it almost felt like freedom.

CHAPTER 39: A MORNING OF REFLECTION

I stirred from a restless slumber, the room around me tinted in soft light bleeding through the edges of the curtains. My gaze slid to the empty space beside me — Emma was already up. Fumbling for my phone on the nightstand, the numbers on the screen blurred into meaninglessness.

The door creaked open, Dougal nosed his way in, tail wagging, his whole body a blur of joy. He bounded onto the bed without hesitation, crashing into me with a wet nose and a heavy thump.

I scratched behind his ears, letting his enthusiasm pull me the rest of the way from sleep. At the doorway, Emma's silhouette appeared, calm and sure.

"I was trying to let you sleep in," she said, her voice warm.

I rubbed my face, a yawn dragging out of me. "Thanks," I muttered. "I was dead to the world."

"Want some coffee?" she asked, already tidying up the room, gathering laundry with easy efficiency.

"Yeah," I said, dragging myself upright. "Sounds perfect, thanks."

As I sat up, the sunlight grew stronger, creeping across the room like a slow tide. Emma parted the curtains wide, flooding the room in sudden brilliance that made me squint and curse under my breath.

"Last night was something else," I said, planting my feet on the floor. Dougal pressed his head against my leg, revelling in the attention.

Emma leaned casually against the doorframe, a smile playing at the corners of her mouth.

"You and Chris seemed to hit it off."

"Yeah," I admitted. "It was good... talking shop with someone who gets it. Even if we work at different prisons."

Stretching the sleep from my shoulders, I made my way to the ensuite. The aches of the week still clung to me, but they didn't feel as heavy this morning.

"Brianna and I made plans for next weekend while you're on shift," Emma called out.

"Funny, isn't it? We both work for plumbing companies. Both married to prison officers. Guess we do get each other."

The rest of the weekend slipped into a familiar rhythm — chores, shopping, ticking off the endless to-do list. Ordinary stuff. But the memory of last night stuck with me like a warm ember, glowing just beneath the surface.

The conversation with Chris, the easy laughter over things only people like us would understand — it had cracked something open inside me.

Sunday afternoon found me in the kitchen, chopping vegetables with a steadier hand than usual. The simple act of cooking felt different. The constant churn of dark thoughts, the instinctive edge I carried after work... it wasn't there.

Talking with Chris had shifted something, loosened the knots inside me. It was a strange comfort knowing that with one call, one text, I could reach someone who understood without explanation or apology. We hadn't worked the same prison yards, hadn't walked the same tiers. But it didn't matter.

Experience had stitched a quiet brotherhood between us — a bond forged not by proximity, but by survival.

It was like finding something I hadn't even known was missing — and now I couldn't imagine not having it.

And for the first time in a long time, I didn't feel like I was carrying the whole fucking weight alone.

But peace like this didn't last long. It never did. Not for people like me.

CHAPTER 40: A DAY OF NEW CONNECTIONS

The train platform glowed faintly under the early morning light, a quiet meeting place for the half-asleep and the already defeated. I checked my watch — 05:01hrs, Tuesday.

Zipping my jacket a little higher against the bite of the morning chill, I glanced around at the other passengers. All of them locked in their own little pre-commute rituals, heads down, earbuds in, lost in the monotony of another working day.

When the train screeched to a halt, I climbed aboard and found a seat next to a bloke already dozing against the window. Pulling out my phone, I settled into my own ritual — building a playlist for the trip in.

Today called for something upbeat. Some of my all-time favourites, a soundtrack for the strangely buoyant mood I hadn't felt in a long time.

Refreshed. Reinvigorated. Energised. It was weird, trying to put words to it.

The sort of feeling that had been missing for years. And while weekends spent with Neil and Caroline were always a good distraction, this was different. Meeting Chris had hit differently — like compressing years of friendship into one night.

At the prison gates, I caught myself exchanging morning greetings with a few officers. Caught a few off-guard — not used to seeing me smile.

Inside the parade room, I scanned the roster and spotted a new name paired with mine: Jacklyn Campbell. A familiar face. She'd worked around the place for years, floating between units, always with a no-nonsense presence. We locked eyes across the room and shared a nod — the silent agreement of people about to be thrown into the same trenches.

After parade, we fell into step crossing the yard.

"Morning, Jacklyn," I said, shifting my bag and papers to my other hand.

"Morning, Mr. Daniels," she answered, formal but not stiff.

"Jacob," I corrected, flashing a grin. "Unless we're standing in front of the prisoners."

She smiled back, brief but genuine.

The day began its familiar grind — prepping the unit, getting ready for transfers, medical runs, appointments. As the unit came to life, prisoners shuffling around half-awake, I watched over Jacklyn move.

Efficient. Organised. No wasted words, no dithering.

I leaned back in my chair, sipping at my coffee, and let myself just observe for a while. The way she managed the prisoners — barking short, clear instructions, keeping them moving, even getting some of the laziest ones to clean their cesspit cells — it was impressive.

Gender didn't mean a damn thing in this job. Competence was what mattered. And Jacklyn had it.

By midmorning it was time for cell inspections. Jacklyn glanced around for a broom handle to check windows — and without saying a word, I pointed toward the spot behind the filing cabinet.

Stick in hand, she moved down the stairs, starting the inspections. Her voice echoed through the unit — authoritative without crossing into overbearing.

"You need to sweep and mop this cell every day," she told one prisoner, deadpan and calm, without having to scream to make her point.

I leaned back again, letting a slow smile creep across my face.

Yeah, I thought, watching her work.

This place needed more people like her.

CHAPTER 41: BONDS FORGED BEHIND BARS

By the time the afternoon sun began to mellow, Jacklyn and I found a rare pause in the day's usual chaos. Files stacked neatly, paperwork up to date, the Unit ran on autopilot for once. We both knew it was a brief reprieve — a new reception prisoner was due any minute, ready to kick off the madness again.

"I've been very impressed with your work this morning, Jacklyn," I said, meaning it.

"Thank you, just doing my job," she replied, her eyes scanning the steady trickle of prisoners still moving about the yard.

Working side-by-side like this, the conversation had started to drift beyond the usual operational chatter.

In this line of work, every word carried weight. Every admission was a potential vulnerability. Officers learned early on how to keep personal details under lock and key, the same way they kept prisoners behind bars.

I found food was the safest ground to walk. Talk about cooking, favourite meals — it was a neutral zone, far from the emotional minefields. Everybody needed to eat.

From there, it was easier. The tension eased. Conversation flowed more naturally. A better feel for the person watching your back.

Jacklyn might have been small, but she carried herself with the sort of authority you couldn't fake. No soft touches here. She shattered any bullshit assumptions prisoners had about female officers being an easy target.

Even her appearance backed it up — short, practical black hair, no fuss with makeup or flashy nails.

Professional to the core.

Time slipped by. Between keeping an eye on the floor, we talked about movies, music, even a bit about sports — all the things that kept you feeling human in a place built to crush you.

Eventually, the conversation veered closer to personal ground. I mentioned being married, careful as always to point out that I didn't wear a ring — not in here. One more thin layer of protection, a boundary, prisoners didn't need to know.

Jacklyn glanced around, making sure no prisoners were hovering close enough to overhear. Leaning in, her voice dropped.

"Just got out of a two-year relationship," she said, almost like she was confessing a crime.

The story spilled out — the dead weight of a partner who couldn't be bothered to lift a finger.

A breakup long overdue.

"She treated the house like a hotel and me like the maid. Glad it's over," she finished, with a shrug that carried more relief than bitterness.

I didn't hesitate.

"I can relate," I said. "Living with someone who won't pull their weight grinds you down."

Jacklyn's whole posture changed — less guarded, less rigid.

Like the pressure she carried on her shoulders had eased up, even if only for a moment.

There, in the middle of all the steel and concrete and desperation, a small thing happened — trust.

Not the naive kind.

The hardened kind.

The kind forged quietly between people who understood just how heavy life could get when you carried it alone.

CHAPTER 42: THE QUIET PACT

Two hours till lockup, and something had shifted.

Jacklyn and I had moved through the day like we'd worked together for years, not hours. It wasn't forced. It wasn't rehearsed. It just… worked. Like the sort of rhythm, you don't build — it just clicks into place.

She answered the phone — I passed her a Post-it ready for her to write something down.

No words. No cue. Just instinct.

By the time the radio snapped with the lockup call, the Unit had settled into a low simmer. Prisoners moved about slowly, like tired ghosts collecting scraps before curfew.

"I'll take the top tier," I said, eyes on the stairs.

Jacklyn gave a nod, already moving toward the dayroom. "Fine."

She passed the Security Officer walking in, nodded without breaking stride, then keyed the front door locked. No wasted motion. Just clean, deliberate steps. She moved like someone who had nothing to prove — and nothing to fear.

Upstairs, I started the sweep. The air was heavier now. Not quite oppressive, but close. The sort of weight that hung around the vulnerable — the mentally unwell prisoners who hovered near their cells. Not quite cave-dwellers, not quite social. They existed in that grey space between function and collapse.

I didn't ignore them.

A nod. A quiet word. A small moment of reassurance — "I'll be here tomorrow, if you need anything." That was sometimes all it took. Just letting them know they weren't invisible.

Empathy wasn't weakness. It was tactical. You didn't show it often, but when you did, it had to be real.

The final cell door clanged shut behind me. I turned, descended the stairs slowly, watching Jacklyn stack her paperwork and bag.

"Hey," I said, voice low. "Can I ask you something?"

She stepped aside, didn't flinch. "Sure."

"What's your impression of Thompson?"

Jacklyn's face didn't twitch. "Honestly?"

"Yeah. Always."

"He's a cunt."

The word landed with a perfect lack of ceremony. Flat. Final.

I couldn't help it — I smirked. "I wouldn't have said it out of respect... but yeah. He's a cunt."

She shifted her bag, like the conversation was one more administrative task.

"I've seen him hitting up new guys for canteen items. Leaning on them."

Jacklyn's voice dropped. "Want me to 'find' something in his cell tomorrow?"

The way she said it... casual. Like offering to grab milk on the way in.

"That's what I was thinking. But only if you're comfortable."

"I am," she said. No hesitation.

"Go for it." I grabbed my bag, careful not to look too interested. "Just don't be the one who finds it."

She smiled at that. Subtle. Professional. "Got it."

"We'll call in Security. Let them make the discovery. Let them write the reports."

She nodded again. A silent pact made under strip lights and steel.

We joined the others to finish lockup. Quick, precise, wordless. We swept both Units, double-checked doors, clicked bolts and locks. The sort of efficiency you couldn't fake.

It wasn't just reassuring — it was rare.

Jacklyn didn't flinch when hard calls had to be made. And she understood something most officers didn't: you don't protect the vulnerable by being kind.

You protect them by being willing to do what others won't.

Outside, the cool night air wrapped around me. The last round of shift-checks dragged on as staff filtered out in ones and twos.

I spotted Jacklyn chatting with two other officers — female, like her — relaxed, casual. She laughed at something. Genuine.

No one came over to me. And I didn't mind. For once, the chatter around me wasn't noise. It was just… comforting. White noise after a storm.

The walk to the train was slow, deliberate. My boots felt lighter. My shoulders too.

I even let a woman cut in front of me at the ticket gate.

Didn't curse. Didn't sigh.

Just smiled. Not that she saw it.

Platform 15 was half-empty. I stood in my usual spot, flicking through my playlist. Nothing too dark tonight. Something with a bit of rhythm. Party music, maybe. Felt right.

I slipped into my seat, pressed play, leaned back.

Then came the buzz in my pocket.

A message from Chris.

'How you doin?'

Simple. Perfect.

The smile it pulled from me was instinctive. I texted back. Told him about Jacklyn. About Thompson. About how she'd offered — without prompting — to "find" something in his cell so we could get him moved.

Chris replied:

'Sounds exactly like something you and I would do.'

And it was.

For the rest of the trip, we messaged back and forth. No masks. No filtered words. Just two men who'd seen the worst of things… finding some sort of light in the shared darkness.

Time passed in a blink.

Back home, I stepped inside. The smell of garlic and tomato from the kitchen. Emma turned at the bench, apron dusted with flour, wine glass in hand.

I pulled her into a hug, kissed her gentle.

She leaned back, smiling. "You're in a good mood. Everything okay at work?"

"Better than okay," I said. "Jacklyn's solid. Thinks the same way I do."

Emma raised an eyebrow.

"Is that a good thing?"

I laughed. "In this job? It's rare."

I told her about the texts with Chris. Mentioned inviting him and Brianna over for a BBQ next weekend.

"Sounds perfect," she said. And meant it.

We cooked dinner together. Chatted about nothing. About everything.

And for the first time in a long time… I felt present.

Whole.

Like the chaos hadn't followed me home.

Emma caught me smiling over the stove. She didn't ask why. She just smiled back.

Because she knew. She'd waited a long time to see it. And now, it was finally there.

CHAPTER 43: GHOSTS AND GRINS

The morning light crept in sluggishly, painting the Unit in soft gold. But the stillness wasn't what caught my attention. It was the air—lighter somehow. The tension that usually hung like static had thinned.

Even the prisoners felt it.

They moved quieter, more casual. No loud demands, no posturing. Some nodded as they passed. A few muttered 'mornin' without a hint of sarcasm. It was subtle—but real.

Maybe they sensed it, too.

That Jacklyn and I had their backs. That we weren't just punching a clock—we were holding the line.

By mid-morning, Jacklyn eased to her feet. No fanfare. Just that calm, deliberate rhythm she carried. I didn't need to remind her about Thompson. She hadn't forgotten. It was already in motion.

I stayed at the desk, coffee in hand. Hot. Bitter. Grounding.

A couple of prisoners loitered nearby. I asked about their day, light check-ins. Nothing deep, just enough to keep a read on their state of mind. In Unit A, you didn't need to dominate the floor. You just needed to be present.

The phone buzzed. I picked up.

"Medical, Grant speaking."

"Yeah, it's Jacob, Unit A. Just following up on that doctor appointment for McLean."

"Let me check with the nurse." Pause. Then, offhand: "Hey, tell Jacklyn she's down for MSO training in the next few weeks."

"Right," I said, masking the jolt. "I'll pass it on."

I didn't like it.

Not because she wasn't capable. She was. But because people like her didn't come around often—and they didn't stay long. Not in places like this.

She passed by just then, heading for the top tier.

"You good?" she asked, reading the change on my face like a roadmap.

I kept my voice even. "Grant just told me you're down for MSO training."

Jacklyn blinked. "Didn't know it'd come up that fast."

"Typical," I said. "Soon as I find someone who gets how I run the Unit... they get moved."

She turned back toward the stairs, smirk tugging at her mouth. "I'm not going anywhere. Just keeping doors open."

That was enough. Said what needed saying.

Time passed. Jacklyn circled back to the desk, giving me a nod—our quiet signal.

Time to move.

I pressed the radio. "Security Senior, Unit A, phone location over?"

"Visits," came the reply.

I dialled quick, cutting through the line noise.

"Visits, Senior Berry."

"Hi Michelle, Jacob. I need a couple of officers to search a few cells. One's a targeted search."

There was a pause, then, "Give me ten minutes—they're finishing a strip."

Perfect.

While we waited, we talked. Not about Thompson. Not directly.

Jacklyn told me more about her training—how medical had always interested her. She'd responded to an expression-of-interest email months ago. Forgot all about it.

"Good for you," I said. And I meant it. "You're the sort of person who'll actually make use of the training."

"I just want to keep my options open," she replied. "Keep moving."

I understood. Better than most.

Ten minutes later, two Security Officers stepped through the front door.

Jacklyn handed them the cell numbers. She said to start with Thompson's.

Smart.

If he'd caught wind of the search, he might've flushed something—or made a play we couldn't unwind. This way, it was clean. Controlled. Quick.

They moved quietly—door closed, no noise.

We observed from the desk. Waited.

Ten minutes.

Then they came back. One of them held a plastic bag—small, but heavy with implication. The other officer hit the phone and called it in.

I enquired, "Found something?"

"Excess medication, and it's not all Thompson's." Came the reply.

Short. Clean.

Just how I liked it.

They moved on to the other cells. But it didn't matter.

We had what we needed.

Thompson would be gone by the afternoon.

Not a single fingerprint on the play.

And all they'll remember is that Security found it.

CHAPTER 44: SHADOWS AND SHIFTS

The snap of latex gloves breaking seal signalled the end of the search.

The security officers stood at our desk, hands empty now, but the weight of what they'd found hung in the air. One of them dropped the plastic bag beside me. It landed with a soft slap.

Jacklyn offered them coffee. They declined. They weren't here to drink coffee. Just deliver consequences.

Supervisor Debrah Jennings entered next. Her boots struck the floor like a metronome, another officer trailing behind her. Standard procedure when things were serious.

Without a word, the two officers collected the bag. A silent nod passed between us. They headed downstairs with Jennings, where conversations happened behind closed doors.

I turned to Jacklyn. "Keep an eye out for Thompson. Let me know if you spot him."

"No problem," she said, already scanning the yard.

The desk gave us a limited view—just enough to catch the edge of the yard, never the full picture. But that was fine. The real picture was unfolding in motion.

Moments later, Jennings returned, this time climbing the stairs halfway, scanning the Unit from top to bottom. Her tone was clipped.

"Have you seen Thompson?"

I shook my head. "He's in the yard. We haven't sent him anywhere."

And there he was—Thompson—ambling back toward Unit A, deep in conversation with another prisoner. Casual. Relaxed. Oblivious.

He didn't see the three officers slip out the front door until it was too late.

They intercepted him like clockwork—one motioned, one flanked, one kept an eye on the surroundings. Thompson hesitated but followed. No choice in the matter.

They guided him back inside. Jennings waited like a ghost at the foot of the stairs, already turning toward his cell. They moved together, a slow procession up to the top tier.

Thompson paused at the door, made the usual noise.

"It's not mine."

Of course it wasn't.

The cuffs came out. Smooth. Clean. No resistance. Jennings radioed ahead.

"Unit G, standby to receive one."

I caught Jacklyn's movement from the corner of my eye. She ascended the stairs behind them, ready to secure the cell. Meanwhile, I began the admin—calls to the box writer, medical, kitchen. The pieces always moved faster once the domino tipped.

I waved down a billet.

"Yeah, boss?"

"Let the others know Thompson's gone. Check if he left anything in the laundry. Bring it to the desk."

He nodded and slipped away. I didn't need to tell him twice. Word would move through the Unit fast—and by the look on his face, it already had.

When Jacklyn returned forty minutes later, she was carrying two bags—one stuffed with clothes, paperwork, personal junk. The other, smaller, packed with canteen items. Chocolate. Chips. A few bottles of drink. And a single, dented tin of coffee.

She dropped the list beside me.

"No coffee in the cell," she said with a grin. "Weird, right?"

I raised an eyebrow. "Strange. Must've been looted."

She reached into the bag and produced the tin, holding it like contraband.

"Think I'll get a prisoner to throw this out. You know, one of the ones Thompson used to lean on."

"Make sure he knows it's coming from us," I said.

She nodded. "Oh, he'll get the message."

She disappeared with the bags, heading to the office downstairs. The door clicked shut behind her.

And just like that—Thompson was gone.

The shift was subtle, but real. The sort of change you didn't measure with noise, but with breath. The Unit exhaled. So, did I.

Some coffee would be 'thrown out'. Some prisoner, somewhere, would be handed back a little piece of dignity.

That was good enough—for now.

But I wondered how long it would last — before someone else stepped into Thompson's shoes.

CHAPTER 45: SHIFTING LINES

Lockup ran like clockwork. No drama, no attitude. Jacklyn and I moved through the unit like we owned it—which, in a way, we did. The Billets noticed. Even if they didn't say it, they felt it. The mood had shifted. The predators kept to themselves, the vulnerable stayed under our watch, and for once, the unit breathed without tension.

Moving Thompson helped. It always takes just one idiot to poison the whole Unit. Jacklyn had spotted a couple of loose meds during her rounds, grabbed them without making a song and dance. Tossed them into Thompson's cell. That sealed it. The paper trail was clean, and Thompson was gone.

We didn't play the game like the prisoners did. We didn't exploit the system for ourselves. We manipulated it to restore order. For the right reasons. And if management didn't like what we did —fuck 'em.

Even Unit B was easier. Word had gotten around about Jacklyn. She wasn't loud. Didn't need to be. One warning from her was enough. Miss lockup call, and you lose your TV. That sort of threat doesn't need repeating. And when the prisoners toed the line, it meant less time we spent repeating ourselves, less time correcting their bullshit.

This place feeds off routine. Every prison does. Doesn't matter if you're a prisoner or staff—you break pattern, and things start to crack. Find the habit, and you control the person. Simple.

Back in Unit A, we packed up. Jacklyn was folding her paperwork when I paused beside her.

"I'm having a BBQ Saturday. If you're not busy, you should come by," I said. "It's not just me—friend of mine from another prison and his wife will be there too. You'd like him."

Jacklyn tilted her head. Thinking. Then smiled. "Actually, that'd be perfect. My ex is picking up some of her stuff that day, and I'd rather be anywhere else."

"Use me as the excuse. I don't mind."

We stepped outside. "I'll text you the address. Say, 1 pm?"

"Sounds great," she said.

I hadn't invited a colleague to my place in twenty years. My old rule said you don't mix work and home. But maybe that rule was just a wall. And maybe I was done hiding behind them. With Jacklyn, it felt right. No warning bells, no second guessing.

In the locker room, I moved toward my locker slower than usual, still riding that post-shift calm. Phillips approached me, voice low.

"Hey, Jacob. Got an update on George."

I swung my bag over my shoulder. "Yeah?"

"Released on bail. Daughter picked him up. His lawyer thinks the charges will be dropped next week."

"Good. He didn't belong in here anyway. Hope he gets some peace."

Outside, I checked my phone. Two messages from Chris. I didn't open them yet. I'll read them later.

Then a tug at my jacket. Jacklyn again, smiling like the fresh air had finally reached her bones. We exchanged numbers. I sent her the address.

A nod, a wave, and we scattered into the night.

The train ride was its usual lull. Headphones in. Messages from Chris. Swapping war stories about the crooks, the daily grind. It was almost therapeutic—the way we debriefed without needing to say it was therapy.

Emma noticed it too. I saw it in her eyes when I walked through the door. She didn't say anything, but it was there—the look. That flicker of relief.

I cracked a joke with her about something I found funny. She laughed. I laughed. I felt like myself again.

And Emma knew it.

CHAPTER 46: SMOKE AND SHELTER

Saturday morning.

Normally I'd sleep in. But not today. Today had to be right.

Emma could tell. She kept straightening things that didn't need straightening. I scribbled out a shopping list on the back of an old envelope, checking supplies, opening cupboards, counting charcoal bags like it was mission critical.

Dougal watched over us both with mild suspicion. When Emma boxed up a few of his toys, he thought it was playtime. It wasn't.

Fridge stocked. BBQ ready. Firelighters, check.

"You want breakfast before you head out?" Emma asked. "Coffee?"

"Coffee would be great."

"I'll prep some salads while you're out," she said. "Brianna reckons Chris isn't big on greens, but I've got a couple he won't notice."

I smiled, glancing down at Dougal. "Don't worry, mate. I'll bring you back a bone."

By the time I arrived back, sunlight cut the yard in half—warm on one side, shadowed on the other. The decking was colder underfoot, tucked just out of reach of the breeze sliding in from the train tracks. It drifted over the back fence like a ghost that never stopped moving.

I lit the charcoal and let the smoke rise. Low and slow—just how Chris liked it. The table was half-set. A few mismatched chairs stood around it like strangers at a wake. No tablecloth. Just a roll of paper towel in the middle like it was standing guard. A couple of glasses—none that matched. Nothing fancy. Nothing staged.

Just enough — for the people who mattered.

By afternoon, the coals were glowing. Dougal barked. Then the doorbell rang.

Chris and Brianna. He carried an esky. She had food. Hugs. Grins. Handshakes.

Inside, 80s music played low in the background. Emma showed Brianna around—where we kept everything, what to ignore, what to use. Chris and I headed straight for the BBQ.

He cracked his esky, pulled out a bottle of vodka and a Coke. "Want one?"

"Already into a Bundy," I said, lifting my can in salute.

He poured himself a drink, took a seat. Dougal wandered over, sniffing his boots.

"Can smell my dog, huh?" Chris chuckled, scratching behind his ears. "Good to finally be here."

As cooking time crept up, I brought out the meat—chicken wings, sausages, lamb cutlets—pulled straight from the fridge, still cold through the plastic. The Tupperware was old, stained with time and spice. I set them down next to the cutting board, along with the knife I'd been using—standard kitchen blade, nothing fancy, but sharp enough for now.

Chris reached for the blade. Rolled it in his hand. Checked the edge like a man checking the balance of a tool he respected, not just used.

"If you want, I can sharpen this for you," he said. "Got my gear in the back of the 4WD."

I glanced at him, smiled. "Yeah, maybe another time. Todays about relaxing. Food. Friends."

He nodded but held the knife a moment longer before setting it down.

"Just so you know," he said, almost casually, "I make knives."

That gained my attention. I looked at him properly.

"Been doing it for years," he went on. "Sort of a hobby. Sometimes sell one if someone wants something custom. Helps cover the materials."

He wasn't boasting—more like letting me in on something few people knew. One of those quiet things a man does to stay sane.

"I've been working on one with an obsidian blade," he added, chuckling. "Black on black. Looks fucking mean."

I laughed, surprised. "Didn't pick you for a bladesmith."

Chris turned, gestured toward the old crab-apple tree in the back corner. The thing had died years ago. Its bark peeled like sunburnt skin, bone-white against the green of the hedge behind it.

"That tree," he said. "If you ever want it gone, I'll take it off your hands."

He looked back at me.

"That wood would make a beautiful handle. Long blade. Something that feels old."

I sipped my drink, considered it. "It's yours. Next time you're here, take it."

Then I smirked, raising my can slightly. "Just make me one out of it."

Chris nodded, no words. Just a look that said *done*.

And just like that, a deal was made. Quiet. Honest.

Didn't know then how much it would matter.

We talked. Shit talk mostly. Work. Life. The usual. Twenty minutes felt like two hours.

Somewhere in the haze of it, I made a comment—half a joke—about getting rid of a few prisoners the way they get rid of people: quietly, efficiently, no tears shed.

Manipulation. Pressure. Leverage. The same game—just flipped.

Chris gave a low chuckle. No surprise. He'd played that game too.

"Best one lately was a piece of shit named Osborne," I said.

Chris's smile disappeared. "That cunt." His tone flattened, like he was remembering something best left buried. "Had a few run-ins with him over the years. Same as everyone."

I nodded. "Got him shifted the other day. Billets helped. Didn't take much."

Chris leaned back. His eyes weren't on me anymore. "Someone needs to kill that fucking prick one day."

It didn't land like a joke. It didn't have to.

I didn't flinch. Just held his gaze.

"Well," I said, slow and even, "if that ever needs doing... I know someone who could make it happen."

Silence stretched out between us. Heavy. Understood. Some truths don't need a punchline.

Dougal barked again — just before the doorbell rang. Like he knew.

Jacklyn.

Bottle of red in hand, smile on her face. I introduced her to Emma, who pulled her into a hug before I could finish the words. I think she whispered something. I never found out what.

We moved through to the kitchen. Brianna greeted her with that polite warmth she did so well. Emma waved toward the cupboards.

"We'll show you once where everything is. After that—help yourself. We want you to feel at home."

Brianna laughed. "Careful—Chris hears that, you'll never get rid of him."

I poured Jacklyn a glass. "Come outside."

Chris stood when she stepped through. Shook her hand. "So, you're the one who's softened this bloke up."

Jacklyn smirked. "Not even close. We just watch each other's backs. That's it."

The conversation picked up like it had never stopped. Work stories. Jargon. Dark jokes that would've made no sense to anyone else. But for us, it was oxygen. Just to talk and be understood.

I ducked inside to grab the meats from the fridge. When I came back out, Jacklyn and Chris were still going—deep in something about Thompson. She was telling him how she'd 'found' a few pills that helped get him moved.

Chris laughed. "Classic. Nothing beats a good, staged find."

The BBQ hissed as the meat hit the grill. Wings sizzled. Steak seared. The smoke carried every memory with it. Everyone dug in. Cajun wings were the standout—Chris couldn't get enough.

Emma and Brianna exchanged salad compliments like two chefs pretending not to compete. Jacklyn thanked us like she meant it.

As dusk set in, I suggested we move inside. The air had cooled.

Emma's hand brushed the small of my back as we stood. No words. Just a look. One of those rare ones that says *this was right*.

Around the dining table, things slowed. Softer tones. Softer light.

"Alright," Emma said. "No more work talk."

She turned to Jacklyn. "Tell us about you."

I picked up Dougal and settled him on my lap.

Jacklyn gave the brief version—background, corrections, family. The stuff you say when you're being polite.

Emma leaned in a little. "Jacob said you're recently out of a relationship. Taking a break, or open to something new?"

Jacklyn didn't even blink. "Break. Definitely. As soon as people find out you're single, it's open season. Some of them—" she paused, "—they act like predators. They don't let up."

"Really?" I asked, surprised.

"You'd be shocked," she said, checking her phone. "I should go. It's been a great day." She turned to Emma. "You have a beautiful home. Thank you."

Emma placed a hand over hers. "You're welcome anytime."

Dougal barked again. This time, it was the goodbye bark.

Chris and Brianna stood as Jacklyn grabbed her bag. Emma hugged her again—longer this time. The sort of hug that feels more like family than friendship.

I walked her to her car, parked beneath the streetlight.

"Thanks for coming," I said.

"Thanks for inviting me. I mean it." She gave a quiet smile, then disappeared behind the wheel.

I stood in the red glow of her taillights until they faded.

Inside, cleanup had already started.

"You two heading off?" I asked.

Chris nodded. "Brianna's driving. Got stuff I need to get on with tomorrow."

"You're welcome to stay. Spare room's ready."

"Next time," he said, already loading up.

At the door, Brianna hugged me. Chris hugged Emma.

"Thanks again," Brianna said. "Today was perfect."

"I'll text you next week," Chris added.

"You always do," I said, watching them disappear into the dark.

I closed the door, looked down at Dougal.

"Come on, mate," I muttered. "Time for bed."

CHAPTER 47: THE CHICKEN OR THE FISH

Tuesday.

It had started like any other day. Quiet. Routine. Which usually meant something was going to blow up.

Jacklyn and I moved like clockwork—no words needed. We read each other like muscle memory. The early hours passed with the usual bullshit. One prisoner shuffled to another unit, and we had one inbound from Psych. I'd been told he was stable. Which in prison terms meant he hadn't stabbed anyone *yet*.

Just keep an eye on him. But don't let him see you're keeping an eye on him.

Easier said than done in a unit this small. No good corners, no blind spots, no backup officer positioned at the right angle to catch the subtle tells. Jacklyn and I had gotten creative. I used Billets as mobile camouflage. Positioned them in front of me while I watched over the real target just over their shoulder. They never knew, and I never explained. I shifted so often, new officers thought I had ADHD.

They found it strange. The way you never held eye contact during a chat. Your eyes were always roaming. Head on a swivel. Never really looking *at* someone, just through them—scanning for the twitchy hand, the side glance, the shifting body weight. A threat.

Jacklyn brought up the weekend. Her voice light. Chris had made an impression.

"He has a big personality," she said with a grin. "You two bounce off each other like brothers."

I nodded. "Yeah. There's something about him. We just… get each other."

She leaned in. "So, when's the next BBQ?"

"Thinking a fortnight. Chris has a mate from Wendarra Prison he wants to bring. Might ask a guy I worked with at Yarra, too."

"That'd be great," she said. "Emma made me feel like I'd known her forever."

I smiled. "She's like that. Once she lets you in, you are family."

And that was the truth. She didn't say much, but I'd told her about Jacklyn. Said she was the perfect partner to work with—sharp, intuitive, and knew when to push and when to back off.

After lunch, our new arrival shuffled in. Twenty-three. Too young for this place. I spoke to the psych unit officer while Jacklyn handled paperwork.

"How's he been?" I asked.

The officer gave a shrug. "Okay now. Last few weeks have been better, so Psych signed off on the transfer. He's manageable—*if* he's medicated."

"And if he's not?"

The officer's face hardened. "Then he picks someone, watches 'em for a while, and one day—*bang*—he lashes out. No warning. If you're in the way, you're getting clocked too."

Got it. Message received.

Jacklyn walked him in, explaining the rules in that calm, firm way of hers. Patient—but not soft. These weren't your garden-variety prisoners—she knew that. They needed clearer instruction, a little more guidance. Like reminding someone how to fill in a form, because they forgot step three again.

Mid-afternoon. I was filing some paperwork when the Unit cracked open.

"I'M GONNA FUCKING KILL YOU!"

The shout tore through the Unit like a gunshot.

I turned toward the dayroom. Carter. Middle of the floor. Hair feral, fists wired tight. Eyes stretched open like floodlights—seeing everything but focusing on nothing.

My instinct barely made it out of my mouth. "What the fuck…"

Jacklyn jumped up; eyes locked on him. I touched her shoulder, calm and steady.

"I've got this. Ring upstairs. Get a Psych nurse. Now."

She hesitated, then nodded and picked up the phone. I wasn't dismissing her—I just knew Carter. And he knew me. I could pull rank. That helped.

I walked into the dayroom slowly. Billets were already backing off. The tension hung like metal in the air—dense, magnetic, waiting to spark.

"Hey Carter," I said softly, "what's going on?"

"I'M GONNA FUCKIN' KILL 'EM!" he roared again, standing in the dayroom like his feet were anchored to one spot.

Chest puffed. Muscles tense. I checked for weapons. Saw nothing, but I wasn't stupid enough to assume he was clean.

"Who's after you?" I asked, keeping my tone low.

"Them. They're after my stuff."

"Alright. How about we sit down and talk about it?" I pulled out a chair and motioned gently. "Just the two of us."

He didn't move.

"Come on. Have a seat." I slowly sat down.

Carter hovered. I could see the wires sparking in his brain. Slowly—like a glitchy robot—he sat down. Shallow breaths. His face flickered like a bad signal—blank one second, twitching the next.

"Want a coffee?" I offered.

"…what?"

"Coffee. You drink coffee, don't you?"

"Yeah."

Jacklyn was watching. I nodded her over. "Two coffees please—my usual. Carter, how do you take it?"

He hesitated. "Milk."

"Sugar?"

"Two."

She walked off without a word. She was smart. Knew the trick—same cups. Different ones would freak him out. Trigger something, we didn't need today.

I leaned forward; arms folded on the table. Calm. Engaged.

"So, do you want to talk to me, or someone else?" I asked gently.

Carter blinked. Confused.

"Let me try again," I said. "You ever been to a wedding reception?"

He looked lost. I kept going.

"You sit down; waitress comes over. Says, 'Chicken or the Fish?'"

His brow furrowed.

"You hate fish, right?"

"Yeah."

"Then it's chicken. Easy. My point is—it's about *two* choices. That's all."

I raised my hand slowly. Pointed left. "Chicken." Then right. "Fish."

He looked down at my hand. Then back at me.

"Do you want to talk to *me*…" I pointed left. "Or to someone else?" Right.

He stared at my hands like they'd solve the war in his head.

Jacklyn returned. Two identical paper cups, placing one in front of Carter. He picked it up slowly. Sipped. No reaction. Good.

Behind him, Nurse Wilson arrived. Quiet. Professional. Waited for a signal.

"Carter, is it okay if Miss Wilson joins us?" I asked.

He turned his head. Saw her. Nodded.

"Hi Carter," she said, easing into the seat beside him, hands visible, voice soft.

"I came here to talk with you, if that's alright?"

He nodded again.

I stood. "Okay Carter, I'll leave you with Miss. I have work to do. But I'll check in on you soon."

He gave a small half nod. That was enough.

I returned to the desk. Jacklyn was already seated. Watching.

We sat together, saying nothing. Just watching the table, watching Carter slowly come back to Earth.

Some days, survival wasn't about brute force or shouting louder than the next guy.

Some days, it was about knowing when to talk about coffee. Or chicken. Or fish.

CHAPTER 48: HOLDING ON TO SOMETHING

It was quiet again.

Carter had calmed. Nurse Wilson had walked him back to his cell like a mother guiding a sleepwalker. He didn't resist. Just shuffled along, cradling his coffee like it was the last warm thing on earth.

The Unit exhaled.

Jacklyn and I sat back at the desk, the silence between us thick with aftershock. Not fear—just the sort of silence that follows a controlled detonation. The kind where you check all your limbs and thank the universe no one lost theirs.

She finally broke it. "You've used that before, haven't you?"

I turned my head slowly. "Used what?"

"The chicken or fish thing. That wasn't off the cuff."

I gave a half-smile. "Not my first time."

Jacklyn leaned in slightly, curious. Not pushing, just… studying.

I took a sip of my now-cold coffee and set it down. "When someone's spiralling out, they're not operating in our world anymore. You can't reason with logic—they're lost in a maze of their own making.

Thoughts don't line up. Everything's loud. Threats close in from every corner. So, you offer one thing. A lifeline. Simple. Tangible."

I paused, watching a prisoner shuffle past the office, eyes down.

"You ever see someone drowning, not physically—but mentally? Their eyes tell you before their mouth does. Like they're reaching out, but not with their hands."

Jacklyn nodded slowly.

"That's when you don't offer options. You don't complicate the *menu*. You say, 'Chicken or Fish?' Two hands. One for each."

She crossed her arms. "And that actually works?"

"Sometimes. Not always. Nothing's foolproof. But when you strip reality down to two choices, you give them an anchor. Left or right. Talk to me or talk to someone else. Sit or don't. It cuts through the white noise. And right at that moment, Carter needed something to grab hold of."

Jacklyn leaned back, thoughtful.

"There was this guy years ago at Yarra," I continued. "Big Lebanese guy. Had done a bashing, Police mainly, but anyone in authority would cop it. Paranoia didn't even cover it. Thought every officer was against him. That the food was poisoned."

One day he's in full battle mode—shouting through the vents, pulling apart his mattress looking for 'whatever'. No one could get near him."

"What did you do?" Jacklyn asked, eyes fixed.

"I stood outside his cell and said, 'Hey mate, chicken or fish?'"

I chuckled, but it was hollow.

"He blinked, like I'd spoken in a foreign language. I repeated it. Then I told him I'd bring whatever he picked. But only *if* he sat down. Only *if* he stopped tearing up his cell. And just like that... he sat."

Jacklyn looked half-impressed, half-disbelieving.

"I brought him two sandwiches from the kitchen. Both chicken. Didn't matter. He needed the *act* of choosing, not the outcome. That moment grounded him."

She rubbed her jaw, processing it. "So, not about the food."

"Nope. It's about focus. Just enough reality to anchor them. Not so much it drags them under."

I stood and stretched, the knots in my shoulders reminding me I wasn't twenty anymore. "This place will always give you chaos. Our job isn't to control it. It's to slow it down. Long enough to survive the day."

"I'll remember that. Chicken or fish."

I nodded, eyes narrowing. "You can use it with family members... anyone."

We both smirked, but behind it was the truth.

You don't reason with madness.

You reach in with steady hands and pull them back—one choice at a time.

CHAPTER 49: SMOKE ON THE HORIZON

Another fortnight. Another payday. Another countdown ticked off in this never-ending dance of routine and watchfulness.

No code blacks. No lockdowns. No hospital runs or med cart brawls. The Unit was running like a silent machine. Jacklyn and I had smoothed the gears so well even the Billets kept their heads down. But they'd never admit it. Respect, like danger in a prison, rarely announced itself.

Still, the calm made me twitchy.

Today was BBQ Day. A breather. Or at least, that was the plan.

I'd prepped early. Chris's favourite Cajun wings had been marinating overnight in a mix of spice and memory. I could already hear him laughing, drink in one hand, cigarette in the other, spinning some warped tale only someone like us could find funny.

Dougal was doing laps around the backyard, tail wagging, waiting for me to throw the ball. His bark was sharp, echoing off the fence, full of that manic energy only dogs and psychopaths truly understand. I tossed the ball half-heartedly—my head already replaying mental checklists for the cook-up.

Inside, Emma had everything looking magazine perfect. Plates, platters, cutlery, all aligned with her quiet precision. It felt like peace. Like the calm before the sort of storm you don't see on a weather radar.

"What time are you expecting everyone?" she asked, catching me mid-swig of coffee number two.

"About twelve. Chris might rock up early." I said, fridge door still hanging open as I grabbed the meat.

"You making salads?" I grinned.

Emma rolled her eyes. "Jacob, not everything's about salads. Brianna and I are on dessert duty. Jacklyn's bringing salad."

"Perfect." I muttered, already calculating grill timings in my head like I was prepping a tactical entry.

Music came next—80s classics, loud enough to stir nostalgia, not so loud Emma would shoot me that *look*. But it wasn't the music that stirred Dougal—it was the sound of tires crunching gravel. He froze, ears alert, then exploded toward the front door like a missile.

Chris. And Brianna.

Dougal bolted through the open door, barking in celebration. I followed, slower, already smiling.

Chris pulled me into one of those bear-hugs that says, 'We're still standing', even with the weight we carry—like backpacks full of bricks.

Inside, Brianna disappeared into the kitchen with Emma, both talking in tones only women with secrets can master. Chris dropped his esky like a lifeline, lit a smoke before his arse even hit the chair.

"Luke might be a bit late. Had someone turn up at his place," he said, flicking his lighter, exhaling vodka fumes and nicotine.

"How's work?" he asked. Straight to it.

"Quiet." I replied, pouring my own drink.

Chris raised an eyebrow. "That a problem?"

"No incidents. Not even a whisper of drama. Nothing." I tapped my glass, eyes scanning the sky. "And that's what worries me."

Chris nodded, blowing out smoke. "Take the win, mate."

"I do. But I don't trust it."

We sat like that—conversation flowed, quiet paranoia—for forty minutes, until Dougal's bark shattered the moment again.

Jacklyn.

I opened the door and pulled her into a hug—an instinctive move, no second thoughts. She smelled like calm, with a glint in her eye that said she'd brought more than salad.

Emma welcomed her like family. Jacklyn beamed. Something about the way she softened in Emma's presence… it just felt right. She'd earned her place at the table.

Chris greeted her like a sister. Dougal barked again. Another car.

Phill.

"Come in, mate," I said, gripping his hand. "Everyone—this is Phill. Worked together back at Yarra."

More hugs, handshakes, polite smiles. Prison stories started flowing like a tap turned full bore. Brawls, stabbings, broken jaws. Normal war stories that made civilians flinch.

Another knock. Another bark. Only this time, I felt something shift.

Two men at the door.

"Jacob?" the one in front asked. "I'm Luke. Friend of Chris. From Wendarra Prison."

I clocked the other man. Something off. Too quiet. Eyes scanning behind me, like he was casing the house.

"And who's this?" I asked, locking my gaze.

He stepped forward. "Mark. Luke said I could speak with you and Chris."

My gut twisted.

"Wait here," I said sharply, and turned without waiting for a reply. Door shut.

I walked fast through the house. Emma saw the shift in my face but didn't say a word. She knew that look.

"Chris." My voice cut through the chatter like a blade.

He saw me and moved immediately, no hesitation. We walked back to the front door together. Opening the door, two men whispering, like they were rehearsing a lie.

"Hey Luke," Chris said cautiously. "Who's this?"

Mark stepped forward, but Luke intercepted. "Can we speak to you and Jacob in private?"

I nodded once. "Outside. Carport."

We walked out into the harsh daylight. Four men, all carrying shadows.

Chris folded his arms, eyes like steel.

"What's going on?" he asked. "Who is this?"

Mark stepped forward, desperation leaking from every pore. "My name is Mark… I need your help."

Chris and I didn't flinch.

"I need you to get justice… for my daughter."

There it was. The crack in the quiet. The tremor before the quake. The storm we'd been waiting for just walked into our backyard.

CHAPTER 50: THE WEIGHT OF JUSTICE

Mark stood there like a man held together by threadbare grief. His eyes were bloodshot, hands twitching like something inside him was ready to snap.

I opened the side gate and led them towards the deck. The others saw us coming—faces turned, chatter cut short. Jacklyn caught the shift immediately. Her body stiffened, posture defensive. She knew this wasn't about ribs and potato salad anymore.

I cracked open the sliding door. Emma looked over, sensing the change.

"Can you give us some space for a bit?" I asked, tone tight.

She stepped closer. "Are you okay?"

I nodded. "Yeah… just work stuff. I'll explain later."

She held my eyes for a beat longer, then nodded and walked away. The door shut behind her, sealing the world out.

I sat beside Chris and faced the man unravelling in front of us.

"Right," I said flatly. "Start from the beginning."

Mark looked like a bomb in a jacket—barely holding himself together. His fingers twitched on his knees. Mouth dry. He opened it once, then closed it again. When he finally spoke, his voice was fragile.

"My daughter was raped."

Silence. That kind that creeps into your bones.

"She went to a birthday party," he continued, breath ragged. "Eighteenth. With her best friend. A normal night. A fucking normal night."

The story came out in fragments—each one sharper than the one before. Drinks were spiked. She blacked out. Woke up in a strange room with a man inside her. Again. And again. Sodomised.

"My baby girl, she's only sixteen" he whispered. "My little girl."

He broke. The sobbing came hard and raw. No one moved. No one dared speak.

When he finally looked up, nothing human in his eyes—just scorched ruin.

"Two months ago. He was arrested. Cops say he's on remand… at Metro."

That peaked our attention. Jacklyn stiffened. Chris flicked ash off his cigarette like a reflex. I just stared at Mark, listening.

Mark pulled a handkerchief from his jacket, wiped his face, and kept going—fuelled now by rage.

"They're saying he might walk with a reduced sentence. 'Mental health.' 'Childhood Trauma.' 'Didn't know her age.' Fucking garbage excuses."

His fists clenched, white-knuckled.

"My daughter can't leave her room. I can't even touch her. Hold her. She won't even look at me anymore."

His voice cracked again, louder this time. "She was a happy kid. She loved school. Music. Now she's just… broken."

Chris turned on Luke. "Okay. First off—not cool, bringing this guy here without warning. Second—how the hell do you know Mark?"

Luke shifted awkwardly, caught off guard. "Mark used to live next to me. Years ago. I was just starting out in the job."

I leaned forward, tone sharp. "And what exactly do you expect us to do? This is my house. My home."

Luke tried to hold ground. "He doesn't expect anything. He just knew I worked in corrections. He's desperate."

I glanced at Chris. He didn't say a word, just nodded. We both knew that look in a man's eyes—the one that says he's staring down the barrel of hopelessness.

"What's his name?" I asked.

"Delany. Raymond Delany."

The name hung there like rot in the air.

I locked onto Luke. My voice went cold. "Look, I get he's in pain. But this isn't how you go about things. He's lucky I didn't throw him back through that gate."

"He just needed to talk," Luke said, softer now. "He's not asking for blood. Just someone to tell him things will be okay."

I sat there looking at Mark.

"Mark," I said, "I'm sorry for what your daughter went through. Truly. But you need to go now."

He looked up, eyes red, pleading. "Can't you do something?"

I stared into him. "Even if I could—I wouldn't be telling you."

Part of me wanted to promise him blood. The other part remembered what it would cost. Both parts knew I'd do it anyway.

"You need to go home. Be with your daughter. That's your job now."

His face fell. The light drained from him. Luke stood and gently helped him to his feet.

"I'm sorry for crashing your BBQ," Mark muttered. "He fucking sodomised my little girl."

He stood; shoulders slumped like the world had crushed him. Turned, and slowly walked back towards the street. I watched over Mark disappear into the dusk.

Back on the deck, the mood had ossified—like concrete poured over the party. Jacklyn sat silent. Arms folded. Chris lit another cigarette. I could feel the fury vibrating beneath his skin. As prison officers, we don't see the victims, unless you work at the courts. We just read what happened to them. No names. No faces.

I stared at the table, then at the half-empty glass beside me.

"So," I said, slow and deliberate. "Does anyone here think that piece of shit deserves to walk?"

No one answered. They didn't need to.

I took the drink. Finished it.

"Time to introduce Raymond Delany to real justice."

I set the glass down.

"Prison justice."

The kind that never makes it into a courtroom. The kind that doesn't need a gavel.

Only silence… and consequence.

CHAPTER 51: TRANSFER OF INTENT

We didn't speak much after lunch. Not after what Mark had dropped on us.

The laughter was shallow. Conversations stalled. The BBQ kept sizzling. But the air had changed—heavier, colder. A quiet storm building just behind the eyes.

But later, after everyone had drifted into smaller pockets of chatter, or stepped away for a smoke or a beer refill—we found the moment. The right moment.

Chris lit a smoke. Jacklyn leaned against the side rail. Phill stayed seated, watching me. Waiting. Like they all knew I was about to speak first.

And I did.

"If we're going to do this—if Delany's going to meet the justice Mark wants—then it starts with control."

I looked at each of them, slow and deliberate.

"I know someone at Yarra Prison. A name I trust. He understands how to make things happen quietly. He can get the job done."

Chris spoke first, "A prisoner? You trust him?"

"I do… when it comes to something like this. He'll do it. Just like he's doing someone a solid."

"But this isn't just about getting a prisoner moved. Normally, no one gives a shit where they end up—just that they're out of sight."

I paused.

"This time, we make sure Delany goes exactly where we want. No mistakes. No detours."

Jacklyn responded. "I can talk to the MSO. Drop a flag about Delany—say he made an inappropriate sexual remark to one of the nurses. Suggest he crossed the line."

She looked at me, dead serious. "You know what MSOs hate more than anything? Someone threatening medical staff. They'll want him out. Fast."

"That might get him removed," I nodded, "but it doesn't lock in *where* he lands. And that's everything."

Chris flicked ash off the edge of the deck. His tone was flat, calm—like he was reading off a grocery list.

"I'll send Intel a report. Say Delany's name's already bouncing around the Wendarra Prison units. Word is some old crew want him flogged over unpaid drug debts. Throw in a threat or two."

I nodded once. "And the other remand centre?"

Luke cleared his throat. "I know a bloke there. I'll get him to mirror the same story. Make Delany look like a liability everywhere *but* Yarra. It's the least I can do."

"Monday," I said. "Intel reports get lodged. Quietly. Jacklyn, speak to the MSOs Thursday—gives time for the flags to register. By Friday, PPU will be looking to move him. And when they do—Yarra will be the *only* option on the table."

The silence after that wasn't hesitation. It was agreement.

I turned to Phill.

"When we get the transfer notification, I'll need you to pass on a message to a prisoner in the Protection Unit."

Phill raised an eyebrow. "What sort of message?"

I looked him in the eye. Cold. No blink.

"Three words: *Delany. Coke Bottle.*"

Phill frowned for a beat—then he nodded.

"He'll know exactly what it means. And who it's from."

"Good," I said. "Then we let the system work the way it always has. Final."

I took another drink. Voice steady. No tremor. "But it won't be quiet."

I paused. "He'll be lucky if he ever walks again."

Chris didn't smile. Neither did Jacklyn.

This wasn't vengeance. This wasn't personal revenge.

It was balance.

The next time Mark sat in court—saw Delany—he'd know.

He'd *see* it.

I knew the line had long been crossed. Maybe it was years ago.

Didn't matter anymore. We were already on the other side.

Real justice. Prison justice.

Our Justice.

CHAPTER 52: PRESSURE LINES

Monday.

The air felt different the moment I stepped off the train. Could've been the clouds. Or the plan already slipping into gear. But it wasn't weather. It was weight.

I kept my head down on the walk to the prison. Didn't want to see faces. Didn't want small talk. Not today.

After parade, I climbed the stairs to Level 3. Main yard. Familiar stretch of concrete. Familiar stench of sweat, steel, and routine. Just before the top, I heard a voice behind me.

"Morning, Mr. Daniels."

I turned as I reached the landing. "Morning." Flat. No warmth.

She smiled. "Hi, I'm Sarah."

I shook her hand without thinking, turned, and kept walking. Didn't catch the surname. Didn't care. She was fresh—maybe two months in. Filling in while Jacklyn did her training.

Jacklyn would be shadowing off-unit for the next two weeks. That meant rotating fill-ins. Different face every day. No rhythm. No trust. No stability. They weren't bad officers—they just weren't her.

They didn't know the Unit. Didn't know the men.

And this Unit? It needed more than presence. It needed instinct.

Just after 9 am, routine done. Cell checks, meds, kitchen orders. The noise of the morning had settled into a low hum. I told Sarah I'd be in the office.

I walked in, locked the door behind me, and sat down. The computer blinked awake, the dull glow lighting the walls. I stared at it. Blank. Unmoving.

All I could see were Mark's eyes. Hear his voice. Feel the way he broke apart when he spoke about his daughter.

That rage... it was still there. Sitting just under the skin, coiled.

I logged in.

Typed slowly. Carefully.

Intel report. Nothing detailed. Just enough. Delany's name—front and centre. I added a line about whispers on the floor—prisoners saying they'd find a way to get to him even in protection. One would volunteer if they had to. Just for the chance to stab him.

I submitted the report. Quiet. Clean. One piece of a much larger storm.

Back at the desk, I sat still for a moment. Let the silence hold. Task complete.

Chris would be handling his part by now. I didn't need to check. He was a machine when it mattered.

"All good?" I asked Sarah. My tone softened.

"Yeah, all good," she replied. "No receptions today, but the Box Writer wanted to know if you were doing any cell moves. Wants a callback."

"You call him," I said. "Let him know—no moves today."

She nodded and went back to work. A few prisoners drifted past the desk, but seeing me there, they kept moving. They knew better than to test the edge of my patience today.

With coffee in hand, I tapped Sarah gently on the shoulder.

"I'll be out front with this. Radio if you need me—double click only."

I moved through the Unit slowly. Dayroom was calm. The usual tension in the air, but manageable.

Outside, sunlight had broken through the grey. Just a small pocket in the corner of the yard. It warmed my face for a moment. Short-lived, like most good things in this job.

I sipped my coffee and let the silence hang.

Then I heard the voice.

"Mr. Daniels, can I talk to you for a second?"

Collins.

His tone was off. Nervous. Hesitant.

"Sure. What's up?"

He stepped in closer, hand in his pocket, like he was about to show me something. That instinct hit fast and hard.

"Stop," I said, raising my hand. "Now follow me."

I opened the Unit door and led him inside. Didn't speak. Didn't explain. I caught Sarah's eye and nodded toward the office. She understood.

Collins followed without protest.

Inside, I locked the door and gestured to the seat. He appeared like a prisoner heading into court for sentencing.

He sat. Slowly. Quietly.

I sat opposite and placed my coffee on the desk.

"Alright," I said. "What have you got?"

Collins reached into his pocket—slowly—and pulled it out.

A fork.

No, not a fork anymore.

It was twisted metal—bent into a crude knuckle duster. Sharp prongs angled forward, perfect for punching through soft tissue, bone, anything.

It was prison work. Quiet. Purposeful. Meant to do damage fast.

I turned it over in my hand. Balanced it. It was crafted well. Too well.

"Where'd you find this?"

"Behind my socks. Top shelf. Last night, after lock-up." His voice shook. "It's not mine. Someone planted it. I don't know who."

I placed the fork on the desk, slid it aside.

Looked him dead in the eyes.

"Alright. I'll take care of it."

He nodded, but he wasn't calm. He was rattled.

"Don't say a word to anyone. Not about this. Not about this meeting."

He nodded again.

"If anyone even hints that you found something in your cell—you tell me. Immediately. Got it?"

"Yeah. Yes. Got it, Mr. Daniels."

I stood. "Head back to your unit. And remember what I said."

He left without another word.

Now I had a new problem.

Someone was trying to move Collins. But not the usual way. No threats. No violence. Just quiet pressure. A weapon left behind. Let the officers do the rest. Classic setup. Controlled. Safe.

That meant someone in the Unit had brains. That made it worse.

Whether they wanted Collins gone, or wanted him somewhere else, I didn't know yet. But it meant I'd have to keep eyes on him.

Not just mine.

Others.

Ones he wouldn't know where watching.

CHAPTER 53: THE BREAKING POINT

I dropped back into the office chair, rubbing my temple, still thinking about the weapon Collins handed over. Everything felt like it was unravelling—too many pieces, all shifting at once. Each problem layered on top of the last. No breath. No pause.

And then the phone rang.

Sarah picked it up, spoke briefly, then turned to me. Her face was unreadable, but her tone was clear.

"It's Psych. For you."

I took the receiver.

The SPO from the Psych Unit.

They had a bed for one of our prisoners. Returning for more treatment. Another psych assessment ahead of his next court date.

Name: Eli Trent.

Didn't ring a bell.

I flipped open the photo ID book, scanned pages until I found his face.

Still nothing.

No red flags. No incidents. Just another number. Clearly one of those guys who slipped through quietly—kept his head down, didn't cause waves. The kind you forget until it's too late.

"Sarah, you seen Trent?"

She looked up. "Think I saw him outside earlier."

I walked down the stairs. That's when I spotted him—drifting past the unit like he didn't have a destination. His walk was slow. Empty.

I opened the unit door just wide enough to call out.

"Trent."

He turned. No expression. No response. Just that dead-eyed stare. Like he hadn't slept in days. Or years.

"Need you back in the unit," I said.

He walked over—slow, robotic. No words.

"Good news," I told him. "Psych called. They have a bed for you. You'll get that assessment before court."

Still nothing. Just the same blank expression. That glassy, vacant look some guys get right before the switch flips.

"Alright," I said. "Let's pack your cell."

I motioned with my right hand toward the stairs. My left hovered behind him. Not touching—just close enough to act.

He moved. Slower than slow. Like every step was an effort. Deliberate. Dragging it out.

At the landing, I called back to Sarah. "Let Psych know we're packing his cell now."

Trent climbed three more steps, then stopped.

I nearly walked into him.

He was muttering. Low. Head down. Couldn't make out the words.

"Come on. Keep moving."

He turned suddenly.

"I'M NOT FUCKING TALKING TO YOU!"

His face twisted. Eyes wild. Lip curled up like a cornered dog about to lunge.

I brought my hand up, palm forward.

"Let's go. FUCKING MOVE!"

He started walking again. I kept my hand lightly on his back as we reached his cell. He turned in, step by step. Slow. Calculated.

Sarah followed close behind.

Inside the cell, I gave him a firm push to create space.

"Fucking sit down," I ordered.

That's when he came at me.

No warning. No buildup. Just rage.

Fists clenched. Arms down. Eyes full of something broken and dangerous.

I pushed him back, hard—palms on his chest. "GET BACK!"

Hands up. Defensive posture. No time to think. Just react.

He charged again. Fists tight now, waist high. Still not swinging—just advancing like I wasn't there.

Another hard push. "GET BACK!"

But he wasn't hearing me. He wasn't here.

He came again.

This time, fists raised. Ready. Locked in.

I couldn't sidestep—tight space. No angle. No time.

I grabbed both wrists. Drove him backwards with everything I had. Shoved him hard toward the bed.

He fell.

Cracked his head against the top bunk on the way down.

But as he hit the mattress, he kicked—right into my elbow. Knocked me back into the bench. My back hit hard. Items flew off. Pain shot down my arm like fire.

I stumbled. Caught myself. Hands still up.

He was holding his head; eyes closed for a moment. Dazed—but not down.

I started backing out. Fast. Controlled.

Sarah was at the doorway. Eyes wide. Silent.

I stepped through. She slammed the door. I grabbed the handle and locked it.

My heart was hammering. Breath ragged. Pain flaring down my arm.

I keyed the radio.

"Security Supervisor to Unit A. Now."

The pain in my elbow was spiking. Sharp. Radiating from the joint to the shoulder.

I walked along the tier to the top of the stairs, trying to steady my breathing. Sarah stared at me.

"You alright?" she asked.

I looked at her. The words didn't come. All I could think was: *are you fucking kidding me?*

Instead, I said, "Yeah."

The supervisor came through the at the end of the tier, seconds later. Saw the way I was holding my arm.

"What happened?"

I told him—step by step. The call. The move. The stairs. The cell.

"Go wait in my office," he said. "You're done here. I'll sort the rest."

"You hurt?"

"My arm," I said. "He kicked me. Hard."

I walked to his office and sat down. That's when Tourney stormed in.

His voice barked before he even shut the door.

"What the fuck just happened?"

I gave him the full story. No sugarcoating.

He cut me off. "Why the fuck didn't you press your duress? Or call a code?"

"I was protecting myself," I snapped. "My hands were up."

He stepped in closer. "Where the fuck was your offsider?"

"Sarah was standing at the door."

"Then why the fuck didn't she call a code?"

I turned away. "Ask her."

The room went quiet. The realisation hit him—I'd done all I could.

"Alright. Sit tight. I'll get the nurse down."

He left. Door half-closed behind him.

I sat there.

That's when I felt it.

The adrenaline dump.

My hand started trembling. Couldn't stop it.

The weight of it all hit at once—the what-ifs. The weapons he could've had. The speed of it. The quiet.

He could've killed me.

The nurse arrived. Checked my arm. Ran through a few stretches. Said it was likely a pinched nerve. A funny bone shot.

Nothing funny about it.

Later, I dictated the report to another officer. Couldn't type properly with the pain. Once it was done, I signed it. The supervisor walked back in.

"You need to go home, Jacob. Can someone pick you up?"

"Yeah. I'll call my wife."

I looked down at the receiver. My fingers still trembled. The sweat on my back had gone cold. I picked up the phone. Dialled.

"Bentridge Plumbing Supplies, this is Emma."

I swallowed hard.

"Hi Emma… can you come and get me?"

"What happened?" Her voice changed instantly.

"I'm okay," I said. "There's been an incident. Just… I need you to come get me."

CHAPTER 54: SILENT IMPACT

Emma gripped the wheel like it was the only thing keeping her grounded.

She didn't speak at first. Just drove. Eyes flicking to the rearview mirror, then across to me. Quick glances. Tight jaw. That quiet tension women get when they're worried but don't want to set you off.

I sat slumped in the passenger seat, left arm resting useless against the door, hand half-curled in my lap. The pain in my elbow was duller now, than sharp. I'd taken hits before, plenty. But this one was sticking. I explained what happened. How I was kicked in the arm.

"You sure you're alright?" she asked finally.

Her voice was low, like she was trying to ease into it. Not push too hard.

"I'm fine," I lied.

"You got kicked in the elbow, Jacob. That's not nothing."

"It's okay. Pinched nerve, that's all. I'll be fine."

She didn't argue. Just nodded once, staring at the road ahead. The wipers cleared a thin streak of drizzle from the windscreen. Somewhere behind us, the prison walls were shrinking in the distance, but I could still feel them in my lungs.

"If you don't want to talk to me about it," she said, "then talk to Chris. Just don't carry it by yourself. I know what you do. I know what it does to you. You don't always have to handle everything alone."

I looked over at her. She wasn't crying. Wasn't emotional. She was just scared. I hated seeing it on her face.

"Keep your eyes on the road," I muttered.

She gave a breathy laugh, the kind that said *fine, be that way*, and didn't speak again.

Which suited me just fine.

Because the hush was better than talking.

But inside, the noise was building.

All I could see was Trent.

The eyes. Empty, dead things. No emotion. No fear. Just a void. Then the sudden switch, the flash of rage like something had short-circuited. One second, he was quiet. The next he was coming at me with clenched fists and wild breath.

It wasn't the first time I'd been attacked.

It wasn't even the worst, physically.

But it felt different.

I kept going over it. Step by step. Trying to slow it down in my head.

His movement on the stairs. The muttering. That moment he turned. The fury in his face like he didn't recognise me. Like he didn't care what I was. Officer. Man. Nothing.

He just wanted to hurt someone.

I couldn't stop thinking about how he came at me. How tight that cell was. What little space I had to move.

He could've had a shiv.

And I wouldn't have seen it coming.

My fingers started twitching—that involuntary kind you can't stop once it starts. Nerves fraying at the edges. My body catching up to what my brain already knew.

He could've killed me.

He could've stabbed me in the gut, the throat—and no one would've reached me in time.

And Sarah… she'd been at the door. Close enough to help. But she didn't.

She just stood there.

Froze.

No duress. No code call. No nothing.

Just wide eyes and silence while I was wrestling with a psychotic time bomb. You freeze in this job, people get hurt. You freeze; people die. That's the worst thing you can do when shit hits the fan—nothing.

I felt the anger creep in. Low and cold. Not rage. Just that slow-burning fury that starts in the chest and spreads behind the eyes.

Had Trent stopped taking his meds? Who was watching that? Where was the warning?

The SPO from Psych Unit knew he was unstable. Knew he was being monitored for court. There should've been something flagged. Something in the file. Some heads-up.

But nothing.

Just another day. Another prisoner. Another box to tick.

And now I had this… weight. Sitting on my chest like concrete.

Because in that moment—in that cramped cell—I felt alone.

Not just physically. Not just logistically.

Alone.

The sort of alone that sticks to your skin long after it's over.

Emma pulled into the driveway, slowed the car, and put it in park.

The rain had stopped. The engine ticked as it cooled.

She turned to say something, but I was still staring forward. Breathing slowly. Eyes unfocused.

She didn't push.

I didn't move.

The rain had stopped, but inside, it hadn't.

CHAPTER 55: WHEN THE EDGES FRAY

Emma unlocked the door first. I stepped in behind her. Still holding my arm close.

We didn't say anything.

There was that brief pause near the kitchen bench—both of us standing there, like we might speak. Like one of us might ask the question neither of us wanted to answer.

But we didn't.

She headed toward the living room. I went straight to the bedroom.

I sat on the edge of the bed and slowly started to undress. Button by button. Moving carefully.

My shirt clung to me in places from the sweat and tension, so I stepped into the walk-in robe and pulled the door mostly shut behind me. The light above buzzed faintly.

That's when the tremble started again. First in my fingers. Then in my chest.

I returned to the bed. I sat still for a moment. Eyes unfocused. Heart thumping. My jaw tightened.

And then it cracked—whatever was holding me together.

I shook. Quietly. Hands gripping my thighs like that might stop the shaking. Shoulders hunched. I stared at the floor, and then the tears came.

No sound. Just heat. Wet down my face.

I kept my mouth shut. Didn't want Emma to hear. She'd worry more. And I couldn't deal with that on top of everything else.

The only one who saw was Dougal.

He stood in the doorway, ears perked, eyes locked on me. Like he knew. Like he *always* knew.

I held out my hand and he walked over. I dropped down beside him and held him tight. Pressed my face into the back of his neck and let it all go. He didn't move. Just stayed there, solid, breathing.

He was the only one I could show this to.

He wouldn't tell.

Dinner was quiet. Forks clinking against plates. Small talk that felt hollow. Emma was trying, and I appreciated it. But I wasn't really there. I just nodded in the right places and kept it together.

She watched over me. I could feel it. She knew I wasn't telling her everything.

And I wasn't.

The next morning, the house was still. I sat with a coffee I barely drank, scrolling through nothing on my phone. Then the message came in. Chris.

'Heard from Brianna. Emma told her what happened. Call me.'

I didn't hesitate. Phone to ear. One ring.

"How are you, mate?" he asked.

"I'm fine."

"Bullshit," he snapped. "Tell me how you're *really* feeling. No spin."

I hesitated. And then it all came out.

"Pissed off. Angry. Still fucking shaking, and I don't even know why."

"There it is," he said. "That's real. And it's exactly how you're supposed to feel. You took a hit, mate. Not just your elbow. The whole fucking system let you down. That leaves a mark."

We talked for nearly two hours. No filters. No bullshit. Just two blokes who've both been through it.

He understood the way fear gets stuck in the bones, how the rage simmers underneath it. By the end of the call, my chest felt a little lighter. Not healed. But held.

Then another call came through. I checked the screen.

Jacklyn.

I answered.

"Fuck, are you okay?" Her voice was sharp. No small talk.

"Yeah. I'm alright."

"Mate, what a fucking shit storm. You should've heard the fallout. Dog Squad had to gas Trent *three times* to get him out. He lost it. Completely off the rails. He had three shivs and a shit bomb in his cell. You were fucking lucky."

"Okay." I let her continue.

"They transported him to Yarra last night—took four hours to vent the Unit. Everyone else was locked in the gym. They were *fuming*. But let's be honest… most of them couldn't stand the fucking prick. Fuck him."

She exhaled, a beat of silence between us.

"You speak to anyone from EAP?"

I told her I hadn't. Just Chris.

"Good," she said. "He's better than any of those EAP suits anyway. He knows what it's like. The real stuff."

And then her voice shifted.

"Listen… I need to tell you something. I'm leaving the Unit."

I went still.

"MSO role. Six months. After that, I'm planning to study medicine. Want to become a doctor."

There was a pause on my end.

"Good for you," I finally said. "Chase that. Don't let anyone talk you out of it."

"I'll miss the Unit... and working with you."

"You'll stay in touch?"

"Only if I still get invited to the BBQs."

That made me smile, just for a second. "Always."

"I'll see you when you're back," she said.

"Might be a week. Maybe two."

"Take whatever you need."

After lunch, Emma called.

"How are you feeling?"

"I'm fine."

Same answer. Still a lie.

She asked if I could pick up a few things from the shop—end-of-month accounts were piling up at work, and she was staying in for lunch. I scribbled down the list, grabbed my keys, and left.

The street was quiet. I walked to the corner, crossed over, and stepped into the small convenience store at the end of the strip.

Lots of cars. More people than usual.

The store looked quiet. Normal. Safe.

I grabbed a shopping basket and pulled the list from my pocket.

Then it wasn't.

Like the walls were closing in.

Everything felt off. Too loud. Too still. Every person in the store felt like they were staring at me. I turned. Looked behind me. Nothing. No one.

But the feeling didn't go.

Neon signs blurred. Fluoro light hummed too loud. My breath scraped inside my chest. The walls weren't walls anymore—they were pressure. Squeezing.

Heart pounding. Hands shaking. Sweat rolling.

My stance shifted. Defensive. Instinct took over.

Basket dropped.

Hands came up.

"Get back," I muttered.

No one had moved. But I had.

I ran. Out the door. Around the corner. Breathing hard, chest tight.

I stopped. Rested against the wall. Eyes darting.

"What the fuck just happened?"

I called Emma.

"Hey, um… I can't get what you wanted."

"You sound out of breath. You alright?"

"I was in the store. Everything just… closed in. I couldn't breathe. Felt like I was being stared at. Started shaking. Ran out."

"Sounds like you had a panic attack."

"Fuck. I've never had that before."

"Just go home. Try and relax. I'll get what we need."

"Do you want me to come home?"

"No. I'll be alright. I'm gonna start working on a new 80s mix for Chris. Keep my hands busy."

"Okay. Love you."

"Ditto."

I walked back, slow, still scanning the street like something might leap out. I didn't like that feeling. I'd spent my whole career learning how to control situations. Predict outcomes.

But in that moment, I was out of control.

That terrified me.

I stepped through the front door. Dougal barked once, then stopped. He knew me.

We sat on the bed again.

I wrapped my arms around him and let it all go.

Head in my hands. Tears hot against my palms.

The second time in two days.

No words. Just the weight.

Then I wiped my face dry.

And made a promise in the dark.

This will never happen again.

No panic. No shaking. Just control—no matter the cost.

CHAPTER 56: REALIGNMENT

The next two weeks gave me a lot of time to think.

And I did. Just not about what people probably assumed.

And then the phone rang.

It was Phill. His voice was low. The sort of low that tells you something's coming—something that can't be unsaid.

"You heard about Delaney?" he asked.

I hadn't.

He exhaled. No lead-in. No prep.

"Big Māori got him. In the Unit. Used a Coke bottle."

I said nothing. Just waited.

"I read the report. He'd filled it with ceramic shards. White and blue pieces from broken cups. Jammed tight. Then…" He paused, like the words physically hurt. "He pushed it in. Real slow. Each time he squeezed, another piece forced its way out. Cut him up inside. Deep."

Still, I said nothing.

"They had to rush Delaney out. Emergency surgery. Tore through his bowel like glass through wet paper. They removed a big chunk. He has a colostomy bag now. For life."

The silence that followed wasn't empty. It pressed down like something physical.

Phill broke it. "How the fuck did you know that Māori would do that?"

I leaned back in the chair; eyes fixed on the wall.

"Years ago," I said. "He came into the unit quiet. Watching. Waiting. Never said much. But one day, he opened up. Told me about what happened to his sister. Some junkie in a halfway house. Beat her half to death. Left her with an ABI. Permanent."

"Jesus…"

"He wanted revenge," I said. "Didn't know how to get it without ending up in the slot for a decade. I gave him structure. Purpose. Set the scene. Just like now."

Phill went quiet again. I could hear him breathing.

"You knew he'd do it."

"No," I said. "I knew what he was capable of if the rules fell away."

Phill exhaled again.

"It felt like a fucking murder scene. Blood everywhere. Delaney screaming, curled up like a crushed spider."

"I get justice, mate… but fuck. That wasn't justice. That was fucking mutilation."

"Just thought you should know," Phill said.

I nodded, even though he couldn't see it. "Thanks."

He hung up. I sat in the dead air that followed. Let the edges of it settle. This was our version of justice. Ugly. Permanent. Effective.

No paperwork. No second chances.

Just consequence.

I stared at the screen. That picture wouldn't leave. Not guilt. Not pride. Just… weight.

And that brought me back to—Trent. The moment. The kick. The fallout. A scar already scabbed over.

But what stayed with me… what *kept* circling like a dog returning to its own vomit… was that feeling.

That I was alone.

Not just physically. I mean mentally, emotionally isolated in a way I hadn't felt in years. Locked in a box with a psychotic, and no one coming through the door. It was like the system peeled away for a second and left me there. Naked.

I couldn't shake it. And it pissed me off.

Worse than the pain. Worse than the adrenaline comedown. It was *that* moment that broke something in me.

The part that still gave a shit.

I used to try. To help. Guide the new ones. Crooks who'd never learned how to *be* prisoners. Because there's a difference. Anyone can be a criminal. That part's easy.

But being a prisoner?

That's about routine. Submission. Structure. Learning the rules—*fast*—before someone teaches you the hard way. With fists.

I used to think I could get to them first. Create order before chaos found them. But I was done.

Done trying to teach discipline to people who'd rather stab their own mattress than follow the daily roster. Done pretending the broken wanted to be fixed.

Time for a change.

Not just in the job. Location. Rhythm. Purpose. I wanted to be somewhere where the routine already existed. Where the prisoners already knew the rules. Where a system was in place. Not putting out fires every shift.

Because we're all creatures of habit. You watch someone long enough—*you'll see it*. Their routine. Their tells. Their pattern.

That's where I wanted to be.

I sat at my desk, coffee gone cold, cursor blinking on a blank screen. Dougal was curled at my feet, his chin resting on the top of my boot. He barely left my side these days. Like even he sensed something had shifted in me.

I picked up the phone and dialled HR.

The woman on the other end was polite, almost too upbeat. She asked when they could expect me back. Next week, Monday. No problem.

She said they'd rotate me through a few different areas when I came back. I didn't care. None of it mattered anymore. My mind was already elsewhere. *Once I decide, that's it.* No one talks me out of it.

Call two. The more important one.

The Ops Manager that handled the HR portfolio. We'd known each other a long time. One of the few in upper management I could tolerate. First ring. No small talk. Just ease—the kind that comes from years in the trenches.

He asked the expected questions. *How are you feeling? Have you spoken with EAP?* I told him I'd made up my mind. I was going back to Yarra Prison. I needed out of there. Too much noise. Too much chaos. And I was done waiting to feel safe in a job that was never meant to be safe.

He was understanding. Said transfers to Yarra were tight. They weren't actively taking on anyone, but a one-for-one swap might be arranged. Could take a few weeks. A month, maybe.

I told him that was fine. I'd wait. But the decision was final.

Next call. The hard one.

Emma.

The phone rang.

"Bentridge Plumbing Supplies, this is Debbie."

"Hi Debbie, can I speak with Emma?"

She transferred me straight through.

"Hi. How's things?" Emma asked.

"Good," I said. "I've made a decision. I'm moving back to Yarra."

Quiet.

Not the stunned kind.

"I figured you might," she said. Calm. Steady. She knew me too well. "When?"

I explained the transfer process. Could be weeks. Could be longer.

"Well, I guess I'll have to start looking for a rental," she said. "Don't worry. It'll be good."

And just like that, she was on board. Like always.

The final call was the easiest.

Chris.

I didn't even get the whole sentence out before he responded.

"Don't blame you one bit," he said. "I couldn't handle remand either. It's a fucking mess. Needy junkies. Slash-ups. Headcases. Every shift, the same fucking shit."

He understood. Like always.

"And if you move down that way," he added, "it just means we stay the night when we visit. Drink more. Eat more. No late-night drives home. Everyone wins."

Chris could be having the worst day of his life and still find a way to spin something good out of it—for someone else. That was his gift. Kept you from drowning by pretending you were already on the shore.

And for the first time in weeks, I felt like things were starting to realign. Like the axis was tilting back into place. It wouldn't be easy. There'd be packing, logistics, maybe stress from Emma or work.

But it felt right.

Like closing a chapter properly. Not slamming it shut in anger—but folding the page down, placing a bookmark, and walking away.

I sat at my desk and opened the audio project I'd been building for Chris. The next 80s mix.

That was my reset button. Always had been. Music from a time that still made sense. Back when supergroups were gods and lyrics meant something.

The 70s had the heartbeat. The 80s had the bones.

I clicked play.

And I let it fill me. The room. My chest.

For the first time since the attack in the cell. Since the fists. Since the stillness—

I was calm.

CHAPTER 57: THE RETURN

The move finally happened.

Boxes stacked high. Emma unpacked at her own pace, treating it like some sort of meditative ritual. I still couldn't believe we had that much shit, even after throwing out what felt like half our lives. Junk we'd dragged from place to place like bad memories boxed up and labelled *fragile*.

Chris loaned me a car through one of his mates. Thing ran like it had emphysema. Rattled like a shopping trolley and coughed before starting in the mornings, but the prison was only ten minutes away. That was enough. It did the job.

It had taken two months, but the transfer had come through.

I was going back.

Back to where it started. My old prison. The real one. The one that stamped you deep.

Faces changed. Layout tweaked. But the bones were the same. That place was carved into me like muscle memory. The State's only *true* maximum-security facility.

The last stop.

Yarra was known for its multi-level segregation units—designed to cage what couldn't be controlled elsewhere—a prison inside a prison. Where they sent the broken, the dangerous, the monsters.

Terrorists. Serial killers. Cartel operators. Gangland enforcers. Outlaw bikies. Child predators. Everyone with blood on their hands or targets on their backs.

This was where the system buried its sins.

And for me… it just felt like home.

Emma didn't mind the move. She'd moved so often before, that she'd grown accustomed to the rhythm of resettling. She said the cleanout was therapeutic. Throwing away clutter, organising space the way she liked it—calm, functional. Minimal.

She believed less was best. I was starting to believe it too. Less to clean, less to worry about, just the things that mattered.

Things that mattered to her—and to me.

Sunday, I spent the day prepping. Bag packed, uniform ironed, boots cleaned, badge polished. Still had to get a new one with Yarra Prison etched across the name badge. But I didn't care. Minor detail.

Monday.

I parked the car in the staff lot. Grabbed my belt and bag. One last check of my reflection in the cracked rear-view mirror.

The walk in felt right.

No more pedestrian dodging through the city. No more staring down sketchy passengers on the early train. No more wondering if some ex-prisoner was going to clock me in front of a 7-Eleven.

This wasn't like Remand—no twitching walls, no screams from unseen corridors. This was order.

This was *clean*. Structured. Professional.

The gatehouse stood tall and still. A wall of authority. The line between freedom and containment.

I walked in and introduced myself at the front desk. A couple of the officers recognised my name, offered polite nods. Then I saw her—Tracey, the SPO. She stepped out from behind the desk, gave me a quick hug.

"Welcome back," she said.

Something eased inside me. A flicker of familiarity. Of belonging.

The rest was paperwork and protocols. Biometrics—fingerprints, eye scan, new ID. Security pass to buzz through the big doors. Same drill, different prison.

Then it was time to meet the HR Ops Manager.

Known for being by the book. Didn't matter if the book made sense. She didn't bend. Just followed it line for line, even if it was upside down and on fire.

She gave me the tour—Gatehouse, Admin, Central Movement. Introduced me to the SPO on post for the day.

Mid-thirties. Shaved head. Tight lips. Security background. Didn't suffer fools, didn't offer pleasantries. His handshake was firm but hollow. I kept my judgement holstered.

He introduced me to the others—faces I didn't recognise. But that didn't matter. I was still watching. Still calculating.

They showed me the ropes, walked me through routines. How movement was done here. The timings. The flow.

It all clicked.

The sights. The sounds. Prisoners shuffling in step, guards watching from behind glass and bars. The distant echo of a steel door slamming shut.

This was my tempo.

Some prisoners looked twice when they passed me. That half-second recognition. Eyes narrowing. *I know you.*

But they didn't say a word. That was fine. I wasn't in the mood for reunions.

End of shift.

SPO came over. No small talk.

"Good job. No issues." Handed me my roster for the rest of the week.

Straightforward.

Different Unit each day. Gatehouse rotation. Weekend in Visits. Absorb how families and criminals tried to outsmart the process. I'd seen it all before.

Still, it struck me how each prison—though run by the same Department—carried its own signature. Same rules on paper. But each one twisted them slightly. Different tempo. Different shade of control.

Lockup done. Staff started filtering out. The long walk toward the Gatehouse gave me time to decompress.

Then I heard them—familiar voices calling my name. Laughter. Handshakes. People from my past. Not many, but enough.

For a brief moment… I smiled.

I was back.

Not fully. Not emotionally. Still cautious. Still scanning the angles. Still expecting someone to swing from the shadows.

But I was here. And for now—that was enough.

Soon I'd be assigned a permanent Unit. One team. One routine. Stability. And I needed that.

I was still fractured, still healing. But I could rebuild now. In silence. In structure. In routine. Because *normal* isn't a destination. It's something you earn back. One quiet day at a time.

CHAPTER 58: THE WARNING

A month had passed.

My new Unit was steady. Mainstream. Full of long-timers. The sort of prisoners who knew the rhythm of this place better than they knew the date. Men doing long bids. Some cycling back in like it was a second home. Others waiting out a sentence so long the idea of daylight was more memory than future.

It was all routine now.

I had a Unit.

A locker.

A place.

The Unit Supervisor was an old head. Grizzled. Walked like every joint had betrayed him twenty years ago. Looked like retirement was calling, but he knew the job inside out. Didn't waste breath unless it mattered. We had an understanding—I ran the floor; he ran the numbers. He'd joke about it, but we both knew the score. I was the presence. He was the paperwork.

The other SPO was four years in the job and already sharp enough to cut steel. Ambitious. Polished. Efficient. The kind who climbed ladders two rungs at a time. I didn't think she'd stab you in the back—but if you stood in her way, she'd go through you in plain sight.

We had different views on prisoners.

She thought structure fixed behaviour.

I knew better.

Behaviour doesn't change. It adapts.

I was nearly back to my old self. Almost. That mask I wore—the one that made me functional—it slipped on easier these days. Routine was the key. The faces didn't change much. Same men. Same eyes. Same fights over nothing. No transfers unless someone had a homebrew or threw a punch.

Prisoners worked in Kitchens or Industries. A few tried to study. Certificates in basic literacy, warehousing, drug rehab. Not because they wanted to change—but because the system demanded they play the game if they ever wanted to leave early.

I knew my billets.

And they knew me.

Took a few weeks to learn where the line was. How far they could push before I pushed back. That line never moved. Not for them. Not for me.

The officers I worked with were solid. Old-school. Professional. Good instincts. But I kept my guard up. Always. None of them were Jacklyn. That bond, that unspoken language—that didn't exist here.

She and I still texted. Sometimes we called. Saturday, we'd finally catch up. Dinner with Emma, Chris and Brianna, and Jacklyn's new partner. Emma was excited—already planning what she'd wear. She'd grown protective of Jacklyn. Treated her like a younger sister. And when Emma cared, she cared with her whole heart.

That night at home, I relaxed the only way I knew how.

Cooking.

Emma had transferred to a new plumbing supply store—now in Southwick Bay's CBD. Longer drive for her. But it gave me time to prep dinner, light the candles, calm the noise.

She didn't mind the commute. Gave her space to breathe. She'd call her cousins, catch up with friends, talk through her day out loud while the traffic crawled by. She liked having that buffer between work and home. She always said it helped her leave the day behind.

Dinner was easy. Pasta with grilled chicken and roast capsicum. A bottle of wine between us, though I barely touched mine.

Emma cleared the table, her usual line: "I'll clean up. You go sit down."

I whistled to Dougal, who trailed me like a shadow now. We settled into the couch. Emma went for a shower.

That's when my phone rang.

Chris.

I smiled before I even answered. "Hey mate, was just thinking about you."

"Looking forward to Saturday," he said.

"Yeah, me too."

A pause. Then, "Hey… I broke Osbourne's nose today."

I sat up. "Fucking *what?*"

He laughed. "Yep. Apparently, he was sent here for some medical thing. Scheduled for next week. But there was an incident—phone use in the Unit got messy, someone hit their duress, I responded."

He continued, voice lighter now. "We were trying to subdue him. I grabbed him from behind, pushed him down with the others… landed with my left elbow—straight into his face. Crack. Blood everywhere."

I could hear the satisfaction dripping from his smile.

"Bet that felt good."

"Couldn't be happier. They admitted him. Officers on bedsit until his surgery next week."

A laugh slipped out—sharp, ugly. Didn't know it was still in me. "Fucking arsehole deserves it. Just wish I could've seen it."

Chris chuckled, but I wasn't laughing anymore.

"You taking any time off?"

"Nah, mate. Back tomorrow. Two more days. Friday off. Then we'll see you Saturday."

"Hey, I finished your 80s mix. Finally. Took longer than I planned, but I wanted to hand it to you in person."

He sounded excited. "Can't wait."

Then my tone shifted.

"Chris…"

"Yeah?"

"Watch your back."

Silence.

"I'm serious," I said. "Osbourne won't let this slide. You humiliated him. He's going to want payback. And he doesn't care how he gets it. It won't be today, or even this month. But it'll come. Could be a prisoner. Could be someone on the outside. Just… watch your back."

Chris tried to brush it off. "I'll be alright."

"No, listen to me."

I leaned forward, gripping the phone tighter. "I've seen what he does. To people who've done less. He's not like the others. This revenge—it'll be permanent."

Another pause.

"I'll see you Saturday," he said.

Then he was gone.

I sat in silence.

My gut twisted. That cold, dead feeling crept in. The same one I felt the day Trent turned on me. That second when you know something's coming—but you can't stop it.

Chris was big. Strong. Smart.

But Osbourne...

He didn't think like normal people.

He calculated.

He planned.

He *waited*.

And now he had a reason.

I stared down at Dougal. He was already watching me, ears slightly raised. Like he knew something was wrong.

"Not this time," I whispered. "We stay ready."

Because Osbourne would come. Of that, I was certain. And this time, I wasn't the target.

CHAPTER 59: THE BLOOD LEFT BEHIND

Saturday — 5:55pm

Emma and I were driving into the city.

One night. That's all we wanted. One night to forget the chaos. A brief escape. A warm bed in Wilson Lane and a dinner in Chinatown. A little luxury to dull the edges of the last few months.

The sort of night you look forward to. The kind you hope becomes a reset.

We crossed the Western Bridge just as the sky started turning amber. I switched on the radio, local FM, hoping for the tail-end of the evening news before the music kicked in.

Then the words came, flat and clinical—spoken without any sense of weight or consequence.

"In breaking news, a man's body has been discovered late this afternoon in an outer western suburb. Police are on the scene in James Street. No cause of death has been confirmed, and police are currently searching the area. More details to follow."

"James Street."

My stomach turned cold.

"Emma…" I said, keeping my voice level. "That's Chris and Brianna's street."

Her hand moved fast—grabbing her phone, flicking through contacts, calling.

Brianna's name.

Straight to voicemail.

Then Chris.

Same thing.

"No answer," she said, watching the screen like it might give her something else.

"Try again," I said. The words came out flat.

She did. Again. Again.

Nothing.

Then she sent texts.

Still nothing.

The stillness between us was louder than any scream. I kept driving, but everything else—everything—was getting smaller. Narrower. The road in front of me blurred at the edges.

I was already bracing for something. My gut knew. My chest knew. But I didn't want to say it. Couldn't say it.

Chris.

No.

No, no, no.

We arrived at the hotel, checked in. The girl at the desk had a smile rehearsed for tourists. She offered a compliment about the weather. I gave her a nod that meant *hurry up*.

She understood the message.

The elevator ride was silent. Emma stood beside me, her face pale and tight. We both felt like we were holding our breath.

Inside the room, I threw the bags to the side. Grabbed the remote. Flicked through channels until I found the late news. No talking. No dinner. No plans.

I texted Jacklyn.

Nothing back.

She was probably doing the same thing. Watching. Waiting.

Emma sat on the edge of the bed, staring at her phone like it had betrayed her.

No messages. No missed calls. Just Silence.

Then the news came on.

There it was.

Footage.

Police tape stretched across the street. Crime scene investigators crouched in the background. And then the worst of it—Brianna, being led away from the house, sobbing so hard her body convulsed with every step. A female cop held her close, guiding her gently. Her face—red, swollen, mascara streaked across her cheek like war paint. Just raw agony.

I dropped to the floor.

I didn't realise I'd moved. I was just… down there. Sitting on the carpet like a child who didn't know where to go.

Emma stayed frozen on the bed.

I couldn't say a word.

I *wouldn't* say the words.

There was nothing we could do. The house was a crime scene. Brianna would be at the station all night. There was no point in being in that hotel room.

I stood. Pulled Emma into a hug. Held her so tight I felt her bones shift under my arms. She didn't resist. She just melted into me like she was waiting for it.

Then we packed. Quietly. Deliberately.

Checked out.

We just wanted to be home.

Where it felt safe.

Where Dougal was.

The drive back was long and wordless.

Not a sound. Just the soft hum of the tyres and our grief sitting heavy in the car like a third passenger. No radio. No thoughts. Just silence and headlights cutting through the dark.

Home.

Drop the bags.

Collapse into bed.

Dougal curled up between us. Emma eventually fell asleep. Her breathing slowed. But mine didn't. I lay there, my eyes open in the dark, staring at the ceiling like it might give me answers.

None came.

Morning.

The curtains glowed with weak light. Dougal jumped up after his usual routine, licking Emma's hand before curling up against me. I slid out of bed. Track pants. T-shirt. Nothing else.

I needed coffee like a wound needed stitching.

The house was silent. The sort of silence that isn't peaceful. The kind that hums with the things you're afraid to say out loud.

TV on.

News reruns.

Still nothing new. Still that horrible phrase—'no confirmed details'—as if saying it enough would make it less brutal.

Emma joined me. Quiet. Eyes soft. She didn't speak. Just sat down and wrapped her arms around me.

She didn't need to say anything.

She was just *there*.

And it was everything.

Then the phone rang.

10:01am.

Private number.

We looked at each other.

Speaker on.

"Hello?" I spoke.

It was Brianna.

Her voice was broken glass.

"I've just stepped out from the police station… I'm outside, having a smoke. I can't talk long."

I leaned in.

"What happened?"

A pause.

"I found Chris… so much blood."

Her voice trembled, like each word might snap her in half.

"Brianna—do you know *what* happened?"

Silence.

Then again, almost in a whisper — "There was… so much blood."

Beep. Gone.

We sat there, staring at the phone like it might call back. But it didn't. Nothing did.

There were no tears yet. Just the ache. The weight. The *stillness*.

Dougal stepped over, his head tilted slightly. I patted my thigh. He jumped up beside us.

And that was it.

The three of us.

Sitting in the lounge room.

Drowning in silence.

No anger yet.

No questions. Just shock. And the cold, horrible truth pressing in from all sides.

Chris was gone.

CHAPTER 60: REST EASY, MY FRIEND

Two weeks later.

The morning felt colder than it should have. Sky overcast. The sort of dull grey that seeps into your bones before you even step outside. I stood at the window, tie half done, collar stiff, staring blankly into nothing. Emma didn't say much. She just moved quietly around the bedroom, giving me space.

I was grateful for that.

But I had one thing I had to do first.

I stepped out onto the back veranda and made a call to the investigating detectives. I had nothing to give them in terms of suspects. No names. No details. But I needed them to understand who Chris was. The woman who answered was calm. Compassionate, even. She let me speak without interruption.

"Chris was solid," I told her. "Reliable. A bloody tank of a bloke. The sort of officer you could count on when everything went to shit. But he wasn't soft. He was measured. Never turned his back on a prisoner unless he trusted them. And even then, he kept them in his peripheral."

I paused, then added, "That's the thing you need to understand about him. He didn't take unnecessary risks. If someone got to him, they either knew exactly what they were doing... or they were sent."

She said she understood. I wasn't convinced she really did. But it didn't matter. I hung up.

We drove in silence. Neither of us had the energy for small talk. I kept looking straight ahead, jaw clenched. I didn't want to be here, not like this. I should've been having dinner with Chris and Brianna, complaining about the food, laughing over 80s playlists, debating who had the better taste in music. Not this. Not a fucking funeral.

The cemetery chapel was small. Intimate. And full of people who mattered.

Friends and family. A few officers. Some dressed in dark suits, all holding the same grief in their eyes. Brianna sat in the front pew, flanked by family. She looked hollow. Like the light had gone out of her. I didn't approach her yet. There'd be time for that.

I walked up the aisle. There it was. The all-white coffin. Stark. Pure. It hit me harder than I expected.

I placed a hand on it. The polished wood was cold beneath my fingertips.

I tried to speak. My voice cracked before the words even came.

"Rest easy, my friend," I said, voice barely a whisper. "No more shifts. No more pain."

I remembered him once, cracking up so hard over a joke. I couldn't remember the joke. Just that laugh—it echoed. Loud. Full. Alive. Now it was gone.

That's when it hit me. Hard. The grief, the rage, the helplessness—all of it crashing down. I broke. Right there in front of everyone. I didn't care. I let it out.

Tears ran down my face as I stepped back and returned to my seat.

The rest of the service moved in a haze. A few officers spoke—stories about Chris on the job, his dry humour, the way he could make a whole room laugh with a single raised eyebrow. But all I could think about was the news I'd heard outside the chapel before the service started.

Twenty-eight stab wounds. All in the back.

That wasn't a killing.

That was an execution.

Later, at the wake, I stood outside under the awning with a few old hands from the job. We shared stories of Chris, as the smoke from cigarettes moved about us.

"This wasn't just some junkie trying to rob a place," one of them said quietly.

"No," I replied. "It was something else."

They nodded, and one of them added, "If we get the chance..."

"We will." I nodded.

We didn't need to say anything else.

As the evening wore on, Emma and I made our way home. The drive was quiet. Words felt irrelevant. Just grief, breathing between us. The heavy kind. The kind that fills every space and settles into the seats beside you.

Once home, I went straight to the bedroom. Kicked off the shoes. Pulled off the suit. Tossed it onto the chair. Loosened the tie, then dropped it on the floor like it didn't matter anymore.

Dougal padded into the room, tail low, ears alert. He knew something was wrong. Always did.

I sat on the edge of the bed. He came over and leaned into me, his weight grounding me. I scratched behind his ear, rested my hand on his back.

"He's gone, mate," I said quietly.

A single tear rolled down my cheek.

And that was the last time I ever cried.

CHAPTER 61: RED BALANCE

Thursday.

The cops made an arrest yesterday. Name was Lee Miller. Didn't ring any bells. But names rarely did anymore. Too many years. Too many files. Too many arseholes. But the faces—I always remembered the faces. Couldn't shake them if I tried. No other details yet. Just a name in the static.

Brianna had moved in with her sister. Gone quiet. Completely. Word was she wasn't speaking to anyone. Couldn't. The grief had her throat in a vice. And who could blame her? Some wounds don't bleed—they just echo.

Grief fades. But anger—that's something different.

It settles in your bones. Slow at first. Then it festers. Boils. Starts to burn a hole straight through your soul. And when it's aimed, pure and true, it's no longer a feeling.

It's a decision.

I went back to work after a few days off. Said the right things. Nodded when people offered their condolences. Made small talk in the break room. But inside—I wasn't there. I was somewhere else entirely. That place in your mind where revenge stops being a thought... and starts becoming a plan.

Mid-morning, I walked out of the Unit under the pretence of needing to update my training record. Instead, I walked straight into the secure staff area, found a quiet corner, and made a call.

Sharon Price answered on the second ring. Still at Metro. Still doing Intel work. Still sharp.

"Sharon. I need a favour," I said, voice flat.

"That depends on what you want."

"I don't have time for games. Just tell me what I need to know."

Silence. Then, "Go on."

"Lee Miller. Look him up. I want history. Any associates. Anyone he shared a cell with. Call me back in thirty."

I hung up.

The minutes dragged like hours. I didn't bother heading back to the Unit. Just sat in the empty room, staring at the wall, hands clenched in my lap.

Phone buzzed.

One name.

Osbourne.

Fifteen years ago, Miller and Osbourne shared a cell. Miller was done for drug possession. Did his time, never came back. Clean record since. Except now, he'd just murdered my best friend—stabbed him twenty-eight times in the back.

I didn't hear much after that. My mind locked onto the name.

Osbourne.

It hit like a fucking freight train.

Of course it was him.

Chris had broken his nose. And Osbourne wasn't the kind to forget. Wasn't the kind to forgive. The guy was a sociopath with a long memory and a taste for symbolic violence.

Overkill. Signature move. He wanted the message to be loud. It didn't matter where you were—inside or out. Osbourne could still get to you. Still hurt you. Still kill you.

No.

Not this time.

This time—I was the message.

That weekend, Jacklyn dropped by. Emma baked banana bread. Dougal snored on the rug. It felt like one of our old catchups—casual, warm, familiar.

But I wasn't the same man she used to know.

As Emma walked back into the kitchen, humming to herself, I leaned forward. Voice low. Calm. Like I was talking about the weather.

"I'm going to kill Osbourne."

Jacklyn froze.

Didn't flinch. Didn't gasp. Just sat in that still, unbearable silence.

It lasted too long.

"Thank you," I said, "for not trying to talk me out of it."

She stared at the floor for a moment. Hands clasped tightly in her lap.

Finally, she spoke.

"You know I'll never say anything. But I can't help you. I can't be involved."

"I know."

Truth is, I never expected her to be. I wasn't looking for help. I just needed someone to know. Someone who mattered. Someone I trusted with the truth.

Jacklyn stood, slow. "Are you doing this alone?"

I stepped toward her. Rested a hand on her shoulder.

"I have a friend who'll help. A few others who'll play small roles. But the less they know... the better for them. And for me."

We stood there. Not speaking. The clock ticking faintly in the background.

Then I hugged her.

A long, slow, final hug.

Not just goodbye.

But a burial.

The man I was—he didn't exist anymore.

The one standing here... was something else entirely.

CHAPTER 62: SMOKE AND SHADOWS

I parked two streets over.

Didn't want to be seen near Roy's place. He still had connections. Old enemies. People with long memories and nothing better to do than stir shit that should've died years ago.

I knocked twice, slow, deliberate. The door opened just a crack.

Roy's eyes appeared first—still sharp, still reading everything. Then the rest of him followed. Thick tattooed arms, weathered neck, black singlet, blacker stare.

"Jacob," he muttered, letting the door swing open.

He was an exceptional tattoo artist. Had a business for years. Lots of loyal customers, like me. Then he was pushed out by Outlaw Motorcycle Gangs. Looking to launder money through his business, while forcing Roy to tattoo all their members for virtually nothing.

He had a face that seemed like he lived for a thousand years. And as an artist, he had an incredible attention for detail.

The room hadn't changed. Dark walls. Old leather couch. Ashtray with more filters than ash. The faint hum of a fridge filled with beer and regret. The place still smelled like ink and Dettol.

Then Anika walked in.

She was originally from South Africa. That pale skin, almost porcelain with the biggest smile, and long straight blonde hair that seemed to always catch the light. Black jeans, tight top, barefoot. Calm eyes. That calm that comes after a storm wrecks your life and you've stopped expecting sunshine.

She nodded once. "Hello darling."

Big warm embrace.

She didn't ask why I was here.

Roy pointed to a chair. "Sit. Let's talk."

I sat.

No small talk. No beer.

"I need him gone," I said.

Neither of them blinked.

"Osbourne."

Anika looked away. Her jaw clenched. "That piece of shit…"

Roy kept his eyes on me. "You serious?"

I nodded.

"You do this, there's no going back."

"I'm already gone."

Silence.

Roy finally said, "I owe you, so you get this one. Just say the word. But I need to hear the full story. All of it."

So, I told them. The stabbing. The funeral. Twenty-eight fucking stab wounds in the back. And one name that sat underneath it all like rot under floorboards.

Osbourne.

I told them about the intel Sharon gave me. That Miller was just a puppet. The signature behind the strings was always the same—cold, detached, calculating.

"Osbourne's not the sort of predator who lunges at you in the dark," I said. "He's the kind that opens the door, smiles, and lets someone else do the killing. Then he watches. He's a social executioner in prison clothing."

Anika sat down slowly across from me. "He's fucking hurt girls. A lot of them. Lap dances that turned into rape behind locked doors. Drugs, threats. Some of them didn't even report it. Too scared. Too broken."

Anika had managed girls working at brothels and strip clubs. She was very protective of every girl she knew. And any attack on them, she took very personally.

Her voice cracked. But only for a second.

"I owe him," she said.

I looked at her. Saw that cold clarity—the kind born from wounds that never closed.

Some men leave bruises. Others leave ghosts.

But Osbourne? He was a cancer.

You don't reason with cancer.

You cut it out—before it spreads.

Roy lit a cigarette and stared at it like it owed him something too. Then he exhaled slow.

"So, what's the plan?"

"He gets parole in two months. Time served on some charges, others dismissed."

"Where?"

We need to grab him. Somewhere quiet. Somewhere no one knows. Then end it. If we try anything with his associates around, they'll attack, then he'll finish the job.

It has to be done quietly. Like he's driving somewhere, but instead, he arrives at his final destination. With us.

"Ok, but if you want to grab him, that won't be easy."

"I know. It will have to be somewhere he feels in control. Like the puppet master, pulling everyone's string."

Anika lit a cigarette, held it high, blew the smoke down…, "He'll be at a strip club. CBD. Monday nights. Industry crowd. Girls have told me they're expecting him back. It's his sort of place—drugs, girls, power. He knows everyone there. Feels untouchable."

Roy smiled grimly. "Perfect."

I leaned in. "We'll need him drugged. Nothing major. Just enough to fog his mind. Get him pliable."

Anika nodded. "I can make that happen. I know a young guy that works the bar. He's gay, been abused and assaulted by Osbourne in the past."

Anika took another drag of the cigarette, blowing the smoke, "I still know a few girls there. Some of them would love to see him bleed."

"Ok, but how do we get him out of the club so we can grab him?"

I leaned forward, "why would someone like Osbourne, straight out of prison, want to leave a club?"

"Cops?"

"Exactly. Even a sociopath like Osbourne won't want to have a confrontation after just being released."

"Ok, but how do we get the cops there?"

Anika spoke in a soft tone, "we tell them there's been an assault on one of the girls."

"Ok. That will get a response but not trigger enough cops that they'll surround the place, or block roads."

Roy added, "I know a way to dispose of him. Final. No trace. But if we want this clean, we need people thinking he's not dead."

"A decoy?"

Roy flicked ash. "Exactly. I know someone. With hair but looks like Osbourne and has similar build. Tattoos can be matched. Can get him to disappear overseas. It'll buy you time. And it'll scatter the scent."

I sat back in my chair.

Roy looked at me, this time with something deeper than just loyalty.

"You really going to go through with this?"

"I've never been more certain of anything in my life."

"It'll change you."

"I've already changed."

He didn't argue.

Instead, he said, "Then let's finish this right."

Anika stood. "I'll set up the club. The girls. I'll get them to watch him. Every move. Until we're ready."

I stood too. Walked to Roy. Shook hands.

Hugged Anika.

Roy put a hand on my shoulder, "I still owe you."

I gave a slow nod.

I looked him in the eye. "Then this is the way you clear that debt."

He nodded again.

Anika grabbed a notebook and started scribbling names. Timelines. Contacts.

We were past the point of no return.

And for the first time since the day Chris was murdered… I felt something I hadn't felt in weeks.

Control.

The balance was starting to shift. Osbourne wouldn't see it coming.

But we'd be waiting. And this time—he wouldn't walk away.

CHAPTER 63: FRACTURE POINTS

Over the next two months, I did what I always did best—I studied weakness. Mapped it. Memorised it. Designed around it.

I treated the plan like a living thing. A surgical procedure. Dissecting it from every angle. Every contingency considered. Every potential fuck-up imagined, and neutralised. I'd been in this game too long to leave anything to chance. If any weakness, I'd find it. And I'd bury it.

I didn't sleep much. Not because I couldn't, but because I didn't want to. Sleep was a distraction. And distractions caused people to be killed.

Roy had been working with precision, too. His decoy—*the double*—was almost complete.

The ink work had taken weeks. Roy didn't just copy tattoos—he replicated them. Every blemish, every faded line, every slight asymmetry that made them unique. Even the ultraviolet Chinese dragon on Osbourne's neck—the one that glowed like a curse under the blacklights in strip clubs—was reproduced to the exact shade.

The decoy even had Osbourne's same gaunt smirk. Same posture. Same thousand-yard stare that told you he'd already killed something inside himself.

Roy wasn't just building a double. He was manufacturing misdirection. A living lie.

And that lie would board a plane to Thailand the night Osbourne disappeared. He'd get seen, flagged on CCTV, confirmed by facial recognition at the airport. Enough to plant the seed. Long enough to grow a story we'd never need to water.

We had the plan.

We had the date.

We had every gear turning.

Except for one thing.

Emma.

She was slipping away from me, and I was the one pushing. Cold hands. Fewer words. Quieter dinners. Less eye contact. And she noticed. Of course she noticed.

But I couldn't let her in. Not into this.

She'd met Roy and Anika a few times, back when things were still light. Still innocent. She liked them—especially Anika. There was a quiet strength in that woman, and Emma respected it. But now? Now this was different. Now it was war. And I wasn't dragging Emma onto the battlefield.

She tried. She kept asking about how I felt. Kept gently nudging me to talk. To grieve. To let it out in a way that didn't involve blood. But every time she said his name, it was like lighting a match inside my chest. All I could feel was rage. And rage didn't want to talk. Rage wanted action. Closure. Justice.

I hated lying to her.

But I hated the idea of her knowing more.

Three days.

Work wasn't helping.

I'd snapped at a prisoner for not stepping back fast enough during a search. Another time I slammed a cell door so hard, it nearly started a fight. The rage was bleeding through the cracks. And the worst part? I didn't even care anymore.

I used to have control. Years of it. Like a wall of reinforced concrete. But now that wall had shifted. Cracks forming. Hairline fractures in my foundation. The wrong word, the wrong look, and I'd feel the pressure start to build behind my eyes. That sharp, warm surge that made everything pulse red.

It was close.

Too fucking close.

But this plan? This would be my release. My recalibration. My therapy.

Because once Osbourne was gone—really gone—the air would feel lighter. My chest wouldn't feel like it was being gripped by a vice. I could go back to Emma. Whole, maybe not. But finished. Resolved. Freed from the weight Chris's murder had left behind.

That was the story I told myself.

That was the lie I needed to believe.

I checked the calendar again.

Two days until Osbourne walked out the gates.

Two days until the plan would no longer be hypothetical.

It was real.

And so was my conviction.

I would end him.

Not with rage. Not with heat.

But with method.

Like every single thing I'd done in my career—

With control. With precision.

And without hesitation.

Even if it meant, what was left of me couldn't be saved.

CHAPTER 64: FINAL ASSEMBLY

Sunday.

Roy's place was quiet when I arrived. The sort of silence that lets your thoughts echo a little too loudly.

The blinds were drawn. The hallway smelled of burnt coffee and stale tobacco. It suited the mood.

Anika greeted me with a warm hug, handed me a mug. Coffee—she knew just how I liked it. She didn't sit at the table. Just leaned in the doorway, arms folded, observing like a silent sentinel. Roy and I sat across from each other, the space between us heavy with what we were about to set in motion.

I set the folder down and started.

"Alright. For this to work," I said, "we work backwards."

Roy blinked at me, puzzled. "Backwards?"

"Yeah. Why do people get caught?"

He shrugged. "Sloppy. Someone talks. Evidence."

"Exactly. Evidence. Evidence buries you. So, this plan has one core rule—no evidence, no crime."

I flipped the folder open. Inside, maps, photos, names, phone numbers, trigger points, entry and exit paths. The sort of blueprint that wouldn't look out of place in an intelligence agency.

"This is what I've been working on."

I walked them through it.

From Osbourne's release date.

To his predictable return to the Strip Club.

To the moment we guide him, gently and unknowingly, to the point of no return.

Every favour I'd asked for, every person I'd roped in through Roy or Anika—they only knew one small part. Enough to complete a task. Nothing more. A whisper in the dark. A favour owed. A debt repaid. Everyone playing a piece, but no one holding the whole puzzle.

Even the hesitant ones—those who flinched at Osbourne's name—were reassured. "You won't be touched. You won't be remembered."

I leaned in closer.

"One more thing. From now on, every time you step outside, I want you to believe you're on CCTV. Every. Fucking. Time."

He didn't flinch. Just gave a small nod.

"No, I need you to *feel* it. Picture it—every corner of the CBD, behind the club, the laneway—cameras are everywhere. You don't need to walk it to know. Just open Google Maps. Street view. You'll see them."

I paused, letting it land.

"Now imagine facial recognition pulling you apart frame by frame. Don't look up. Don't draw attention. Just flow. Seamless. Invisible."

Roy was quiet. He nodded again, slower this time. Message received.

We spent hours on it.

Refining.

Tightening.

Tearing it down, rebuilding it, then doing it again. Over and over. Until it became second nature. Until it became muscle memory. The smoke thick in the air. Our coffee cold by the time we remembered to drink it.

Anika didn't say much. But she didn't need to. She was watching every detail. Processing it like a machine.

Chris used to say, 'You don't plan for what goes right. You plan for when it all goes to shit.' I didn't just remember the words. I felt them in my spine.

Finally, Roy stood. Crossed to a cluttered desk and pulled out a folder with an old map taped together at the creases.

"This," he said, laying it flat, "this is where it ends."

It was isolated. The roads not marked on any map. An old track a farmer once used on land now abandoned, near an old oil refinery. Nothing for miles. One road in. One road out. Blocked by timber and old concrete blocks. He tapped the map.

"We clear the blockage tomorrow morning. Drive through. Once we're in, we reseal it. No one stumbles in. No one finds us."

I nodded.

"You'll have everything I need?" I asked.

"Every last thing on your list, plus more."

"Good," I said. "Don't worry. I'll bring the weapon."

Roy hesitated.

"You sure you won't be missed?" he asked.

I leaned back in the chair. "No one's looking for me. Not that day. Not that night. Not for a while."

He nodded. "Alright. But your phone stays home. No contact once this starts. You understand me? No last-minute calls. No adjustments. This train only runs one way."

"I understand," I said. "This ends tomorrow night."

He turned to Anika. "We'll do our part."

Anika gave a small smile. Not warm. Not kind. Just resolute.

"I owe him," she said, her voice low. "For the girls. For what he did. I've waited years for this."

Her eyes were glass. But her tone was steel.

I stood.

Shook Roy's hand.

Hugged Anika—tight. Like the world was about to split down the middle.

And then I left.

As I drove home, the rage that once burned uncontrollably was now cold.

Coiled. Purposeful.

My spiral had shape now. My grief had fangs.

My conscience, long since buried beneath a blueprint of blood and calculation.

The wait would kill me.

But the act?

That would bring peace.

Not just for Chris.

But for me.

CHAPTER 65: THE QUIET BEFORE THE KILL

I returned home. Locked the car. Stepped inside.

The crumpled pieces of paper in my jacket pocket—scribbled notes, last-minute adjustments—pressed against me like tiny explosives. I shoved them deeper, out of sight.

Dougal was the first to greet me, as always. Tail wagging, tongue hanging out. Emma followed from the hallway.

Her voice soft. "Hi. How were Roy and Anika?"

"Yeah, good," I said flatly, already moving past her.

"Do you want to talk?"

"Not at the moment. Got a lot on my mind."

She watched as I sat down at the computer, her concern hanging in the air like smoke.

"I made dinner. Do you want something?"

"No thanks." My eyes were fixed on the screen.

I pulled up the plan one last time. The strip club. The laneway. Google Maps open in full screen. Every detail laid out like a battlefield. I checked the time stamps on the street view images. Angle of the shadows. Position of the rear cameras. It was all there. I'd rehearsed this a dozen times. A hundred. But my gut still twisted, a slow-burn acid turning certainty into doubt.

Too many people. Too many moving parts. What if someone pulled out? Froze? Went rogue?

What if someone was caught?

Suddenly, Dougal barked. High-pitched. Something outside, probably just a possum on the fence.

"DOUGAL! SHUT THE FUCK UP!"

The silence that followed was instant—and awful.

I heard him retreat under the kitchen table. Tail down. Ears pinned.

Emma stepped into the room; her eyes lit with fury. "Jacob—what the fuck? He's just a dog. He doesn't know what's going on. I don't even know what's going on."

Then she was gone—bedroom door closing behind her. Not a slam. But enough.

I sat there in the flickering light of the monitor. A cold weight settling in my chest.

Then I saw Dougal's face peeking out from under the table. Eyes wide. Head low.

I knelt. "I'm sorry, mate." I patted my leg. "Come here."

He stepped out slowly. Cautious. Head down.

I reached down and stroked his head, his soft fur between my fingers. "Didn't mean it, little guy. You bark all you want. You're the best guard dog."

I shut down the computer. Stuffed the notes back in my pocket.

Time to apologise again.

I opened the bedroom door. Emma was lying on the bed, scrolling her phone, pretending not to notice me.

"Hey," I said. "I'm sorry."

She didn't look at me. Not at first.

"I said sorry to Dougal, and now I'm saying it to you."

She finally set the phone down. "Jacob don't shut me out. You can talk to me. About anything."

I stepped closer. "Actually… I'm going to be away for a couple days. Three, max. After that, things will go back to normal. I promise."

Her eyes locked on mine. "Jacob, you're my rock. I need you." Her eyes filled with tears.

"You used to tell me everything. I can't compete with whatever's going on in your head. I'm worried that something is going to happen to you. I don't want you to get hurt." A single tear rolled down her left cheek.

"I need you to look after me and Dougal. The same as I need to look after you."

"I know, I mean it, this will all be over soon."

Emma didn't wipe the tear away.

She exhaled, her breath shaking. "Chris's murder changed you. I get it. It changed all of us. But I'm worried, Jacob."

I reached out and took her hand. Squeezed it softly.

I'd dragged her into a war she didn't even know she was fighting.

"I love you."

She half-smiled. "Ditto."

Dougal jumped up on the bed and curled into his spot.

"One more thing," I said. "I have to swing by Chris's place in the morning. Something I need to pick up."

"Does Brianna know?" Wiping the tears away.

"Yeah. She's still with her sister. I told her days ago."

I prepared myself for bed. Washed my face. Brushed my teeth. Looked in the mirror, not liking the man staring back.

Laying down beside Emma, I reached down and scratched Dougal behind the ears. He nudged my hand with his nose, soft and cold.

I closed my eyes, but it didn't bring peace. Just echoes.

And then I heard it again—Brianna's sobs at the funeral. Not the kind that fade politely into a tissue. The kind that come from somewhere deeper. Raw. The sound of a soul tearing loose.

It crawled into my head and stayed there, just under the skin. I turned on my side, but it followed.

That sound didn't just haunt me.

It fuelled me.

This was it.

Everything was in place.

All I had to do was keep breathing. Stay quiet. And finish what I started.

CHAPTER 66: THE FINAL TURN

I pulled up to Chris's house and killed the engine.

It felt wrong stepping onto the driveway without hearing his laugh. Without that dumb grunt he made when his knee cracked as he slipped out of a chair. But now… nothing. Just the wind in the trees and the creak of the old side gate.

I made my way down the narrow path toward the back of the property. The garden was overgrown. Brianna hadn't been back since. I didn't blame her. Who the hell could walk past the house where they found his body and keep breathing?

The shed loomed ahead like it had grown out of the dirt itself. Solid. Boxy. Square-jawed. Just like him.

I stood at the door for a long time, not quite able to put my hand on the handle.

Thinking about the last time Chris was here, working on his knives.

I opened the door.

Inside, it was exactly how he'd left it. Tools hanging like surgical instruments on pegboards. Vices bolted to benches. Everything had its place — sharp, polished, obsessively arranged.

Chris didn't just build things in here. He restored order. This was where he made sense of the world. Where things could be measured, cut, shaped. Unlike prison. Unlike the shit storm outside these walls.

I stepped in.

I stood at the bench, taking in the place where he felt most at home. And all I could feel was anger.

Anger. That my friend was taken from me.

I slammed my fist down on the workbench.

A chisel jumped and clattered to the floor.

Dust puffed off the surface and settled into the air like ash.

I bent down, opened the lowest drawer — the one with the military-grade lock Chris used. Inside, wrapped in a black cloth, was the reason I'd come.

I didn't unwrap it. I didn't need to.

I just held it in my hand, the weight of it pulling at my soul. A goodbye wrapped in darkness.

My voice cracked when I spoke aloud.

"Tonight. You die tonight."

I slipped it into my back pocket. Locked the shed behind me.

Didn't look back.

Later that day.

17:00hrs

Roy and I met at a hole-in-the-wall café tucked between two laneways off Grant Street. Metal chairs. Rusted signage. Dust on the menus.

He was already there. Back to the wall. Watching the door like I knew he would. I nodded. Sat down opposite him. We didn't shake hands. Didn't need to.

Anika wasn't with him.

A waitress came over. I ordered out of habit. Roy already had a coffee.

We made small talk. Something about construction works on Foster Street. Some bullshit about footy scores. He made a joke. I gave a small laugh that died in my throat.

Eventually, Roy slid a small black pouch across the table under a paper napkin.

He didn't look at me when he said it.

"Everything you asked for. Burner too. Number is clean. Been tested."

I nodded. Slipped it into the inside pocket of my jacket.

"Sure, you're good?" he asked.

"No," I said. "I just want it to be over."

"It will be. Tonight, it's done."

"I want to go home after this, Roy. Really go home. I want to open the door and not have Dougal flinch at the sound of my voice. I want Emma to stop searching my face like there's someone missing behind it."

"She deserves that," Roy said. "We all do. But you already know there's no going back to before. You do this, you don't come out the same."

"I don't care anymore."

My left hand started to shake. Just a tremor at first, like something inside me was shorting out. I didn't even notice. But Roy did.

He kept his eyes on the passing crowd, then said, calm as ever, "It never gets easier. You just go through the motions until it's done."

He took a sip of his coffee. "Don't worry. You'll get there. I'll make sure of it—after all, I owe you."

He looked at me, eyes dark beneath his cap.

Roy finished his coffee in silence. We sat there in that grim peace for another ten minutes. Watching the world blur past the dusty front window.

Nobody cared. Just two men at a table.

When I stood to leave, Roy gripped my wrist.

"You have one shot at this. One. Don't let rage make you sloppy."

I stared back at him, the weight in my jacket pocket suddenly colder.

"No rage. Just purpose."

I straightened my jacket, and put on my cap. "I'll see you soon."

And then I walked out. Down the alley, across the street, into the crowd.

The people around me were alive, oblivious, loud.

I felt none of it.

I was already somewhere else.

Already halfway to a kill.

CHAPTER 67: FIRST PIECE

The corner felt colder than it should've. A breeze hissed through the streets. I kept one hand buried deep in my jacket pocket—wrapped around the weight that said this was really happening.

Club 262 wasn't a nightclub. Not really. Just an old building in the CBD, painted matte grey, windows blacked out like eyes punched shut. A single neon sign flickered above the door—blood-red. It didn't look inviting. It looked secretive.

Wind pressed in. Cold. Knife-edged. I pulled my collar higher, but it still seeped in—like everything else lately.

The street was thinning. Fewer headlights. Fewer faces. But I scanned each one—checking for a pattern, a break in rhythm. I wasn't watching for threats. I was hunting the moment.

My phone buzzed once. A text from Roy.

You good?

I replied. *Yep.*

I flexed my left hand. That tremor again—same one that had started when I first planned this. Microfractures in my control. A fault line running through my bones.

This was what the moment before the first shot felt like.

Across the street, the club's sign surged brighter. The security guard stepped out front—massive. Bald. Jacket stretched across bulk and arrogance. A man built for intimidation, not discretion. I observed him from under the shadow of a café awning. Didn't move. Didn't blink. Just counted my heartbeats and focused on the weight of the bottle tucked inside my coat.

Inside, Osbourne would be upstairs soon. VIP area. His little throne. Surrounded by strippers, sycophants, maybe a wannabe bikie or two. The predator holding court while the girls laughed too loudly and flinched too slowly.

I thought of the girls Anika had told me about. The ones who cried in back rooms, then powdered their noses and went back out smiling.

He didn't just break them. He filmed it.

10:13 PM.

Anika had said between 10:30 and 11. He liked to arrive late. Watch people squirm when he entered. The night was his. Always had been.

I stepped inside the café behind me, nodding to the barista—she knew my order by now. Gave me one last coffee before closing. I took it without speaking and moved back outside to the corner.

And then I saw him.

Not Osbourne.

The first piece.

Young guy. Slim build. Nervous energy in a cheap blazer and shiny black shoes. Trying hard not to look like prey.

He paused just short of me. Fidgeted. Cleared his throat.

"You Jacob?"

"Depends."

He glanced around. Swallowed. "I… I work the upstairs bar. Club 262. Someone said… you had something for me?"

I said nothing. Just stared.

"They said it was for Osbourne."

There it was. The trigger phrase.

"What about him?"

The kid's face twisted. "He's a prick. Harasses me. Calls me names. Makes fun of me being gay. He tried to make me touch one of the girls once. He's even hit me a few times. Laughed about it with his mates."

His voice cracked a little. But it wasn't fear I saw in his eyes.

It was hatred.

"He filmed me once, I think," the kid said. "Didn't say it, but... I saw him holding his phone, smirking while I cleaned puke off the carpet. Just—like I was nothing."

I reached into my coat and pulled out a black cloth pouch. Shielded it from the streetlight. Inside: a glass bottle with a dropper lid. Clear. Potent.

"Liquid GHB," I said, my voice low. "One drop per drink. No more."

He looked at it like it was a holy relic. Or a loaded gun.

"You sure he won't know?"

"He won't. But I'll know. You can do this."

He nodded, stuffing the bottle into his inside pocket. Hands trembling slightly.

"What if he sees me?"

"He won't."

I stepped closer to the kid, placing a hand on his shoulder. Reassuring.

"Just keep it hidden behind the bar. You know how to be discrete. We just want him a little more drunk than usual."

"But what if he suspects something?"

"Smile. Serve him. And tell yourself that tonight—he's not the one in control."

"Now, give me your phone."

The kid looked puzzled, "Why?"

"Cause I need to give you my number, just in case."

His eyes widened, "What do you mean, just in case?"

"Relax. If you need me, just text me. I'll help you through it."

He nodded again, sharper this time. Not brave. Just resolved. Then crossed the street and slipped past the bouncer with a slight nod.

First piece—in place.

I sipped my coffee. It was cold now. This wasn't planning anymore. This was the first cut.

Measured. Controlled. Like surgery on something diseased. You don't hesitate when you're cutting out cancer.

A light mist had started falling. The kind that crept down the back of your neck and reminded you were alive—barely.

I tilted my head back and stared up into the sky. The clouds were moving fast. No moon. No stars.

No witnesses.

"For you, Chris," I whispered.

And then I stepped out from the corner, into the dark, toward the next piece.

CHAPTER 68: THE LANE

I crossed the street.

Every step forward now was a choice I'd already made.

Club 262 loomed in front of me—its blacked-out facade like a mouth that didn't speak, only swallowed. The neon sign flickered, coughing red light into the night. Still pulsing. Still alive.

And then I saw it.

The black Mercedes.

It glided to a stop like a predator settling in the grass—quiet, composed, lethal.

Two men stepped out. Suits stretched tight across muscle. Sunglasses still on, even under streetlights. Security, maybe. Or something meaner.

Then came the third.

Osbourne.

He slid out of the car with the sort of casual arrogance that comes from getting away with things too many times. He adjusted his jacket. Scanned the street like he owned it. Not worried—waiting to be feared.

He lived for that twitch in people's eyes.

He nodded to the guards, and the three of them disappeared through the club's door. No ID check. No questions. Security just nodded like loyal dogs.

I watched as the door closed.

Enjoy it while it lasts, I thought. *This is your last fucking night.*

I turned and made my way toward the laneway behind the club.

Dark. Damp. Silent.

The buildings leaned in like they were eavesdropping. Light leaked through a few frosted windows. Everything else was shadows and puddles. Industrial bins lined one side of the lane. Rubbish and empty beer bottles scattered near doorways.

I kept my walk steady. Casual.

There were CCTV cameras—cheap, glitchy ones mounted on the rear of buildings—but I kept my head down. Just a guy taking a shortcut through the alley. Nothing to see.

I reached the end of the lane, closest to the club and checked my watch.

He was late.

I waited. Pacing slowly from one side of the lane to the other. Watching the traffic roll past on the main road. Every car, every pedestrian, every flick of brake lights tightened the screws.

Then finally—headlights.

A white delivery van slowed and turned in.

I moved to intercept as it pulled up beside me.

The driver wound the window down. Late twenties. Stubble. Tired eyes.

"You know why you're here?" I asked.

"Not really. Just told to do a delivery," he said, glancing at the empty back. "But there's nothing to deliver."

"That's fine. Just back into the lane. Park behind the first building."

"That's it?"

"Just say you're waiting on a mate for a signature. Keep the engine running. No questions."

He frowned. "What if they want me to move?"

"You don't move for anyone. Not unless it's the cops. Got it?"

He paused. Then nodded. "How long am I sitting here?"

"Until you see a limo behind you flash its lights. Then you're done. You go home."

"Okay…"

He eased the van into the alley and parked. Engine still running. Lights dimmed. A blockade in plain sight.

I examined him for a moment, then turned and walked to the other end of the lane.

Everything felt tight. The air. My jacket. My skin.

Another set of headlights approached.

Long, low, and slow.

The limo.

It pulled into the lane with the grace of a hearse, and I stepped toward the driver's side. Knocked once.

He rolled the window down halfway.

"Evening," I said. "Pull all the way down. Cut the engine. Someone'll come out in a bit. You stay in the front. One of the girls from the club will hop into the back. Later, four of us will get in the back. When we're in, we'll give you the address."

He looked at me, face unreadable. A beat of hesitation. Then he nodded.

"Yeah, alright."

The limo rolled down the lane like a funeral procession, taillights casting a faint red glow against the brick walls. When it stopped behind the van, it felt like part of the darkness—just a silhouette now. Waiting.

The trap was half-built.

I stood there for a few minutes, watching. Making sure no one came out the back of the club. No smokers. No stray staff. No noise.

Then—another horn. One short beep.

Second van.

Right on time.

I waved him in.

He pulled up beside me and leaned out the window. "Hey. Supposed to be doing a delivery?"

"Kind of. Park here. Wait. Someone'll bring you a slab. After that, you can go."

"How long?"

"Hour, maybe. Just sit tight. That's all."

He raised his eyebrows but didn't argue.

"Alright," he muttered, cutting the engine.

I nodded, but something felt off. That itch at the base of your spine. That whisper in the back of your brain telling you something's about to crack.

Sweat crawled down my back. My hands clenched and unclenched like they had their own heartbeat.

This had to work.

No fuck-ups. Not tonight.

I checked my watch.

Time to move down the lane. Find cover. Wait for Roy and his friend.

I took a breath that didn't go all the way down. My chest felt hollow. Not with fear. With certainty. The kind that tightens your muscles like wires and hollows out your stomach.

The lane was sealed now. A blockade in plain sight—brazen, like it dared someone to ask why it was there.

Osbourne had no idea what he'd just walked into.

But he would.

Soon. Very soon.

CHAPTER 69: THE WAIT

I found a doorway two doors down from the rear of Club 262—recessed, shadowed, just enough to disappear into. From the lane, no one could see me. That was the idea.

I waited.

Couldn't tell if it was the cold or the nerves, but I'd started to shiver. Jaw tight. Shoulders coiled. My back was wet. Not from rain—sweat. And the night air was getting colder.

I checked my watch again.

Still nothing. Every second dragged like a knife across my spine. I kept picturing the inside of the club. Osbourne holding court. Laughing too loud. Someone crying in the toilets.

So many things could still go wrong.

Then I heard it—footsteps down the lane. Light. Controlled. One pair. Then another. I leaned out slowly.

Two silhouettes. One sparked a lighter mid-step, casting a flash of orange against a familiar face.

"'Bout fucking time," I muttered under my breath.

Roy exhaled smoke and waved a hand like it was no big deal.

"Relax," he said. "Dropped off two slabs for the delivery guys. Told the one down near the end of the lane he'd better share, or we'd know about it."

He grinned. "Think we scared him a bit."

The second figure stepped forward.

Jesus.

I froze.

Even in the dark, he appeared like Osbourne. Not just similar—uncanny. Bald now, same build, same posture. I'd seen old photos, but this… this was something else.

I had to double check it wasn't him.

"Roy?" My voice was quieter than I expected.

"Yeah," he smirked. "Good, right? Wait till he walks. Even got the fucking swagger right."

The decoy nodded silently and stepped back into the shadows behind a dumpster. Hidden. Waiting.

Roy turned back. "How much longer?"

"Not sure," I said. "But if everything's on track, one of the dancers will come out soon. She'll hop in the limo. That's our cue. Once she's in, Osbourne won't be far behind. I'll text my friend. She'll make the call."

"Rear exit covered?" I asked.

"Yeah. Friend on the inside. Knows exactly what to do when Osbourne gets there."

"Alright. Then we wait."

We stood side-by-side in the dark. Our backs against cold brick. The street at the end of the lane moved in slow motion. A car, then silence. Everything felt like it was holding its breath.

My phone buzzed.

"Fuck," I hissed. Glanced at the text on the screen.

It was the kid.

'Osbourne is drinking Coronas. Watching me open them. Watching the lemon wedges go in. What do I do?'

I froze.

Think.

Quickly, I typed:

'When he walks away from the bar, dose two lemon wedges—two drops each. Keep them separate. Use those.'

Sent.

"Fuck," I muttered.

Roy leaned in, voice low. "The kid will handle it. And the girls will keep Osbourne distracted. Just hang on a bit longer."

"Yeah," I breathed. "I hope so."

He lit another cigarette. The tiny ember cast shadows across his face. Calm. Steady.

Me? My hands wouldn't stop clenching. The tension sat just beneath my skin like something crawling.

Finally, I pulled the cloth from my back pocket. Felt the weight inside. Slipped it inside my jacket.

Thirty minutes passed like thirty hours.

I checked my watch again.

Then the rear door of Club 262 slammed open.

She came out fast—heels clacking against the concrete, silver sequined skirt barely covering anything, matching bra catching flashes of streetlight. Black stilettos stabbed the pavement like she wanted to hurt it.

Didn't need to be a body language expert—she was pissed. Shoulders stiff. Eyes locked straight ahead. Lips tight with rage.

She yanked open the limo's back door, threw herself inside, and slammed it shut hard enough to rattle the frame.

I exhaled through my nose. "Guessing she just had another run-in with Osbourne."

Roy scratched the side of his face, watching the door settle. "Yep. She knows him all right."

"Time," I said.

Roy nodded.

CHAPTER 70: THE SNATCH

Roy flicked the last of his cigarette into a puddle, the ember hissing out like a fuse cut short.

I sent the message.

Make the call. Now.

Two minutes later, my phone rang.

"Jacob. It's done. Call's made. Cops'll be there soon. Good luck."

Jacklyn hung up.

Didn't give me time to reply. Maybe she knew I wouldn't know what to say.

Thanks. Good luck to you too.

Now all we had to do was wait.

I pulled the black pouch Roy had given me earlier. Opened it slow. No noise. No mistakes.

Inside—one loaded syringe.

I held it up for a second, watching the way it caught the faint light.

"You sure this'll work?" I asked.

Roy nodded once. "Enough Ketamine in there to drop a horse. Just hit him behind the collarbone—deep muscle."

I nodded.

"And don't forget," he said, eyes locking with mine, "push the fucking plunger. Or we're all fucked."

"Alright. Won't be long now," I said. "Let's move."

We crept forward to the next building, still hidden in shadow, one wall away from the rear club door. Just close enough. Just far enough.

Roy leaned in, voice barely above a whisper. "Anika said the second the cops show up, the girl on front desk hits a button. Alerts the VIP rooms."

"Yeah?"

"Yeah. Usually gives the coke-heads time to flush their stash. Zip up. Pretend to be civilised."

I scanned the lane. "Not this time."

"Nope. This time, Osbourne gets told about a limo out back."

"And he walks right into it," I said.

Roy nodded once.

I gripped the syringe tight. Thumb on the plunger. The weight of it felt heavier now. Realer.

Three minutes.

Then the banging started.

Loud. Abrupt. Angry.

BANG. BANG. BANG.

"What the fuck..." I hissed.

The rear door cracked open. A beam of interior light spilled into the alley, then the silhouette stepped out.

Osbourne.

Security had a grip on his arm—not quite dragging him but guiding him like someone who couldn't walk a straight line. He stumbled sideways, caught himself. Swiped a sleeve across his mouth like a man already tasting bile.

Then he spotted the limo.

His posture changed. He straightened, adjusted his pants. Like he was about to be rewarded.

Security pointed.

Osbourne walked toward it. Heavy. Sluggish. But determined. He reached for the handle—missed it. Swore. Reached again.

This time, it opened.

He stood there—one hand on the door, one on the roof—peering inside. That grin spreading across his face like grease. Thinking he was about to get serviced.

That was my cue.

I moved.

Fast. Quiet.

He was still smiling as I approached him. Still leering at the girl in the back seat. Mouth half-open. Already salivating.

Then I drove the needle in. Thud.

Right into the muscle below his collarbone—deep.

And I pushed the plunger. Hard. All the way in.

He jerked. His grin collapsed.

He turned toward me—slow, confused. I slammed my left arm across his, pinning him to the roof of the car.

His eyes locked on mine.

Recognition.

That flicker of shock.

Then rage.

Then fear.

"Remember me, cunt," I said.

The moment twisted. His body tensed, trying to fight. Too late.

His fists curled. Then loosened.

His eyes rolled back.

His knees gave out.

Osbourne crumpled—folded like wet cardboard—and dropped, head bouncing off the base of the limo door before slumping sideways onto the concrete.

Roy was there. So was the decoy. Security looking on.

"Fuck," Roy muttered. "Didn't think he was gonna go down."

I stared at Roy. "You didn't think he'd go down?"

The girl climbed out from the other side of the limo, stormed around the back in those towering heels. She looked down at Osbourne, unconscious and limp.

Then she kicked him. Hard. Right in the gut.

"Fucking pig," she spat.

Roy grabbed her arm. "Careful, sweetheart. You'll break your foot before he feels anything."

He gestured to the rear door. "Go on. Get inside. We'll take care of it. He's going on a nice long trip overseas."

Security opened the door for her. "Thanks Roy, I'll see you in a week for that tattoo."

She looked at us once more, fire in her eyes, then stormed off toward the door.

They both disappeared back into the club.

I looked down at Osbourne.

Dead weight.

"Jesus," I groaned. "He's heavy."

Roy took one arm. I took the other.

The decoy climbed into the limo, reaching to grab from inside. We struggled. Pulled. Hauled.

Osbourne flopped halfway onto the seat, one leg dangling out like a corpse caught mid-exit.

"One more—push!" Roy grunted.

We heaved him in. Then pushed him onto the floor.

Roy climbed in after. I paused. Scanned the alley.

Empty.

Still ours.

I slid into the back seat and shut the door.

Tapped the glass between us and the driver.

"Flash your lights at the van. Let's go."

The engine growled to life. The limo rolled forward, slow and steady, nosing out of the alley like it didn't want to be seen. It eased up beside the delivery van. I glanced at the signage stamped on its side — Bentridge Plumbing Supplies.

Legit enough to disappear in plain sight.

Then—traffic.

Just like that, we were moving.

In a limo.

In plain sight. And we had him.

Osbourne.

Drugged. Contained.

His time wasn't just running out. It had already started bleeding.

CHAPTER 71: THE DISAPPEARING ACT

I switched seats with the decoy and slid in beside Roy. The back of the limo was dim, the sort of dark that made your thoughts louder.

Osbourne's body lay at our feet—crumpled, unconscious, breathing like a dying animal. Roy casually rested one boot against his back. Not hard. Just enough weight to remind us he was still there. Still real. Still a problem.

No one spoke.

Outside, the city passed like a dream I couldn't wake from—traffic lights washing the interior in red and green hues, people walking dogs, laughing. Living.

And here we were—hauling a man to his final address.

Every block we passed felt like a choice we couldn't undo.

The tension sat between us like a live wire.

Then, from the other side, the decoy looked at Roy, leaned forward and mumbled, "I'm hungry."

Roy didn't even glance over.

I exhaled. "Maybe we should hit Macca's drive-through?"

We all laughed—short, sharp, offbeat.

It helped. Not much. But enough to loosen the grip around my throat.

Roy looked at me. Gave a small thumbs up.

Everything's fine.

But it wasn't. Not really. There were still a hundred ways this could collapse.

Someone could recognise the decoy. A neighbour could see too much. Osbourne could wake up and start screaming bloody murder before we had him inside.

I pulled the parole note from my jacket—creased, damp at the edges. I ran my thumb across where Chris had circled Osbourne's address. Handwriting—faded now, but still angry. Thinking about my friend drawing on the paper. Like it was a target. Maybe it always was.

I folded it back up. Tight. Like that might hold the weight of what we were doing.

Forty minutes later, the limo pulled into a quiet coastal street. Upscale. Wide lawns. Curated hedges. Houses with names instead of numbers.

Osbourne's townhouse was near the end of the row. White rendered walls. Silver Mercedes out front. The sort of place built to hide sins in plain sight.

Roy leaned down, searched Osbourne's jacket. Pulled out keys, a black leather wallet, and a phone. He handed me the phone. I searched through text messages, deleted a few.

He tossed the wallet to the decoy. In a low voice, just for us.

"Driver's licence is inside. If anyone asks, you're him."

I tossed the phone across. Keeping the conversation private.

"When you land in Thailand, don't forget to send a few messages."

He nodded.

"After you get your picture taken at The Pink Pussy Gogo bar, leave the wallet and phone behind where you're staying. After that, you change back to yourself. Fly to Singapore and return home in a few weeks."

The decoy grinned.

He pulled on Osbourne's jacket—cheap cologne still soaked into the lining—and grabbed the black carry-on he'd packed hours earlier. Nothing fancy. A toothbrush, some old receipts, burner phone, a couple of shirts. Just enough to sell the illusion.

I looked at him. "Walk out the front gate. Security cams will pick you up. Then straight back to the limo. You'll be a ghost in ten minutes."

He nodded.

I turned to the driver. Calm. Direct. Knocked on the glass partition.

"He'll be back in ten. Airport run. Wait here."

He nodded, eyes in the mirror. No questions.

Roy stepped out first. The keys clicked in the front door like teeth grinding.

We pulled Osbourne out together. He sagged between us like a drunk after a twelve-day bender. Roy and I held an arm each, with the other one grabbing Osbourne's belt. Still out cold. Still snoring. That sound crawled up my spine. The decoy followed.

The foyer was marble and glass. Everything smelled expensive.

We laid him on the tiles like a pile of wet laundry.

The decoy nodded in silence to Roy, walked out. As he reached the gate. He paused—just a heartbeat too long. Long enough for a neighbour to wonder. Long enough for fate to grow teeth.

A curtain twitched across the street. I didn't breathe until the limo began to move. Roy and I observed as the taillights of the limo slowly disappeared from our view.

All good.

Inside, gloves on. Every move measured. Minimal contact.

There could be no trace of us here. No smudged handles. No shadows left behind.

This was a house about to lose its master. And for once, the world would be better for it.

CHAPTER 72: GHOSTING THE PAST

The house was silent when we stepped in, but it wasn't peace.

It was *sterility*. A curated illusion—floors too polished, air too neutral. The sort of silence you'd expect in a morgue, or a rich man's secrets.

The door clicked shut behind us. Roy reached back and bolted it out of habit. I clenched my hands a few times. My hands were sweating.

Osbourne lay crumpled just inside the threshold. One arm trapped under his body, drool spiderwebbing down to the polished tile. He didn't look human—just a collapsed thing.

Roy nudged him with a boot. "Still with us?"

I didn't answer. I couldn't. My chest felt like a fist was tightening inside it.

I scanned the space—a townhouse in an upscale coastal suburb, but the kind that only looked lived-in if you squinted. Designer furniture. Clean. Soulless.

Everything was expensive and empty.

We moved like phantoms, careful not to disturb anything that didn't need disturbing. Not because we were afraid of being caught—because we didn't want to leave a single fingerprint on this man's life. He didn't deserve the dignity of a legacy.

Roy went first, heading toward what felt like an office. I paused in the living room.

Photos lined one wall—Osbourne with celebrities, politicians, athletes, musicians. Grinning like he belonged. Like he was one of them. Like the filth he was inside had been scrubbed clean by association.

He wasn't proud of who he was. He was proud of who *they* thought he was.

And they had no fucking idea.

Roy called from the hallway. "Found his playpen."

I followed. Office. Sleek, masculine, lifeless. Glass desk. Matching chair. No clutter.

Roy had the top drawer pulled out, flipped in his hand. He pointed. A strip of black tape beneath it.

He peeled it back. Silver key.

"Bastard hid it like a child hides porn mags," he muttered.

We found the safe in the walk-in robe—behind a false panel, magnetic latch.

Roy slid the key in. The lock clicked with an almost polite little *snick*, like the house was welcoming us.

Inside: rows of bundled cash, three bricks of tightly wrapped white powder, two flash drives, and a Glock 17 resting on a folded microfibre cloth like it was part of a museum exhibit.

"Jackpot," Roy whispered.

I said nothing. Just stared.

Roy grabbed the cash first, then the bricks. Held one up to the light. "That's not stepped on. That's pure."

He tossed it in a bag he pulled from under his jacket like it was laundry.

"I've got debts to pay," he said flatly. No apology. No shame.

I was still staring at the gun.

"Leave it," I said.

"You sure?"

"Yeah. It's traceable. Leave it."

"Suit yourself."

He zipped the bag, slung it over one shoulder.

I looked down the hall. The snoring had changed. A lower rumble now. Less human.

Like Osbourne was already being dragged downward.

We stood over him. He hadn't moved. Still face-down on the tiles. One shoe off. His hand twitching slightly, like a dying insect.

"You think he's dreaming?" I asked, quietly.

Roy shrugged. "Hope it's a fucking nightmare."

I turned away. Couldn't look at him like that anymore.

Roy disappeared out the side door.

Five minutes passed.

Then headlights flared against the lounge room wall. The sound of a motor, soft and low. A Holden Commodore—beige, dented, the sort of car no one remembered seeing.

Roy reversed it into the driveway. Opened the boot.

Time to move the body.

We dragged Osbourne out of his house like a rolled-up carpet. His weight shifted awkwardly—limp and unhelpful. He grunted once as his hip caught the edge of a doorway, then went silent again.

We move him to the boot. Dropped him in. Hard. A wet *thump* against the spare tyre.

Roy folded his arms over his chest, like some parody of a funeral. The kind where no one cried, and the dead had what they deserved.

Then he slammed the lid shut.

That sound again. Not just an ending.

An erasure.

We stood in the garage. Listening to the engine tick. The scent of pine air freshener and sweat hanging in the air like smoke.

Roy looked at me. His eyes darker now. Less smirk, more calculation. "Still time to back out."

"No," I said.

The word came easy.

Too easy.

I was already too far in.

Roy climbed into the driver's seat. I slid into the passenger's seat.

Neither of us spoke for a while.

Osbourne groaned once, muffled through steel and fabric.

Roy smirked. "Not long now."

The garage door rolled down with a soft mechanical whine.

And just like that, we were gone.

Taking the past with us.

CHAPTER 73 – THE FARMHOUSE

We didn't speak for the first 30 mins. Just the sound of tyres on bitumen, city lights giving way to long black stretches of highway. The sort of dark that starts peeling back your skin from the inside. One layer at a time.

Eventually Roy broke the silence.

"Jacob… about Collins."

I turned to him. That name brought something old and raw to the surface.

"My nephew. You remember."

"I remember," I said. "That scared little kid at the Metro."

Roy nodded slowly. "He's getting out in three months. Got a job lined up. Forklift licence. Warehouse out west. Says he wants to go straight."

"That's good."

"He will. Because of you. You protected him when he didn't even know he needed it. You kept him alive. I'll never forget that."

I looked back out the window. Couldn't look at him. "I didn't do it for thanks."

"I know," he said. "That's what makes it mean something."

Nothing else needed saying. We let that truth hang between us. Heavy. Final.

The road narrowed, fractured. Gravel took over. Then weeds. Then memory.

There was no driveway. Just a break in the scrub where nature had reclaimed the forgotten. One crooked fencepost. Faded wire coiled around itself like something strangled and left to rot.

Roy swung off the road without slowing.

The tyres bumped and crunched through debris—branches, beer cans, a broken pallet. I climbed out at the choke point and pulled the old barrier into place. Sheet metal. Timber. A rusted sign that once said *Keep Out*, now just pitted steel and faded red.

We drove in a little farther. The farmhouse emerged like a tumour on the land—swollen, broken, rotting from the inside. Every board a splinter. Every nail rusted through.

The roof sagged like a dying breath.

Windows smashed. Graffiti crawling across the walls in tags and slurs. A mattress in the corner, stained and deflated. Burn marks on the floor. Blood, maybe. Or oil. Or something worse.

"This it?" I asked.

Roy killed the engine. "Yeah. It won't be missed."

The silence was suffocating.

We stood for a moment. Not moving. Listening. The wind threaded through the trees like it had a secret. No birds. No insects. Just the sound of a place that had been abandoned not just by people—but by time.

We popped the boot.

Osbourne was curled like a child, knees drawn up. His breathing shallow. Face slack. The ketamine had done its job, no elegance to it. Just dead weight.

Roy kicked the sole of his shoe. Just checking.

We lifted him, silent. His limbs flopped uselessly as we carried him through the side of the house—what used to be a laundry door. Now just hinges and air.

The room was ready. One chair. Bolted. Metal loops anchored to studs. Floorboards reinforced with planks. A lightbulb hanging by wire. No power.

Roy turned on a lamp sitting on the floor next to a box of things he prepared earlier.

We sat Osbourne down and started the tape.

Ankles. Wrists. Thighs. Chest. Gaffer screaming as it peeled off the roll. It echoed through the empty house like something being flayed alive.

I wrapped each layer tighter than the last. Not just to restrain. To silence. To punish.

His mouth lolled open. A string of spit slid down his chin.

I didn't wipe it away.

We finished. I stepped back.

Roy lit a smoke. His fingers trembled. He didn't try to hide it.

"You know," he said, staring at Osbourne, "I used to believe in karma. Thought people like this got what they deserved."

"Turns out karma needs help," I said. My voice sounded hollow—like it had to crawl through miles of grief to reach my mouth.

I walked over to the window—what was left of one. Just a jagged square framing the bushland. I could see the coast from here. A line of black where the sea met the sky.

I didn't want peace. But I wanted it to end.

The chair creaked. Osbourne shifted slightly, his body twitching through the last stages of sedation. Almost time.

Roy blew a puff of smoke out. "You ever think about what comes after?"

I didn't answer. Not because I didn't know.

For me, there was no *after*.

There were only the next few hours. The fire. The silence. The lies we'd tell ourselves so we could sleep again.

If sleep ever came.

Roy looked over. "Last chance to change your mind."

I nodded. "You prepped this. I'm just finishing it."

He didn't smile. Didn't joke. Just flicked his smoke into the dark.

We stood there—two men, two ghosts—watching the sky fold in on itself.

It wasn't just about revenge anymore.

This was about erasure.

About taking back something that had been stolen. About giving voice to the screams no one else heard. About finishing what grief and law and justice never could.

Because ghosts don't leave.

You bury them. Or you burn them.

And when the flames came, I wouldn't look away.

CHAPTER 74: FINAL INSTRUCTIONS

We didn't speak as we moved through the gutted frame of the farmhouse. The place had been hollowed out by time and squatters. Plaster peeled like dead skin. Floorboards creaked under our weight like they remembered violence.

Roy held a lamp, its dim beam swaying with each step. "Watch where you put your feet," he said quietly.

I stepped through what used to be the kitchen—just two old copper pipes left in the wall. Someone had drawn cartoon eyes around them. Crude. Mocking. Like the house was watching us now. Judging. Or amused.

The back passage was barely there—just a gap between walls and rotted timber. We emerged into the yard. Fencing on both sides, most of the palings gone. Probably burned in backyard fires long ago. At the far end, the skeleton of a collapsed shed slumped into itself. Refusing to fall any farther. Just waiting.

Beyond that, the black outline of the bay. A single marker buoy blinked in the distance like it was waving at the dead. To the right, the oil refinery glowed in the night—an industrial Christmas tree pulsing with heat and chemicals.

Roy pointed with the lamp. "This is the drum."

I stepped closer. A large steel barrel, blackened and scorched in places. Inside, he'd lined the walls with ceramic tiles. Rough, cracked, heat-resistant.

"It won't burn as hot as a crematorium," Roy said, "but it'll get close enough."

I ran a hand over the rim. "And the fuel?"

Roy popped open a second drum. "Aviation fuel. Two full barrels. It burns clean, hot, and fast. Plus, with the refinery just over there, no one will question the smell. Just don't light the fucker during the day. Someone might get curious. The fence will block most of the flames if you're careful. To anyone watching, it'll just look like squatters torching the place again."

I stared at the fuel barrels. Slick black drums with red hazard labels and faded serial stamps.

"This'll do," I said.

Roy knelt beside the drum, tapping the side like he was proud of it. "When the body's done cooking, give it time to cool. Then—" he paused, grinning now, "—you use this."

He pulled a tarp off what appeared like a modified cement mixer. No. Not a mixer. A rock crusher.

I stepped in closer. "Fuck me," I said, crouching beside it. This wasn't improvisation. This was surgical.

"Industrial grade," he said. "Feed the bones in here, the drum underneath catches everything. Got a small generator to run it, and a backup container of fuel if you need to top it up."

I crouched and ran my hand over the steel hopper. Cold. Rough. Efficient.

"If not," Roy said, "tip the fuel around the place when you're done. Soak the walls. Burn everything."

"Got it."

"There's more." He pointed behind a stack of timber—an old sieve, blackened at the edges. "Go through the ash. Just in case this arsehole had screws in him. Plates. Bolts. I've seen stranger things."

I nodded.

He tossed me a small magnet. "Wave it across the remains. If anything sticks, throw it in the barrel and light it again."

I looked at him, silent.

Roy lit a cigarette, the ember flaring in the dark. "I told you I had experience."

We stood there, inspecting the equipment. The tools for ending a man so completely the world would forget he ever existed.

Roy took a drag, exhaled slow. "Call me in a few days. When it's done."

I nodded. "We'll talk about the tattoo then."

"Something for Chris?"

"Yeah. Nothing obvious. No name. No picture. Just… something that's mine. Something that's his."

Roy flicked ash off the end of his smoke. "I'll give you a discount."

"No," I said. "You cleared your debt. You paid it back the night you said yes."

"Maybe. But friends don't charge friends."

I stepped forward. Held out a hand.

He took it—but I pulled him in instead. A brief hug. Real. Unspoken.

"Thank you," I said. Barely above a whisper.

Roy stepped back. Nodded. Walked around the side of the house, climbed into his little Hyundai, and turned the engine over. The headlights swept past the shed, catching a shimmer off the fuel drums. Then he pulled away, taillights glowing red until the dust swallowed them.

Gone.

I stood there alone, the air suddenly heavier.

Then—behind me—a groan.

Low. Wet. Close.

I turned.

Osbourne.

Still taped to the chair. Still drifting between sedation and pain. His head lolled forward. His chest rose shallow.

I stepped into the doorway and faced him.

My fists clenched without thinking.

No more talking.

No more questions.

Just the last chapter of a story no one would ever read.

And it was nearly time to write the final line.

CHAPTER 75: THE VOICE IN THE DARK

Osbourne stirred.

First it was just breath—shallow, irregular. Then a twitch in his fingers. A shift in his neck. Like something crawling back into the world that should've stayed buried.

His head rolled to one side. Eyes half-closed. Confused. His mouth dry and cracked. He coughed once, gagged on the taste in his throat, then muttered the name like it meant protection.

"Tony...?"

It came out hoarse. Barely a whisper. A question without context.

He blinked slowly, trying to place himself. Trying to understand the walls. The smell. The cold air against his skin. This wasn't the club. There were no lights, no music, no dancers. Just rot. Dust. Dread.

His head lolled forward.

Then he saw me.

A shape at first. A silhouette backlit by the lamp on the floor. No features. Just shadow.

"Who the fuck...?"

I didn't move. Didn't speak.

Not yet.

He squinted, eyes twitching in the dim glow. Breathing harder now. He pulled at his arms. Heard the gaffer tear slightly under the tension.

He tugged again. Harder. The chair creaked beneath him. His voice rose with it.

"Hey! Let me the fuck outta this! I swear to God, I'll kill you, I'll fucking kill you!"

He thrashed, spit flying from his mouth. Muscle strained against the tape—veins bulging in his neck, cords in his arms pulling tight like wires ready to snap.

Still, I stood there.

Still, I said nothing.

Until I raised a hand.

Slow. Deliberate.

Then the voice came—low, cold, measured.

"This is the end for you."

Osbourne froze mid-struggle. Breathing hard. Staring into the black.

I stepped forward once. Just enough.

"You didn't just have him killed. You had him butchered. Stabbed twenty-eight times."

He shook his head violently. "Don't know what the fuck you're talking about. I didn't stab anyone."

He jerked again, chair rattling. "Let me go! You hear me?! You're fucking dead, whoever the fuck you are! I'll rip your heart out, you fucking dog!"

I didn't flinch.

"You didn't stab him," I said calmly. "You had someone do it for you. After he broke your nose at Wendarra Prison."

His face changed. A flicker—not fear, but memory. Wendarra Prison. The broken nose. The voice.

I turned and walked back. Picked up the lamp.

Lifted it slowly—until the light caught my face.

Osbourne's eyes locked on.

"Ffffuck…" His breath hitched. "You!"

I said nothing.

"I'll fucking kill you, Daniels."

"Not this time."

He recoiled, head twitching side to side like denial could reverse reality.

"You've been a plague," I said. "Feeding on the weak. Getting girls hooked, fucking them up, pushing gear to kids, bleeding every lost soul for your amusement. You ruin people. And you enjoy it."

Osbourne laughed. A wet, bitter sound. "What, you here for revenge? Huh? Is that it? You want money? I've got money, you dumb fuck. Let's make a fucking deal."

I stepped closer. The light shifted. His face was soaked in sweat now. Eyes wide. Desperate.

"No," I said. "I want you to die."

He went still.

No more bargaining. No more rage.

Just silence.

And for the first time, I saw something real in his eyes.

Not fear of pain.

Fear of *consequence*.

Fear of facing something he couldn't manipulate. Couldn't out-talk. Couldn't buy.

Me.

He swallowed. The sound loud in the quiet room.

"You don't have to do this," he said.

"You already did."

I lowered the lamp again, casting my face back into shadow.

His voice broke.

"Wait… wait…"

He pulled at the tape again, weaker now. The fight gone out of him. Or maybe just starting to understand the rules had changed. He wasn't in control anymore.

I stepped back.

Turned to the doorway.

And left him there—

Taped to a chair in the guts of a rotting house, staring into the dark.

Knowing he wasn't going to make it out alive.

CHAPTER 76: THE ONE THAT COUNTS

I stood just inside the other room.

The walls were breathing. At least that's how it felt. The cold came in through the cracks like it was watching. Waiting.

Osbourne was still ranting.

"Let me out, you gutless fuck! You hear me?!"

The voice cracked—part threat, part panic. He was wearing down. His words were slurred. Too much adrenaline, too much fear. His body knew something his brain wouldn't accept yet.

I didn't answer him.

I reached into my jacket and slowly pulled out the black cloth. My hands didn't shake.

Not anymore.

Osbourne's voice carried through the rotting walls.

"I've got money. People! You don't know who you're fucking messing with!"

I unfolded the cloth. One side. Then the other.

The obsidian blade caught the faint lamp light.

It was beautiful. Sharp as a secret. Smooth as silence.

Chris had made it for me—his last real gift before everything fell apart. He'd worked it by hand. Shaped it with the sort of care most men reserve for people they love. There weren't many bladesmiths left like him. Fewer still who gave a damn about the meaning.

Underneath the blade was the photo.

The last one I had of him.

Us at the pub. His arm around my shoulder. Vodka in one hand, that massive dumb grin on his face—like he was about to tell a joke that would get us both punched.

I stared at it.

My smile came without effort. Like muscle memory.

I rubbed my thumb across the picture, brushing off a smear of dust. A tear slid down my cheek. Salt reached the edge of my lips. I tasted the truth of it.

"I miss you," I whispered.

I tucked the photo back inside my jacket.

And when I closed my eyes again, the sadness was gone.

Replaced by something sharper.

Something earned.

Osbourne's voice broke the silence again.

"Fuckin' let me go! You don't know who I am!"

I turned toward the sound.

No more patience.

I picked up the lamp and walked back into the room. Each step deliberate. Final.

I set the lamp down in front of his feet. The light cut up through our faces—casting shadows that stretched like guilt across the walls.

Osbourne blinked through the glare. His face soaked in sweat and spit.

"Wait, wait—listen to me. There's a shipment coming in. Two weeks. Five hundred million in product, another fifty mil in cash. I can give you all of it. Everything. You just have to let me walk."

Still bargaining. Still thinking this was about leverage.

Still thinking he was in control.

I held the obsidian blade low beside my leg. Then slowly raised it. Let the light catch its edge.

Osbourne's eyes went wide.

"This—" I said, "—is the only thing I want."

He opened his mouth, but I cut him off.

"You had my friend stabbed. Twenty-eight times. Left him to bleed out in the bathroom like a fucking dog."

His lips quivered. "It wasn't me. It was just business. I didn't—"

I stepped closer. Calm. Intent.

"But I'm only going to stab you once."

His eyes darted left and right. No exits. No miracles.

"This is for Chris."

I didn't wait.

My left hand gripped his shoulder. Firm. Anchored.

Then I drove the blade into his chest—fast and brutal. No ceremony. No speech. Just *justice*.

It sank deep. The sound was ugly. A wet thud, flesh giving way, bone catching halfway down the blade before splitting apart.

I let go.

The handle stayed. Only the hilt remained visible. That was enough.

Osbourne screamed.

His head whipped back against the chair. The sound rang through the farmhouse like a siren for no one.

Then silence.

He looked down at the blade in his chest. His eyes found mine.

He tried to speak.

Only a cough came out. Wet. Ragged. Full of blood and regret.

His chin dropped.

His eyes fluttered.

One final breath slipped out. A soft exhale, like a balloon surrendering its last bit of air.

Then... nothing.

Osbourne was dead.

I stood there. Watching. Waiting.

Making sure.

The house didn't move. The world didn't shift. No thunder. No divine reckoning.

Just quiet.

And the dark.

And me.

CHAPTER 77: THE CLEAN-UP

I don't know how long I stood there, staring at Osbourne's body.

Maybe minutes. Maybe hours. Time had stopped keeping track the moment his heart did.

He was slumped forward now—head tilted, mouth half open, eyes glazed in that final dumb shock. The blade was still buried in his chest, its obsidian handle slick with the last of him. It looked peaceful. But that was a lie.

Nothing about this was peace.

Eventually, I moved.

Out through the side door, past the crumbling walls and dirt-caked windows, into the cold breath of the night. I grabbed the first fuel drum. Aviation grade. The sort of burn you don't walk away from.

I unscrewed the lid and poured a few litres into the steel drum lined with ceramic tiles. The smell hit instantly—sharp, chemical, unforgiving.

Then I went back inside.

To finish what I'd started.

I crouched in front of him. His skin was starting to cool. Muscles losing tension. Just a bag of meat and memory now.

I reached for the blade.

Wrapped my fingers around the handle.

Pulled.

It came free with a sick little pop, the kind that stays in your head longer than it should.

I looked at it in my hand. The edge glistened. The blood clung in a single ribbon. Still beautiful. Still his.

"You and I have work to do," I muttered.

And then I proceeded.

Arms first.

I cut through the gaffer tape with a ripping sound that echoed like a scream that couldn't get out. I rolled down the sleeve. Found the joint. Pressed the blade in.

It slid through the muscle like it was nothing.

The bone was harder. I hacked, twisted, leaned my weight into it until it cracked. Not clean. Not elegant. Just *done*.

I carried the first arm out and dropped it into the drum.

Came back.

Did the second.

By the time both arms were gone, the floor was spotted in blood. Not spurting—just slow, heavy drips. Like the house itself was bleeding now.

Next were the legs.

Heavier. Thicker. Harder to manoeuvre.

I grunted as I worked—sweat now stinging my eyes, breath fogging in the cold.

But the blade didn't care.

It kept slicing, chewing, splitting through him like it was born for this.

Eventually, I had both legs in the drum. Bent at the knee, wedged into the metal like firewood.

I poured more fuel.

The liquid hissed as it soaked into the tissue, pooling in the bottom.

Then I stepped back.

Deep breaths.

I reached into my jacket pocket. Pulled out the box of matches.

Held it in my hand like it meant something more than it did.

Ceremony, maybe. Or just the weight of knowing what came next.

I struck a match. The sound was small. Final.

Then I tossed it in.

WOOSH.

The flames exploded upward—angry, orange, alive.

I flinched from the heat, staggered back, felt the warmth hit my face like a slap.

I stood there, watching the fire twist and dance, licking at the sky. Smoke billowed upward, thick and black, curling into the night like something trying to escape.

But no escape here.

Not for him.

Not anymore.

For the first time in months, I smiled.

Not from joy.

From release.

From knowing something was finally—*finally*—over.

I turned back into the house.

Osbourne's torso was still on the floor. Head lolled to one side.

Time to finish it.

I dragged him by the arms—what was left of them—his weight scraping against the floor, leaving a thick, red trail.

Out the door.

Through the weeds.

To the drum.

The flames reached for him like they'd been waiting.

I fed him in, bit by bit.

The fire didn't judge.

It just burned.

And I let it.

Because that's what this was now.

Not revenge.

Not justice.

Erasure.

CHAPTER 78: THE ERASURE

Morning crept in without permission.

The sky shifted from black to steel, not light but less dark. The wind had a bite to it now, slicing through my jacket, but I barely noticed. My eyes were locked on the drum. Osbourne was gone—what was left of him still flickering just above the rim, a final twitch of flame licking at the sides.

I found an old crate near the shed. The wood was dry, splintered, half-rotten. I turned it over and sat down.

Next to me, a small duffel bag.

I reached in. Pulled out a can of Bundy.

No toast. No words.

Just the hiss of the ring-pull.

That sound was enough.

I raised it toward the fire. Toward nothing. Toward Chris.

Took a drink.

The rum burned, but it didn't warm me. Not really. Only the drum did that. The heat radiating off it wasn't comfort—it was closure. Charred, chemical closure.

Beside me, the obsidian blade. The same one I'd buried in Osbourne's chest.

I picked it up.

Turned it in my hand.

It was beautiful. Still. Even now.

But it was filthy—blackened, sticky, tainted.

I grabbed an old rag and wiped it down, careful around the edge. The cloth came away streaked in red and soot.

Not clean. Just *cleaner*.

I heard Chris in my head, that mocking tone he used when something wasn't good enough.

"You're not going to leave it like that, are you? Go clean it properly."

Always the perfectionist. Always the craftsman.

Even now.

The flames started dying down. Less noise. Less movement.

Time for the next part.

I waited until the heat dropped enough to get closer. Then I leaned in, using the blackened BBQ tongs Roy had left behind. They were warped, twisted at the end. Looked like they'd been used for this sort of thing before.

Wouldn't surprise me.

I pulled out what was left—chunks of bone, rib, spine, socket. White-hot and brittle. They didn't even look real anymore. Just... objects.

I carried them to the crusher. An old machine Roy had rigged with a generator and a custom container underneath.

I fired it up.

The motor screamed to life.

Loud.

Ugly.

Perfect.

I fed the first rib cage in. It cracked like brittle wood. The grinder chewed through it with mechanical indifference—grinding, spinning, pulverising.

Dust and bone mist swirled in the air, catching the rising light like ash from a crematorium.

I kept going.

Vertebrae. Shoulder. Femur.

Didn't think. Just processed.

Like I was breaking down a junked car. No identity. No weight.

Just material.

The skull was last.

I stared into the holes where his eyes once were.

Didn't flinch. Didn't blink.

Then tossed it in.

It shattered louder than the rest. The final insult. The last indignity.

Good.

I turned the crusher off. The silence after that motor stopped was deafening.

I pulled the container out from underneath. A mess of grey powder and bone fragments. All that remained of the man who had murdered my friend.

I brought the container to the fence line. Sat down again. Pulled the sieve beside me. Took a deep breath.

Then I went to work.

Handful by handful, I dropped the ash into the sieve, gently shaking it side to side, watching the dust fall like sand in an hourglass. The wind picked it up, carried it into the scrubland like it was nothing. No burial. No headstone. No legacy.

Just dispersal.

I rubbed my fingers through the grey as I went—feeling for anything solid. Anything that didn't belong.

Eventually, I found them.

Two tiny screws.

Surgical, maybe. A fracture once. A reminder he was still human once—barely.

I held them up, turning them in the light.

Little reminders.

"I should give these to Maintenance," I muttered. "Might hold a hinge or something."

Chris would've laughed at that.

The bastard anchored to the prison forever. Right where he belonged.

I gave the sieve a final tap against the side fence.

Tink. Tink.

Then dropped it.

That was it.

No prayers.

No music.

No fucking eulogies.

Just dust.

And silence.

And one more job left.

Erase the farmhouse.

Burn it to the fucking ground.

CHAPTER 79: NOTHING LEFT TO FIND

I treated the place like a cell search. Like I was back inside, sweeping the corner of a max unit after an incident.

No assumptions. No shortcuts. No forgiveness.

Every room.

Every gap between the floorboards.

My eyes weren't just looking for evidence—they were tuned to absence. Things that didn't belong, and things that should've been there but weren't. That was always my edge. My talent.

I could walk into a room and *see* what no one else saw.

That loose screw in the vent. That torn corner behind the mirror. That trace smear near the drain that shouldn't reflect light.

Now I used that same skill to erase everything.

The chair—gone. Dismantled, stacked in the front room, soaked in fuel.

No gaffer tape left behind.

No stray fibres.

No DNA.

No second chances.

I collected the last of the aviation fuel and dragged the barrel into the main room—what used to be the living area. Where Osbourne died. Where justice was done.

That barrel would be the heart of the fire.

Then outside—to the perimeter. The crusher was doused in petrol, the generator unplugged and smashed. I gave it one last look.

No part of this operation would survive.

I checked for footprints—mine. Drag marks. Nothing obvious. Weeds had already begun reclaiming the ground.

I went room by room again.

Not just looking.

Feeling.

Anything that might breathe suspicion. Anything that felt out of rhythm.

If I had a doubt, it went on the burn pile.

By 5 p.m., the light had turned copper. The sun was low, but it was still strong enough to reveal what mattered.

Time to finish it.

I walked back to the main room and tipped the final drum over. Aviation fuel splashed across the floor like blood. It spread fast, rushing into cracks, hugging walls, creeping like it knew what was coming.

I created a trail—thin, deliberate—out the front door, all the way to the car.

I emptied the last container of fuel into the dirt outside the door, completing the trail. Flung the can back inside. Took off my gloves. Tossed them too.

No residue.

No trace.

I stood at the edge of the trail, staring at the house.

It looked peaceful now. Empty. Like it was waiting.

Like it *knew*.

I struck the match.

Watched the flame bloom.

Then dropped it.

The fire raced up the trail like a fuse, whispering across the dirt. It hit the door frame and *woof*—ignition.

I didn't wait.

I eased myself into the car.

Started it.

Pulled away slow.

Didn't floor it. Just rolled down the gravel path.

Dust in the mirrors.

Behind me, the farmhouse began to cough smoke from every gap. Then flames. First licking at windows. Then eating them.

In the rearview, I saw the whole house inhale and then start to scream.

Orange. Red. Black.

The sort of fire that doesn't ask for permission.

The kind that *consumes*.

I viewed it until the road curved, and the flames were gone.

Then I kept driving.

Eyes forward.

The saying came back to me. One I'd once told Chris after a late shift while we were on the phone.

"There's a reason your rearview mirror's smaller than your windscreen," I'd said.

"Because what's in front of you, is more important than what's behind you."

"And like any good rearview mirror, it's okay to look back sometimes."

"Just to see how far you've come."

But not tonight.

Tonight, I drove forward.

No more looking back.

CHAPTER 80: NOTHING TOO SERIOUS

The porch light was on.

It always was when she knew I'd be coming home late. Emma believed in that sort of thing. A beacon. A way to say, "You're safe now. You made it."

The key turned like it always did.

The lock clicked open like nothing had changed.

But everything had.

Dougal was first—ears up, barking, full sprint across the hallway like I'd been gone for years. He launched into my arms, tail a blur, body shaking. That little mutt knew exactly what I needed. He always had.

Then Emma.

She stood in the hallway, barefoot, eyes wide but soft. About to ask— but something in her stopped. Maybe it was the way I stood. The weight I carried.

I stepped forward and pulled her into me. Hard. Like I wasn't letting go. Like if I did, something might break loose that I'd never get back.

She didn't speak.

Didn't need to.

"I'm home," I said into her hair. "It's done."

That was all I ever gave her.

No names. No places. No timelines. And not what the fire smelled like.

Over the week that followed, sometimes she'd ask in her own way. A look. A silence. A question without a mark at the end.

But I never talked about *him*.

Only about Chris.

The man who still walked beside me, even if no one else could see him.

Dinner was waiting. She'd kept it warm, like always. I ate like I hadn't touched food in days. Maybe I hadn't. Dougal sat beside me, paws on the edge of the chair, eyes flicking between the two of us like he couldn't believe I was real again.

Emma reached across the table a few times. A hand to my forearm. A brush down my back. Not to comfort me—just to reassure *herself*.

That I was back.

That I was still me.

Plate emptied, I stood. "Shower. Bed. Early start tomorrow."

She nodded, watching me like she was trying to read pages she hadn't been given permission to turn.

But I smiled. That was enough.

She hadn't seen that smile in months.

"Before you crash," she said, reaching into a drawer. "I have something for you."

She handed me a few brochures. Home builds. Acreage. Dream-house shit.

"It's time," she said. "Let's find our forever place."

She kissed my cheek, turned, and walked back to the couch.

Dougal followed her.

I stepped into the ensuite.

The water ran hot. Steam on the mirror. My face slowly reappearing. Less haunted now. Still me—but different.

I fell into bed. No tossing. No thoughts.

Just sleep.

And it came like a blackout.

Morning.

Dark outside. Cold enough to bite through your jacket.

My routine kicked in like muscle memory.

Uniform.

Lunch from the fridge.

Bag packed. Keys.

Door creaked open.

Dougal at my feet, like always.

I bent down and scratched his ears. "See you this afternoon, buddy."

The drive was short. Familiar. But everything felt heavier.

Like I was carrying something that no longer needed carrying.

I pulled into the staff car park just as the sun crested over the Gatehouse roof. Pale light cracked the clouds open.

I sat for a minute.

Pulled out the picture of Chris.

Held it.

Stared into that ridiculous grin. That pub night. That laugh—I could still hear it if I closed my eyes.

Then I put it away.

Grabbed my keys.

Opened the door.

Stepped out.

The sunlight hit me full in the face. Cold wind at my back. Clouds shifting.

I turned my face to the sky. Let it warm my skin. Let it *reach me*.

"Rest easy, brother," I whispered. "It's done. Finally."

I stood still, one hand on the car roof, my head bowed.

Another officer approached. Young. New. One of those eager types that hadn't seen what real evil appeared like yet.

"You alright, Jacob?" he asked.

"You, okay?"

I didn't look at him.

Just slid on my sunglasses.

Eyes forward.

Back straight.

Smile, slow and small.

"Nothing Too Serious."

And walked into prison.

The End

(In memory of those who never had justice. And those who carried it alone.)

About the Author

Bruce McLeod is the pen name of a former Senior Prison Officer with over 20 years of frontline corrections experience. His firsthand knowledge of high-security facilities, emergency responses, and the emotional toll of institutional life shapes the raw authenticity of his storytelling.

This debut novel is inspired by real events, transformed through fiction to explore justice, grief, and revenge with psychological grit and brutal honesty.

Thank You

Thank you for reading Justifying The Means.

Your feedback is invaluable as I prepare the sequel — *Justifying The Silence*.

I'd love to hear your thoughts. What stayed with you? What do you want more of?

Your voice helps shape what comes next.

✉@ Email: bruce.mcleod.author@gmail.com

🌹 Twitter(X): @AuthorBruceMcL

📰 Facebook: Bruce McLeod – Author

www.ingramcontent.com/pod-product-compliance
Lightning Source LLC
Chambersburg PA
CBHW080716020726
47501CB00010B/2446